THE VILLE RAT

THE
VILLE
RAT

Martin Limón

Copyright © 2015 by Martin Limón

Published by
Soho Press, Inc.
853 Broadway
New York, NY 10003

Library of Congress Cataloging-in-Publication Data

Limón, Martin, 1948–
The ville rat / Martin Limón.

ISBN 978-1-61695-685-1
eISBN 978-1-61695-609-7

1. Sueño, George (Fictitious character)—Fiction. 2. Bascom, Ernie
(Fictitious character)—Fiction. 3. United States. Army Criminal Investigation Command—
Fiction. 4. Americans—Korea—Fiction. 5. Young women—Crimes against—Fiction.
6. Murder—Investigation—Fiction. 7. Korea (South)—History—1960-1988—Fiction.
I. Title.
PS3562.I465V55 2015
813'.54—dc23   2015009880

Interior design by Janine Agro, Soho Press, Inc.

Printed in the United States of America

10 9 8 7 6 5 4 3 2 1

To Aaron, with hope for a brilliant future

THE VILLE RAT

Ville \ ˈvil \ noun: GI slang for village, usually in Asia.

-1-

We left the Main Supply Route and turned onto the two-lane blacktop that led toward the village of Sonyu-ri. The road dropped off precipitously and we both held onto the overhead roll bar as the jeep bounced downhill. When we reached ground level, the tire chains caught and began to crunch reassuringly on freshly fallen snow. Still, even though the time was already an hour past dawn, visibility was poor. Ernie switched on the headlights.

"Are you sure you're using the right map there, pal?"

"Official army map," I told him, slapping the folded sheet.

"What's the date on it?"

I aimed the beam of my flashlight and checked. "Twenty years ago."

"Right at the end of the Korean War," Ernie said. "This area north of Seoul has changed since then. Half the roads probably aren't even listed."

And half the villages, I thought. With two million dead out of a population of twenty million at the end of the war, the Republic of Korea was only now beginning to recover. And they were still nervous about another North Korean invasion. With 700,000 bloodthirsty Communist soldiers on the far side of the Demilitarized Zone, just a few miles from here, who could blame them? On the trip from Seoul, we'd passed two ROK Army checkpoints and driven around a mile-long row of armor-blocking cement pilings, and rolled beneath tank traps set to explode if the northern hordes ever decided to come south again.

My name is George Sueño. My partner Ernie Bascom and I are agents for the 8th United States Army Criminal Investigation Division in Seoul. The call had come in at oh-dark-thirty. Our presence was requested at a crime scene some fifteen miles north of the capital city in a village known as Sonyu-ri. Said presence was requested *now*. Or, as 8th Army liked to say, immediately if not sooner.

We continued to roll down the snow-covered road, passing the Paju-gun County Health Clinic on our right and then a few idle three-wheeled tractors parked along the edge of a four-foot-high berm. Rows of small farmhouses sat cozy in the brisk winter breeze. Fifty yards farther along, just where the map told me they would be, a cluster of blue police sedans waited atop a rise. As we bounced up the dirt pathway, all eyes were on us, even Mr. Kill's.

His real name was Gil Kwon-up, chief homicide inspector for the Korean National Police, but "Kill" is what the American Army MPs had taken to calling him. Changing "Gil" to "Kill" made some sort of sense, at least in GI minds. Whenever they could turn a Korean name or word into something American, they did it. Ernie and I had worked with Mr. Kill before, on more than one case, and somehow we had won his grudging respect. Ernie for his ability to blend in with GIs everywhere, under any conditions, and me for my facility with the Korean language and interest in Korea's five-thousand-year-old culture.

Ernie drove up closer to the other vehicles, turned off the engine, and set the emergency brake. We pushed open the stiff canvas doors, climbed out of the jeep, and trudged to the top of the rise.

Mr. Kill wore a broad-brimmed fedora and a dapper overcoat made of thick material. He stood with his hands shoved deep into his pockets, staring at us. He was tall for a Korean but at six-foot-one Ernie loomed over him. I was three inches taller than Ernie, but to show respect for Mr. Kill's rank, I stopped lower down on the ridge. We were eye to eye. I nodded a greeting. So did Ernie. Kill pulled his right hand out of his pocket and motioned for us to follow. We did, downhill to the ice-encrusted banks of the Sonyu River.

In the stray beams of a half-dozen flashlights, it was the splash of color I saw first. Bright red. Ernie saw it too. We both stopped. Mr. Kill took two steps forward and then crouched, both to get himself a better view and to give us time to absorb the scene. The rays of illumination coalesced around her, like a spotlight introducing a star. It was then I saw the stiff flesh and the raven black hair.

She was beautiful. Like an ice princess.

Somehow her body had been washed up against the shore and any further drift had been stopped by a foot-high shelf of crystalline white snow. She was wearing a *chima-jeogori*, a traditional Korean dress made of flowing red silk. The skirt had been tied breast-high, as was the custom, and embroidered with white cranes flapping broad wings to the sky. The short blouse was made of a sturdier material and was canary yellow and tied in the front with a long blue ribbon. Her eyes were open, staring into the opaque grey sky, and the smooth flesh of her face seemed to have been bleached pure white by death. A cold breeze blew down from the north. I shuddered. So did Ernie. So did every cop milling about the crime scene, except for Mr. Kill.

He was known to be impervious to petty feelings. Heartless, some called him. But I knew that when he was on a crime scene he didn't have time for emotions, only thought. And the processes of his mind, coupled with his vast investigative experience, were not good news for the perpetrators of any crime scenes he was assigned to.

I stared at the woman again. Who could have done such a thing? Who could have so cruelly abandoned her in this frigid, unrelenting stream?

The Sonyu River does not run deep. No more than three or four feet now and even less in the dry summer months. But due to the cold snap that had drifted down from Manchuria in recent weeks, it was frozen almost solid, except for the five or six inches of frigid water that rushed by beneath the ice. The river was about twenty feet wide and at its center, for a width of about two yards, it ran quickly and freely.

Ernie looked upstream. "How far did she drift?" he asked.

Mr. Kill nodded at the question but didn't answer.

Upriver, a basketball-sized chunk of ice broke free and swirled toward the body. It spun madly and crashed into the red skirt, lifting it lewdly up pale legs.

"No underwear," Ernie said.

Which was unusual. Part of the traditional female outfit during the winter was a wool tunic and long underpants and warm socks under cotton-stuffed slippers. All designed to combat the long Korean winter. None of these appurtenances were worn by the Lady of the Ice.

The silk string that was used to secure the wrapped skirt was loose, trailing limply in the slow current.

As if we were thinking the same thing, both Ernie and I turned and gazed upriver. The meandering stream ran through rice paddies and past small animal pens and near farmhouses, and although we couldn't see it from here, we both knew that just over the rise was an installation we were both familiar with: Camp Pelham, home of the 2nd of the 17th Field Artillery, which maybe explained why Mr. Kill had called for us. Even though he was the chief homicide investigator of the Korean National Police, under the Status of Forces Agreement signed between the US and the Republic of Korea, he had no jurisdiction on American military compounds.

A large van pulled up and a team of forensic technicians climbed out. They all wore blue smocks and a few of them toted metal briefcases. Stenciled on their backs in block *hangul* script was the word *kyongchal*. Police. Mr. Kill left us and gave them a quick briefing. Soon, they were plotting their grids and slipping on knee-high rubber wading boots.

Another group of cops had apparently been canvassing the neighborhood and reported back to Mr. Kill. He listened to them and nodded and then barked further orders, pointing at the homes off in the distance. The men saluted and left.

He walked back to us. Wearily, he nodded toward the corpse. "Your thoughts," he said.

I let Ernie go first.

"Nobody but a madwoman would leave her house dressed like that, not in this weather."

Mr. Kill nodded.

"And the knot holding her skirt came loose," Ernie continued, "probably tied in a hurry." He paused. "Do we know the cause of death?"

"No," Mr. Kill replied, "but did you see her neck?"

We all turned and studied the body. Mr. Kill switched on his flashlight. The technicians were closing in on her now, one of them examining the silk skirt.

"Bruises. She was strangled," Ernie said.

"Yes," Mr. Kill replied. "The river is much too shallow for her to have drowned."

Ernie glanced toward the invisible compound upriver. "I bet Eighth Army won't see it that way."

If an American GI was in any way involved, the powers that be at the 8th Imperial Army would do their best to deny it. A young woman, maybe inebriated, staggers around in the dark. She trips and falls into the frigid waters of the Sonyu River, she struggles, maybe hits her head against a rock. She's disoriented and starts gulping down water. She passes out. Before you know it, she's history.

Was that scenario possible? Barely. But all cops, military or otherwise, play the percentages. And with a battalion full of horny American artillerymen just a couple of hundred yards upriver, the percentages were that one of them had something to do with this.

One of the technicians squatted in the stream. Wearing plastic gloves, he searched the dead woman's clothing. We waited expectantly. At first, he found nothing. No jewelry, no money, no laminated Korean National Identification Card, nothing that would make our lives easier. Finally, from the inner sleeve, he pulled out a piece of paper. He waded out of the water and handed it to Mr. Kill. The paper was wet but appeared to be made of cloth vellum. Thick. The type of paper used for official documents.

Kill, having similarly slipped on plastic gloves, unfolded the paper.

We held our breath.

Finally, he twisted the dripping paper toward us. It was a torn shard. Some of the ink had run but it was still legible, composed of the phonetic *hangul* script interspersed with Chinese characters.

"What does it say?" Ernie asked.

"You might recognize it," Mr. Kill said. "It's about a night and a meeting and something being stretched." He surveyed our blank faces and almost smiled. "It's poetry," he said. "I'll have it identified."

"And the calligraphy," I said.

"Yes, another key point. It's clearly written with ink and a brush, not a ballpoint pen. That in itself is a lead. Very few people write this way anymore."

Except for Mr. Kill himself. He was an expert calligrapher. He'd been educated in classical Korean, which included Chinese characters, and he'd attended university in the States, which was why he spoke English so well. And it probably explained why he so quickly recognized this snippet of writing as a fragment of a longer work of poetry.

"So maybe we can leave now?" Ernie said.

Kill stared at him quizzically.

Ernie glanced back toward Camp Pelham. "None of those guys is an expert calligrapher, or is likely to have anything to do with anybody who is."

"How can you be so sure?"

"They're nothing but a bunch of know-nothing GIs. Lowlifes." Ernie jabbed his thumb into his chest. "I ought to know. I've been working with them all of my adult life."

"You harbor such a high opinion of your fellow soldiers?"

"I'm being generous. These are guys who read comic books and watch cartoons on AFKN on Saturday mornings. Hell, anybody who can pass a fifth-grade spelling test, like my partner Sueño here, they think he's a freaking *genius*."

"Still," Kill said, looking back at the body floating in the frozen river. "She was a beautiful woman. They are men. They would've been watching her."

"Maybe," Ernie said, "but the Second D MPI isn't going to like it."

He was referring to the 2nd Infantry Division military police investigators. They controlled the three-hundred-or-so-square-mile area in which the US 2nd Infantry Division operated. Even though the 8th US Army was the higher headquarters, and theoretically in charge of all operations in Korea, the 2nd D cops wouldn't want us 8th Army investigators poking our noses into what they would consider to be none of our business. A jurisdictional dispute could be overcome, but it would take some high-level phone calls. And the Division would like even less the Korean National Police sniffing around one of their compounds.

"We will let the evidence lead us," Mr. Kill said. With that, he turned and started to walk back to his blue police sedan.

Ernie called after him. "So that means we can't leave?"

"No," he replied without looking back. "I've already made some phone calls. Your fate is being determined as we speak."

"Shit," Ernie said, turning to me. "Division's going to have a case of the ass."

We'd dealt with the honchos of the United States Army's 2nd Infantry Division before, and it hadn't been pleasant. In fact, with all that firepower at their disposal—tank battalions, howitzer batteries, and gung ho infantry units—it could be downright dangerous.

The banks of the Sonyu River became muddier and more treacherous the closer we came to the outskirts of Sonyu-ri.

Ernie balanced himself by holding on to a clump of reeds.

"Why does Kill want *us* on the case?" Ernie asked. "What did we ever do?"

"We worked with him before," I answered, hopping from one stone to another over a thin crust of ice. "He appreciated our efforts."

"We didn't do anything anybody else couldn't have done. Except for you speaking Korean, that is."

"Maybe," I replied. "But he knows we don't give a shit about what Eighth Army thinks. That's what sets us apart."

Ernie didn't answer. He knew I was right. We both refused to brownnose to get a promotion, especially when it involved overlooking crimes that were considered embarrassing to the 8th Army command. It was an attitude that had gotten us in trouble more than once, and even got me busted down a stripe. But it was an attitude that, no matter how hard we tried, we couldn't shake.

Ernie had spent two tours in Vietnam. He'd seen death and he knew he was lucky to be alive. And as such, he lived each day without worrying about tomorrow, and he sure as hell didn't care what anyone thought about him.

I had a different take. I didn't care what most people thought, but the opinion of those I respected was desperately important to me. Mr. Kill, for example. He'd somehow survived the Machiavellian politics of the South Korean government and managed to rise to top homicide investigator of the Korean National Police, all the while maintaining a reputation for impeccable integrity.

I wasn't sure if that was possible for me, not in the 8th US Army, but I was trying. I'd been orphaned at an early age and grown up as a Mexican-American orphan in an indifferent Los Angeles County foster care system. What kept me from giving up were the very few people who had inspired me to do better. That's what I was trying to do here and now in the US Army. And I believed that's what Mr. Kill was demanding of me—to do better—because we owed it to that woman who'd been left to float all night, alone in a river of ice.

"There it is," Ernie said, pointing. "Sonyu-ri."

A muddy walkway ran parallel to the water as it curved along an almost unbroken wall of wood and brick. Each building was dirty and run-down, and now the river was littered with trash: empty tin cans, a tiny shoe bobbing in muddy water, a dead rat. Every twenty yards or so a crack appeared between buildings, barely wide enough for a person to squeeze through, and I knew from previous visits that these ran uphill about a hundred feet until they reached the same two-lane blacktop that led back to the MSR—the Main Supply Route.

On the right bank stood Camp Pelham, protected by a ten-foot-high chain-link fence held up by sturdy four-by-four wooden beams and topped by rolled concertina wire. Every fifty yards or so, stretching all around the perimeter, were guard towers with floodlights and a wooden ladder leading up to a roofed platform. At each one, the muzzle of a .50-caliber machine gun poked out from behind a sandbagged firing position. Backed up against the fence were rows of round-topped tin Quonset huts, all of them painted the army's favorite color: olive drab.

Ernie pointed straight ahead. "That must be one of the bridges over the River Seine."

Actually it was nothing more than a utilitarian flat wooden bridge, similarly lined with chain-link fence and concertina wire. It led from Camp Pelham's main entrance onto the compound proper. We climbed to our left toward the walkway that lined the river, slapping mud off of our hands and off the sides of our trousers.

"She could've emerged from any of these pathways," Ernie said, "run down to the river and fallen in."

"Or been pushed."

"If it was nighttime and nobody witnessed anything, she could've been held under in the center of the river where there isn't much ice, and she could've floated downstream."

"Maybe," I said. "But if that's the case, if the perpetrator was a GI here in the village, somebody would've seen something."

"People around here are frightened of all the things that go on at night. They keep their doors shut and their windows locked. And more importantly," Ernie added, "they don't trust the KNPs."

When the Korean War ended with a ceasefire more than

twenty years ago, Korea was economically flat on its back. People were desperate for food and shelter and medical supplies, and to make matters worse, the Syngman Rhee government was notoriously corrupt. That corruption included the Korean National Police, the one police force in the country. The citizenry didn't trust them, and for good reason. The average cop on the beat was underpaid and looking for ways to supplement his income and support his family. Bribery was endemic. But with the advent of the Pak Chung-hee military dictatorship, the KNPs were trying—albeit slowly—to change their image. Trust was growing between the average citizen and their national law enforcement agency, but it still had a long way to go.

The KNPs were working their way up the river, knocking on every door, interviewing every farmer and housewife they could find. Within an hour or two they would reach the village of Sonyu-ri. Mr. Kill had called for more cops, but it would probably take them the better part of the day to interview all the people who lived along the banks of the river. North of Camp Pelham was nothing but a couple of other small military compounds and then countryside, so chances were good that the Lady of the Ice had entered the river somewhere around here.

"They have MP patrols here at night, don't they?" Ernie asked. He meant in the village of Sonyu-ri.

I nodded.

"We'll have to look at their duty logs and talk to them. Especially the gate guards."

"That's why Mr. Kill asked for us. He knows we can get that information a lot easier than he could."

"Maybe," Ernie said. He was staring up at the bridge. I turned to follow his gaze. An MP jeep had stopped in the middle of the bridge, and two MPs climbed out. They were facing out through the chain-link fence, staring at us, hands on the hilts of their .45s.

Ernie grinned and waved.

Neither of them returned the greeting. In fact one of them kept his hand low, just in front of his web belt, and flipped us the bird.

"Same to you, Charley!" Ernie shouted. Then he turned to me, still grinning. "Welcome back to the Second Infantry Division."

"Second to none," I replied.

-2-

The main drag of Sonyu-ri was lined with tailor shops, brassware emporiums, nightclubs, and chophouses, all catering to American GIs and most sporting neon signs in both *hangul* script and even larger letters in English. It was mid-afternoon by the time we met with Mr. Kill again, this time at the Red Dragon Tea House. He ordered a green tea. Ernie and I both stirred cups of Folgers instant crystals.

"What did you find out?" he asked.

"Nothing," Ernie replied. "The Camp Pelham MP commander chewed our butts for even asking questions."

Kill frowned. "My superiors have contacted the Eighth Army commander."

"It takes a while," Ernie said, sipping on his coffee, "for shit to roll downhill."

"You mean your Eighth Army commander hasn't yet ordered the Second Infantry Division to cooperate with our investigation?"

"That's exactly what he means," I said. "And even though

Division knows they'll have to go along eventually, what they're probably doing is trying to convince Eighth Army to assign their own MPIs to the case. Not me and Ernie."

Mr. Kill set down his handle-less cup of tea. "That way they'll have more control."

"Exactly. If it turns out a Division GI was involved in this death, they'll be able to present whatever evidence they have the way they want it presented."

"How do you think this will turn out?" Kill asked us.

Ernie shrugged. "It's up to the honchos."

"When will we know?"

"Probably before close of business. They won't want us staying up here if we're off the case."

"Tonight," Kill said, "some of the MPs who were on duty last night will be on duty again, won't they?"

"Most likely."

"And the same gate guards?"

I nodded again.

"And the same dollies at the nightclubs," Ernie said. "They stand at the front doors and watch everything that goes on."

"They'll trust you," Mr. Kill said, "more than they would trust me. You know how to get them to open up."

Ernie drained his coffee. "We can try," he said.

"I've watched you work," Mr. Kill said. "You two are better at that than any of your colleagues. The other American investigators are . . . How do you say . . . ?"

"Stiff," I offered.

"Exactly," Mr. Kill said.

"Corncobs up their butts," Ernie added.

Mr. Kill gazed at him, puzzled.

"An old expression," I said. "So you want us to stay up here tonight and investigate, whether we're recalled or not?"

"Yes. I'm asking that favor of you."

We could get in trouble for it, but Ernie and I had been in trouble before.

"How soon will you have the autopsy report?" I asked.

"A few days, but preliminary conclusions tomorrow."

"And your canvassing so far?"

"We've found one housewife. She heard something. A man and a woman arguing. They were in one of the alleys here, heading toward the river. She had the impression that the woman was trying to get away from him."

"Did she see anything?"

"No. There are so many drunks in this village at night. The local people stay very much behind closed doors."

"What language were they speaking?" Ernie asked.

"She thinks English but she's not sure."

"Your men will keep working?" I said.

"Yes. And depending on what you find tonight . . ."

"By tomorrow," I said, "you might have enough evidence to convince someone higher up to keep us on the case."

He nodded. "That's the idea."

I was sometimes startled by Mr. Kill's use of American colloquialisms and had to remind myself that he'd spent almost four years in the States.

"Even if we stay on the case," Ernie said, "Second Division isn't going to want to cooperate with us any more than they are with you."

"But you know your way around."

We'd both been in the country for going on three years. I was the only American in law enforcement who could speak Korean and Ernie had a knack for communicating with the druggies and the business girls.

Ernie grinned. "I guess we do."

I plopped a shiny hundred-*won* coin onto the counter of the Red Dragon Tea House, paying to use their phone. It was a big, bulky job, painted pink, and it sat on a hand-knitted placemat.

I dialed. It took me fifteen minutes to get through to the 8th Army exchange. A Korean woman's voice said in English, "Extension please." I told her the number. Ten seconds later a gruff voice answered, "Eighth Army Criminal Investigation, Staff Sergeant Riley speaking."

"Riley," I said.

"*Sueño!* Where in the hell are you?"

"Doing what we were told to do."

"You're supposed to get your asses back here, right now. The provost marshal hasn't decided whether or not you're going to be assigned to the case."

"What's the holdup?"

I could almost hear the veins popping on Riley's neck. "That's none of your *freaking* business," he yelled. "You get your asses back here and you get them back here *now!*"

I thought of the beautiful, red-robed woman floating faceup in the Sonyu River. I took a deep breath. "Ernie's jeep broke down."

"Don't give me that shit!"

"It's in the shop now. I'll keep you posted."

"Don't give me that *shit*, Sueño. You get your butts back here and you get them back here—"

I hung up.

When I returned to the table, Mr. Kill said, "You have the clearance to stay tonight?"

I nodded. "They agreed wholeheartedly."

Mr. Kill paid for the coffee and the tea. He left the shop first.

The main drag of Sonyu-ri stretches about two hundred yards from the front gate of something called RC-4, Recreation Center Four, all the way to the front gate of Camp Pelham. Ernie and I killed the next couple of hours on RC-4 at the tiny Quonset hut that housed the base library, and later at the RC-4 snack bar that featured a hot grill and a scratchy-sounding jukebox. RC-4 also housed a movie theater, a military credit union, a gym, and a small arts and crafts center. The idea was to have all the recreational facilities serving the scattered military compounds near the Demilitarized Zone in one place. A green army bus pulled up in front of RC-4 every hour or so, and GIs and any dependents—usually Korean wives—disembarked and made a beeline to the main attraction on RC-4, the post exhange. Once they loaded duffel bags full of freeze-dried coffee, soluble creamer, maraschino cherries, instant orange juice, cigarettes, and canned meat products, they climbed back on the bus and returned to whatever compound they'd come from.

"Free enterprise is a wonderful thing," Ernie said.

He was actually referring to the black market. With the Korean economy still hurting, there was a huge unfulfilled demand for imported American products. A GI, or more often his Korean wife, could sell almost anything they bought in the PX at twice what they paid for it.

We finished listening to a song called "Mandy" by some Stateside singer, swallowed the last of our cheeseburgers and coffee, and headed toward the front gate of RC-4. Already the sky was dark. On either side of the narrow two-lane highway, neon began flickering to life.

Ernie inhaled deeply. "Do you smell it, pal?"

"Smell what?"

"Kimchi fermenting in pots," he replied. "Honey buckets on their way to the field. Brown OB bottles chilling on ice."

"You can't smell cold beer," I said.

"I can," Ernie replied.

He exhaled and we strode into the Sonyu-ri night.

Our first stop was the Red Dragon Nightclub. The sound system was turned up so loud that we could hear the rock and roll from ten yards out. Scantily clad Korean women held the bead curtain parted and waved us in with polished nails. Ernie led the way, forced to duck a little to pass through the curtains. Both he and I were several inches taller than most of the GIs in the room, and a few looked up from their pool game, glancing in our direction. We took seats at the bar.

"You buy me drink?" one of the girls asked Ernie.

He stared at her as if she was out of her mind.

"You Cheap Charley GI?" she asked.

"That's me," Ernie replied. "Cheap Charley to the max."

"Where's your compound?"

"Itaewon," Ernie said.

"You come from Seoul?"

Ernie nodded. There was no point in trying to hide it. Division GIs could spot a GI assigned to 8th Army headquarters in Seoul from ten kilometers away. For one thing, we didn't spend all our time in the field, in the dirt and mud and snow, and we were soft, in their eyes, from all our luxurious rear-echelon living. "Rear-echelon motherfuckers" was what they called us, when they were being kind.

"Why you come Sonyu-ri?" she asked.

That's what these bar girls were, little intelligence-gathering machines. Despite the hot pants and the halter tops that barely covered their bosoms and the heavily made-up faces, they were always gathering data and calculating odds, looking for ways to make money. I didn't blame them. There were no safety nets in Korea. Once a young girl was of age and hadn't made the cut to get into high school, the chances of her finding a job were slim to nonexistent. Her family needed her out of the house. But despite all this, many of these girls still sent money home to help support their parents and brothers and sisters. More than two thousand years ago, Confucius had demanded filial piety. Most of the business girls here at the Red Dragon Nightclub were still listening.

Ernie answered her question with another question.

"What's your name?"

"Cindy," she said.

"Your Korean name?"

"Not your business."

"How much you want for an overnight?"

"Twenty dollars," she said, without hesitation.

Ernie feigned falling off his stool. "Twenty dollars? You think I'm a newbie?" New to Korea.

"No, you rich GI from Seoul. Make lotta money."

"How I make lotta money?"

It went on like that, the banter back and forth, and once the other business girls figured Cindy had Ernie cornered, they turned their attention to me.

I asked the one standing next to me, "The girl last night, did you see her?"

She didn't understand and so the taller girl next to her translated. When she was done, they both turned to me. "What girl?"

"The girl wearing the *hanbok*." Korean clothes. "All red. Did you see her?"

They turned away from me and conferred for a few seconds, whispering, and with the loud rock music I couldn't understand what was being said. But the concerned looks on their faces told me that they weren't completely baffled by my question. Finally the taller one turned to me and said, "We no see."

"Who did see?" I asked.

The shorter girl glanced quickly toward the door, her eyes aiming across the street and about ten yards to the left.

The taller girl shook her head in opposition. She grabbed the shorter girl by the arm and pulled her away. I was left alone at the bar, sipping on my bottle of OB beer. I decided not to finish it. Instead, I elbowed Ernie and we rose to leave the Red Dragon Nightclub. Cindy escorted us to the door and, as we left, instead of saying goodbye, she once again called Ernie a Cheap Charley.

There were two bars across the street, so we tried them both. The first was a dead end, but at the other we found a barmaid willing to talk. She was an older woman, maybe in her mid-thirties, and went by the name of Angela. She spoke English with a voice ravaged by tobacco.

"She run," she said, pointing out the door toward the main drag of Sonyu-ri.

"Running away from someone?" Ernie asked.

"I don't know. Just run. Then she go down alley across the street."

"Toward the river?"

She nodded.

"Where'd she come from?" I asked.

"I no see. But somebody say she at main gate. MP say she gotta *karra chogi*." Go away.

"She was at the front gate of Camp Pelham and the gate guards told her to leave?" I repeated.

The barmaid nodded.

"Why was she running?" Ernie asked.

"I don't know. Maybe somebody chase."

"Who?"

"I don't know. Nobody know."

"Had anyone ever seen her before?"

"No. I no hear."

"And the dress," I said, "the *chima-jeogori*, does anybody in Sonyu-ri wear those kind of dresses?"

"On *chuseok*," she said. Korean Thanksgiving holiday.

"But in the bars," I continued, "or in any of the nightclubs. Do any of the girls normally wear that kind of clothes?"

She shook her head vehemently. "Not in Sonyu-ri. Any GI around here, they like hot pants, miniskirt. Maybe in Munsan. Korean soldier there. Maybe somebody there dress up like *kisaeng*, real nice. But not in Sonyu-ri."

Kisaeng were Korean female entertainers, a group that had faded in relevance since the advent of the profession in ancient Korean kingdoms. While modern *kisaeng* houses were often a front for prostitution, true *kisaeng* were high-class and expensive, not something likely to exist in a low-rent GI village like Sonyu-ri. Munsan was a larger city, about two miles away on the far side of the MSR, and since it was closer to the Imjin River and closer to the Demilitarized Zone, it was surrounded by dozens of ROK Army compounds. But the Lady of the Ice had been carrying a snippet of poetry in her sleeve. In classical times, *kisaeng* were educated women—musicians and performers—and some of the most famous *sijo* poetry had been written by them. I tried to relate all this to the current circumstances, but I didn't get very far. Why would a high-class *kisaeng* wearing only her outer garments be running through the low-rent streets of a GI village?

"So nobody knew her," Ernie said, "or knew why she was running through Sonyu-ri?"

"No. Nobody know."

"And now," he asked, "now that everybody knows she's dead, isn't anyone talking?"

"KNP ask anybody," she said, waving her hand to indicate the entire village of Sonyu-ri. "Nobody see nothing."

"How do you know that?"

"In Sonyu-ri," she said, lighting up another Turtle Boat cigarette, "nobody never see nothing."

I left her a tip—one thousand *won*, about two bucks—and told her how to get in touch with me if she heard anything. The money disappeared.

On the way out, Ernie said, "That was a waste of *won*."

"You don't think she'll ever call?"

"Not a chance in hell."

The MP at the front gate of Camp Pelham was ready for us.

"No, I *don't* talk to rear-echelon motherfuckers, and *no*, I wasn't on duty last night, and no, I didn't see *nothing*."

He stood tall with his hands on his hips, a .45 in a polished black leather holster hanging from his web belt. The embroidered name tag on his fatigue blouse said Austin. His rank insignia was Specialist Four.

"You wanna talk to somebody," he continued, "you head your rear-echelon butts right over there to the head shed and talk to Lieutenant Phillips. He's the officer on duty tonight."

A contract-hire gate guard, a middle-aged Korean man in a khaki uniform, stood behind the MP, his face turned away from us. I spoke to him in Korean.

"Ajjosi, ohjokei ku yoja boasso-yo?" Uncle, did you see that woman last night?

He didn't answer, or even turn his head our way.

The sound of the Korean language seemed to enrage the MP.

"None of that shit!" Specialist Austin held out his palm as if stopping traffic. "No Korean around here. You wanna talk to somebody in the Second Division, you speaky English, you *arra*?" You understand? "You don't talk to my man here."

"Was he on duty last night?" Ernie asked.

"None of your freaking business."

Ernie stepped up close to Specialist Austin. They were nose to nose.

"A woman's dead, Austin. Found almost naked in the frozen

Sonyu River. If you were on duty last night, you talked to her, only minutes before she died."

"I didn't talk to nobody."

Ernie stepped around him, reached into the open window of the guard shack and snatched a clipboard off a nail. Austin shoved him, but before he could get his hands on the clipboard, Ernie tossed it back to me.

I twisted it and held it up to the light of the huge overhead bulb. Quickly, I scanned the dates on the left and found Austin's name and read the name right above it. As he was unsnapping his holster, I tossed the clipboard back to Austin. He caught it on the fly.

"Groverly," I said. "Buck sergeant. He was on duty last night. Where can I find him?"

By this time, Austin had stepped away from Ernie, tossed the clipboard clattering back into the guard shack, and the business end of his .45 appeared in front of him.

"*Back off!*" he screamed. "*Back off or I'll fire, by God!*"

Ernie and I both raised our hands and stepped away from the gate. As we did so, the Korean guard appeared at Austin's side. In the reflected light, I read his brass nameplate.

We backed away into the darkness, Austin still swearing. Once safely around the corner of the nearest building, we trotted away. No sense waiting around to see if he called an MP patrol to come after us. He probably wouldn't though. It would be embarrassing to admit that two unarmed guys from 8th Army had snatched his clipboard away from him. GIs can be relentless in their teasing. Austin probably wouldn't want to give them the opening. We slowed to a brisk walk.

"You got the name?" Ernie said.

"Yeah. And the name of the Korean gate guard."

"What is it?"

"Kim."

"That doesn't narrow it down much."

A third of the country was named Kim. Another third was named Park or Lee.

"No," I said, "but it's a start."

After lying low for a while and downing a couple of shots of soju, Korean rice liquor, we set off through the narrow alley Angela had pointed to, heading for the banks of the Sonyu River.

There were no lights down here, and as we walked single file down the muddy lane we kept our hands on the grease-stained bricks on either side of us. Finally, we emerged onto the runway that paralleled the river. Moonlight reflected off the frozen expanse. To our left, about fifty yards away, the glare of floodlights illuminated the flat bridge leading into Camp Pelham.

"The MPs patrol back here?" Ernie asked.

I shrugged. "That's what the business girls tell me."

"They should know," Ernie said.

We wrapped our coats tighter around our shivering bodies and settled back to wait.

-3-

The MPs emerged from the darkness beneath the bridge.

There were three of them. Black helmets glistened, reflecting rays from the Camp Pelham floodlights.

"No ROK Army," Ernie whispered.

In Seoul, 8th Army always has a Korean MP and an American MP patrol together, usually accompanied by a representative of the Korean National Police. The idea is that whatever miscreant they might come across—be he Korean military, American military, or civilian—one of the cops would have jurisdiction over him. Apparently, here at Division, they didn't worry about such niceties.

As the MPs moved down the far edge of the Sonyu River, Ernie and I stepped back into darkness. About fifteen yards from the bridge, the lead MP stepped into what I first thought was running water, but when his lower leg didn't disappear, I realized that he was following a line of stepping stones. Deftly, the three men lunged and hopped from one stone to another until they were on our side of the waterway. As they approached, they shone their flashlights into the narrow alleys, but having anticipated this, Ernie and I had each stepped into recessed stone doorways on opposite sides of the pathway. Beams of light slithered up the muddy walkway and disappeared as quickly as they'd appeared. Ernie and I emerged from our hiding places and looked out on the banks of the river just in time to see the last MP turn up a lane at the far end of the row of jumbled buildings.

"They're heading for the main drag," Ernie told me. "Come on."

We followed quickly.

I expected them to pause once they reached the bright lights of Sonyu-ri and from there start their patrol of the bars and nightclubs. Instead, they surprised us and continued across the two-lane road. After winding past a few storage sheds, the patrol found a meandering pathway that led through a clump of chestnut trees at the far end of the village. We had less cover here, so Ernie and I proceeded cautiously, letting the MPs gain a lead until they were out of sight. After a steep incline, the pathway emerged onto a plateau. I turned around. Behind us, in the valley below, the neon of Sonyu-ri sparkled. Ahead, scattered across neatly tended lawns, were dozens of egg-shaped hills, each about six feet high.

"Burial mounds," Ernie said.

We wound through them. Many were adorned with stone carvings of ancient patriarchs, some with bronze tablets embedded into mortar. I would've liked to stop and read them, but we didn't have time. At the far end of the plateau, we heard the rushing, gurgling noise of a huge volume of water. Ernie held out his hand. I stopped. Below us rolled the dark, murky waters of the Imjin River. North of here was the Demilitarized Zone and beyond that, Communist North Korea.

"Where are they?" I asked.

Ernie pointed.

In the distance, the beam of a lone flashlight flickered. One by one, moonlight revealed three helmets.

"That pathway," Ernie said. "It leads back toward the village, to the rear of the buildings lining the main drag."

"First they surround Sonyu-ri," I said, "then they invade it."

Ernie shrugged. "They've probably caught GIs smoking pot up here before. An easy bust."

With our Olympian view, we decided not to follow the MPs any longer but to sit back and observe their progress. As we'd expected, it was time to start the exciting part of their evening's activities: patrolling the nightclubs. They started at the RC-4 end of the strip; first a nightclub, then a bar, and after that a teahouse. We knew how it worked. One MP waited out back, cutting off any means of escape, while the other two entered through the front door, checking for drug use or unruly behavior and walking into both the men's and women's *byonso*, the bathrooms, to make sure there was no untoward activity going on in there. Once they were through, they moved on to the next joint.

"Let's go to the main gate," Ernie said. "We'll wait for them there."

I agreed. We scurried downhill, careful to avoid the MP patrol as we made our way toward the front gate of Camp Pelham. We didn't want to confront Specialist Austin again, not yet, so we lingered about a hundred yards from the main gate itself, near the rolling carts that had appeared with the night. They were filled with souvenirs and hot snacks and bottles of soju for the off-duty

GIs parading out of the pedestrian exit after a hard day's work in the 2nd Infantry Division.

One old woman wore a wool scarf and three or four heavy sweaters as she stirred a vat of simmering oil heated by a charcoal briquette. "You eat," she told me as I approached. "Number *hana* French fry." Number one.

"How much for onion rings?" Ernie asked.

"Same same French fry," the old woman said. "Fifty *won*."

"Too much," Ernie replied.

"Big bag," the woman countered, holding a folded paper container about the size of a splayed hand. There was printing on the paper. numbers and letters in English. Probably printouts salvaged from the compound itself and then recycled for a more practical use. There'd been times when top-secret documents had been retrieved, folded neatly, grease-stained, and used to serve four ounces of deep-fried cuttlefish.

Ernie nodded his okay. The old woman reached beneath her cart and pulled out a generous handful of sliced onion. She plopped them into an earthenware bowl thick with batter, then lifted them again and dropped them dripping into the boiling oil. Steam and burning grease sizzled into the air. A few seconds later, using metal chopsticks, the old woman fished the onion rings out of the hot oil and deposited them into the paper holder. Ernie munched on an onion ring to see if it met his approval. When it did, he handed her the money. He offered me an onion ring. I accepted it and asked the old woman if the young girl in the red *chima-jeogori* had bought any of her food last night.

"She no have time," the old woman replied.

Ernie's eyes flashed but he said nothing; just kept chomping on the onion rings.

"You talked to her then?" I said.

"No talk. She talk MP. Crying."

"What'd she say?"

"I don't know. My English not so good."

"Did she come from the ville?"

"I don't know. I busy, sell French fry. I look up, she talk MP. How you say . . ."

"*Hankuk mallo heiju-seiyo,*" I said. Say it in Korean.

Her eyes widened. "Hey, you speaky Korean pretty good."

"She talked to the MP," I prompted in English.

"*Sallam sollyo,*" she say.

"She asked for help?"

"Yes."

"Why?"

The old woman shook her head. "I don't know. She scared something."

"What?"

"I don't know."

"How long did she talk to the MP."

"Maybe one minute. Pretty soon she *karra chogi.*"

"She left. Which way?"

"That way." The old woman pointed along the main drag of Sonyu-ri.

"Did you see where she went?"

"I no see. Do you want French fry now?"

I contemplated buying some just to keep her talking, but Ernie elbowed me in the ribs.

"Company."

The MP patrol was about halfway down the strip, but apparently they'd spotted us. They stopped entering the bars and nightclubs and marched three abreast, heading straight for us. One of them held a walkie-talkie to his ear.

"Should we un-ass the area?" Ernie asked.

"Naw. We have to talk to them anyway. I want to ask some questions."

By now, the old woman had seen the MPs coming and begun to roll her cart toward safer ground. They were still about ten yards away when, from the main gate, a roar arose from the engine of a vehicle whining at full torque. We turned. Specialist Austin raised the vehicle barrier just in time to avoid it being smashed by an MP jeep barreling out of the compound. The vehicle must've been doing thirty miles an hour and was aimed right at us. There was nowhere to run, so Ernie and I stood our ground. At that last second, the driver slammed on the brakes and the vehicle swerved sideways in a cloud of dirt and exhaust, stopping just three feet in front of us. Before the engine stopped whining, a tall MP leapt out of the jeep and charged directly at us.

Discipline in the army is a malleable thing. Sometimes, for example in basic training, it's as inflexible as a Prussian riding crop. Other times, as in a headquarters garrison unit, it can be a set of unwritten rules and gentlemanly agreements, sort of like a country club full of trust-fund babies trying not to annoy one another.

But in the US 2nd Infantry Division, discipline can be brutal. Regardless of the hour, one is expected to appear within minutes of an alert siren being sounded, and if you're not present, you can face court-martial. You're expected to be standing tall before dawn for the physical training formation, and if you're late you can face non-judicial punishment. Enlisted men are restricted to their compounds like prisoners unless an off-duty pass is granted, and that pass can be rescinded for the most minor of infractions—or on a whim. As the NCOs love to say, "A pass is a privilege, not a right." The 2nd Infantry Division officer corps and senior enlisted non-coms can force a young enlisted man to do just about anything—scrub a floor, clean a grease trap, pull guard duty all night—and justify it as either needed to accomplish the mission or, when that rationale grows thin, as additional training that is beneficial for personal development. After a few months, or even just weeks in the heady atmosphere of the 2nd Infantry Division, even a lowly first lieutenant can begin to believe he's a young god gifted with mighty powers.

And it was just such a young god, with an MP helmet on his head, a single silver bar on his lapel and a name tag that said Phillips, who exploded out of the still-sputtering jeep and strode toward us, face aflame, pointing his forefinger at Ernie and then me like an avenging demon, shouting at the top of his lungs.

"*You don't mess with my people!*" With that one shout, his voice was already hoarse. Doggedly, he kept at us. "You don't *mess* with my people! Do you understand me, Troop?"

He was nose to nose with Ernie. Too close. Ernie grimaced but let the silence stretch for a moment. Then he said, "You think you're hot shit, eh, Phillips?"

Phillips leaned in closer. "You will address me as Lieutenant Phillips or *sir*. Is that understood?"

Phillips must've had bad breath. Ernie leaned his head back

slightly but then, without warning, snapped his skull forward and butted the helmet of Lieutenant Phillips, hard. Lieutenant Phillips's head bounced back like a bowling ball and, startled, he took a step backward, instinctively reaching for his .45. The MP patrol closed in, at least one of them unsnapping the leather cover of his holster. Specialist Austin, the MP at the gate, had stepped outside of the guard shack, along with the Korean guard named Kim, and both men were staring at us. All of the food and souvenir vending carts had disappeared. Along the strip, made-up faces craned out of bead-covered doorways. Some of the bar girls were walking forward now, arms crossed, but oblivious to the cold night, craving an exciting show.

Lieutenant Phillips reached for his forehead. "You *hit* me," he said, incredulous.

"No," Ernie replied. "I headbutted you. There's a difference. If I'd hit you, you'd be flat on your ass by now."

One of the MPs reached for my elbow. I shrugged him off. Another MP started to reach for his handcuffs, but Lieutenant Phillips held out his open palm and waved them off. By now, word had spread throughout the nightclub district of Sonyu-ri; bar girls and teahouse dollies and half-drunk GIs were streaming our way like a small parade.

Phillips reached toward the center of his chest, undid one of the buttons on his fatigue blouse and reached inside his shirt. Grinning, he pulled out a sheet of paper.

"Message for you boys," he said. "Straight from the head shed." Without taking his eyes off of Ernie, he handed it to me. It was a strip ripped from a larger roll of teletype paper. A "twixt," the army calls it. A telegraphic transmission.

"I can't read this," I said.

Obligingly, one of the MPs pulled out his flashlight and held it steady for me. I read the message and sighed.

"What is it?" Ernie asked.

Before I could answer, Lieutenant Phillips said, "You CID pukes are hereby ordered back to Seoul, immediately if not sooner. You're off the case. Your services are no longer required. So get the hell out of the Division area." He turned toward the MPs. "You three men, escort these two to their vehicle. No bullshit this time. Make sure they leave Sonyu-ri."

Lieutenant Phillips adjusted his helmet and turned to walk toward his jeep. On the way, he waved his forefinger at Ernie. "Your assault on a superior officer will be noted in my report. And I've got *witnesses*."

He hopped in his jeep, started it up, and backed away in a swirl of burnt gas.

"*Bite me!*" Ernie shouted after him.

One of the MPs snickered. Another stared at him sternly and the offending MP straightened his face.

"Where's your jeep?" one of the MPs asked.

"This is your village," Ernie said. "Don't you know?"

I grabbed Ernie by the elbow and we walked up the MSR away from the village of Sonyu-ri. The MPs watched us. About a hundred yards east of the Camp Pelham gate, on the opposite side of the road, was a small nonappropriated fund compound known locally as *maekju chang-go*. The beer warehouse. It was a transshipment point for the food and beverages used by the Division officer and enlisted club system. The guards were Korean contract hires. Not MPs. I'd tipped them with some PX-purchased cigarettes and they said they'd keep an eye on our jeep, which they did. It was waiting for us just inside their compound near the small guard shack.

"What's the message say?" Ernie asked.

"Nothing much. We're ordered back to Seoul immediately."

"It doesn't say if we're off the case or not?"

"Not specifically."

Ernie started the jeep and we rolled out of the NAF compound, waved to the gate guard who was smoking happily in his shack, and turned west on the two-lane road. We passed the Camp Pelham gate on our left. Austin and gate guard Kim seemed to be hunched down in their shack. The MP patrol had disappeared and the bar girls were back at their stations, standing beneath neon, waving and cooing to potential customers. The village of Sonyu-ri, and the universe, rolled on.

We had almost reached RC-4 when a dark shape darted into the road. Ernie slammed on his brakes.

"What the . . ."

A man stood in front of us, holding both hands out. He was young, Caucasian, about five-foot-eight and extremely thin. He was wearing a collared shirt, brightly colored like something designed to replicate a psychedelic dream. His hair was reddish and curly and worn in a bouffant that was beyond what was allowed by military regulation. He had a scraggly mustache that drooped around the corners of his mouth, and he seemed not to have shaven for a couple of days. When he saw that we'd come to a full stop, he approached Ernie's side of the jeep. Ernie shoved the canvas door open.

"What the hell's the matter with you?"

"I had to stop you," the man said, breathless. His voice was hurried. Green eyes darted from side to side. "He shouldn't have done it," he said.

"Who?" I asked.

It was as if he hadn't heard me.

"She just wanted her freedom, that's all."

"Who are you talking about?" I shouted.

"The red dress," he said, nervously gathering the front of his shirt in his hand and glancing toward the village. "It wasn't even hers. *He* gave it to her. She was forced to wear it."

Ernie switched off the engine and started to get out of the jeep, but the small man was quick. He backed away and darted in front of our headlights. By then I was opening my door, but we were parked next to a line of kimchi cabs, some of them with Munsan license plates, and many of the drivers were standing outside of their cabs, smoking, and watching the little display in front of them.

The man slid deftly between two of the cabs.

"You can talk to us," I shouted. "We'll listen!"

"You were there," he shouted back. "You were almost there!"

And then he disappeared into one of the narrow alleyways.

Ernie and I glanced at one another, coming to an unspoken agreement, and as Ernie padlocked the jeep, I leapt out of the passenger side and gave chase. But there wasn't much lighting in the alleyway, and by the time Ernie had grabbed his flashlight from the jeep and caught up with me, I'd come to a complete stop because I couldn't see a foot in front of me. He switched on the "flash," as Koreans call it, but the narrow pathway in front of us was empty. We followed it five yards back, where it split into three more passageways. We followed one, but it wound through the backs of tightly packed hooches. All we heard was the shouts of mothers berating their kids and pots being clanged and radios blaring the songs of Patti Kim. We returned to where we'd started and checked another passageway but found nothing.

"He knew where he was going," Ernie said, "even in the dark."

"Right. He stopped us at that spot so he could say what he wanted to say and then get away."

We walked back to the jeep. The cab drivers stared at us curiously. In Korean, I asked loudly if anyone had seen that skinny American guy before. Uniformly, they all shrugged. One of the drivers chomped a wad of gum, grinning at us. I asked him specifically if he'd ever seen that American. "*Mullah nan,*" he replied. Don't know, me. The other drivers smiled more broadly, enjoying our discomfort, and enjoying the disrespectful way the driver was speaking to us.

Ernie and I climbed back into the jeep.

We drove off slowly, checking the side of the road, half expecting the skinny guy with the red Afro to appear again at the side of the road. About a mile on we reached the MSR. A sign pointing right said JIAYU TARI, FREEDOM BRIDGE, 2 KM. It led across the Imjin River and on into the Demilitarized Zone. The sign pointing left said SEOUL, 27 KM. Ernie turned left.

As we rolled down the MSR, Ernie said, "Who was that guy anyway? A civilian?"

"I don't know."

"And what was he trying to tell us?"

I tried to remember his exact words. "He said it wasn't right that 'he' had killed her. That she had been forced to wear the red dress she was wearing when we found her."

Ernie nodded. "And that she wanted her freedom. But he said something else."

"He said we'd been close."

"Yeah. I wonder if this means we missed something today."

I gazed out the window. Dark rice paddies rolled by. About fifteen klicks farther south, we rolled to a stop at the last 2nd Division security checkpoint. The American MP checked our dispatch.

When he handed it back, he said, "Been waiting for you guys."

"Why?" Ernie asked.

"I guess somebody's anxious to make sure you depart the area." Apparently, the word had been put out via field radio.

"Well, we did," Ernie snapped.

He gunned the engine as we headed for the distant lights of Seoul. It felt good being away from Division, as if a burden had been lifted from our shoulders. As if we were free.

Seoul was empty, the streets filled with nothing but howling ghosts riding the backs of swirling winds. It was past midnight, during the nationwide midnight-to-four curfew. Nothing moved during these hours. No vehicular traffic, no pedestrians. And if you were by some circumstance on the street, you were not only subject to arrest and prosecution but, more importantly, if you didn't halt when a soldier or curfew policeman told you to halt, you were subject to being shot on sight. The supposed reason for such draconian measures was to stop any infiltration into the country by North Korean Communist agents. That's what the ROK government told the world. But I believed the real reason was because the military government of President Pak Chung-hee wanted to demonstrate its iron-fisted control over the general populace—and to make it clear, on a nightly basis, that no dissent would be tolerated.

We passed through Seoul and reached Yongsan Compound on the southern edge of the city. The Korean gate guard checked our dispatch. It was an 8th Army Criminal Investigation Division emergency dispatch and, as such, we were amongst the elect who were authorized to be out during curfew hours. He waved us through.

The barracks were dark and quiet, but as I walked down the long hallway I heard someone talking in a deep baritone voice. When I opened my door I realized what it was. My roommate, Ricky Harrison, had left his stereo system on full blast. It was an inspirational speech by Martin Luther King, Jr. I closed the door behind me, walked through the small room, and switched off the stereo set. Harrison didn't move. He was sound asleep.

What a lullaby.

I took off my clothes and climbed into my rack. The sheets were crisp and clean because my houseboy, Mr. Yim, was paid to keep them that way; along with doing my laundry and shining my shoes and performing additional errands like taking my clothes in for alteration or having unit patches sewn on, all of which I paid him extra for. As I leaned back and relaxed, I thought that life for a GI in 8th Army wasn't bad, unless you were on night patrol along the DMZ. Before I could contemplate that difference, exhaustion overtook me.

■   ■   ■

"Where the hell you guys been?"

Staff Sergeant Riley hunched over his desk, a sharpened pencil behind his ear, the padded shoulders of his green dress uniform sticking out from his rail-thin body like the wings of Icarus. In the back of the office, a stainless-steel coffee urn pumped steady blasts of fragrant steam.

Ernie plopped down in the chair in front of Riley's desk and grabbed the morning edition of the *Pacific Stars and Stripes*. As he snapped it open, he said, "We got your twixt, we came back."

Riley pulled the pencil from behind his ear. "I sent it at fifteen hundred hours. You shoulda been back here by close of business."

"Are you nuts?" Ernie asked. "We would've never made it through the Seoul traffic."

"Besides," I added, heading for the coffee urn, "we didn't receive it until that night."

"Why the hell not?"

Ernie slammed the paper down. "Because we were out in the ville doing our jobs and not sitting on our asses inside the MP station, like some other investigators around here do."

Riley jabbed his pencil toward Ernie's nose. "Some other investigators around here know how to follow the provost marshal's orders."

"And they know how to brownnose."

Riley shoved his pencil back behind his ear and stared down at the stack of paperwork in front of him. "There's that," he said.

As I walked toward the coffee urn, Riley shouted at me, "It's not done yet."

"Close enough for field soldiers," I said and drew myself a mug.

Riley grunted. "Some field soldiers."

I sipped on the coffee. He was right; lukewarm and insipid. Still, I didn't want to let him know he'd been right, so I drank it down.

Miss Kim, the statuesque admin secretary, busied herself checking a list and pulling files out of grey metal cabinets. When she had what she wanted, she returned to her desk and sat down in front of her *hangul* typewriter. I set my coffee down and approached her.

"*Anyonghaseiyo?*" I said.

She smiled, nodded and said, "*Nei. Anyonghaseiyo.*"

She wore her hair short and businesslike, just below her ears. Her heart-shaped face was pale and unblemished, and her figure was well-respected enough that MPs occasionally made excuses to come into the CID office just to ogle her. It was difficult for her because she was shy and the attention embarrassed her. On her way to work, she usually scurried from the main gate to the office and seldom ventured outside during the duty day; too many foreign eyeballs caressing her. She and Ernie had been an item for a few months, but when she found out his affections weren't directed toward her exclusively, she dropped him flat. The fact that they still worked together didn't seem to bother Ernie. When I brought it up, he didn't understand what I was getting at. But Miss Kim was tormented by the almost daily proximity; I could tell by the way she glanced at him furtively, her face turning red as she did so, and the fact that she always found something to do as far away from him as possible. Still, she couldn't quit her job. In the early seventies, the Korean economy was still flat on its back from the devastation of the Korean War, and employment opportunities for a young woman were few and far between.

I tried to be friendly to her. Not pushy. I even occasionally left her a small gift, like hand lotion from the PX or a jar of instant coffee, which I knew her mother liked. I'd never asked her out, and I believed she appreciated that too.

Riley treated Miss Kim with indifference. She was just a working colleague to him. Prim and proper wasn't his style. He liked 'em raunchy and drunk. Where he found his girlfriends I wasn't quite sure since he worked long hours, but find them he did. I'd get my first hint of a new Riley girlfriend by seeing her scurrying from the men's latrine to Riley's room at about two in the morning. He would hide her there, in the barracks, along with a bottle of Old Overwart. That's all he needed to attain nirvana. At least temporary nirvana, until morning came and the hangover kicked in.

But he was a workhorse, Staff Sergeant Riley was. He kept the office running, even if he was a constant thorn in Ernie's—and my—side. He completely identified with the provost marshal and with the United States Army. To him, their pronouncements were the revealed word of God, and 8th Army regulations were holy scripture. Ernie and I, he was certain, were apostates and thereby destined for military hell. To us, 8th Army was self-serving and run by careerists who only wanted to safeguard their own paths to promotion. Of course, we usually didn't say that to Riley. There was no point. We wouldn't change his mind, and besides, sometimes we needed him.

Like right now.

"Who's Lieutenant Phillips?" Riley asked.

Ernie turned the page of the newspaper. "Some asshole from Division," he said.

"Well," Riley said, "it looks like this asshole from Division has made a formal complaint. Says you assaulted him in front of witnesses."

"If I'd 'assaulted' him," Ernie said, "he wouldn't have been able to make a complaint."

"He says you headbutted him in front of the main gate of Camp Pelham."

"He headbutted me," Ernie said.

Riley glanced at me. "Which was it?"

I strode away from Miss Kim's desk back toward the coffee urn that had stopped brewing. "Like Ernie says," I replied, "Lieutenant Phillips headbutted him."

Riley wrote some notes that I knew would be relayed to Colonel Brace, the 8th Army provost marshal. "You're gonna have to sign a statement," he said, "both of you."

"Write it up," Ernie said, still studying his paper.

"Second Division pukes," Riley said, muttering beneath his breath. Then he said, "Zero nine hundred. Mandatory formation in the JAG conference room. Be there."

"Bite me," Ernie said.

"*Mandatory,*" Riley said, glaring at him. His favorite word.

-4-

"Attention to orders!"

All the JAG officers and the clerks and the MPs and the Criminal Investigation agents stopped their milling about and snapped to attention. Colonel Walter P. Brace, the 8th Army provost marshal, stood at the front of the judge advocate general's conference room, and next to him were two of our fellow CID agents, Jake Burrows and Felix Slabem. Margaret Mendelson, a female second lieutenant, read the citation, mimicking perfectly the slow drawl of 8th Army officialese. I'd seen her before, a new JAG officer. She had long, reddish-brown hair that she tied atop her head when she was in uniform. She wore the knee-length skirt and tight green jacket of the US Army female dress-green uniform and most of the men in the room were happy to watch her rather than the Sad Sacks who were being honored.

Burrows and Slabem were brownnosers from the word go. Everybody knew it, but their career strategies seemed to be paying off. What they'd done was spend the last three months auditing 8th Army's Non-Appropriated Fund activities—NAF, for short—in a comprehensive review required by an act of Congress every ten years. They'd looked at the records covering the post exchange, the commissary, the Central Locker Fund, the Defense Youth Activities center, and both the 8th Army officers' club and the half-dozen or so NCO and enlisted clubs.

"Mainly they audited the steam and cream," Ernie whispered to me. He was referring to the on-base massage parlors also run by Non-Appropriated Funds, but he said it loud enough for a few frowning faces to turn and glare at us.

The DPCA, the Director of Personnel and Community Activities, stepped up to present the award: the Meritorious Service Medal. Not bad for a couple of junior enlisted men. Although as CID agents our ranks were technically classified, everyone knew that both Burrows and Slabem were staff sergeants, the same rank as Ernie. But Burrows and Slabem had been slated for promotion to sergeants first class, something that pissed Ernie off royally.

"All they do is shuffle paper," Ernie'd told me, "and make sure they get the results the honchos want."

And in their review of what amounted to hundreds of thousands of dollars' worth of NAF activity, the only anomaly Agents Jake Burrows and Felix Slabem had found was the misappropriation of the football pool by one of the part-time bartenders at the officers' club. The total dollar value of which was less than seventy-four dollars.

"For this they get an award?" Ernie asked.

I elbowed him to shut up. Reluctantly, he did, scowling around the room as if he wanted to choose somebody to pop in the nose. Lieutenant Mendelson's voice droned on. When she was done, the DPCA pinned the medals first on Jake Burrows and then on

Felix Slabem. Then he shook their hands. When the ceremony was over, most of the attendees stood in line to congratulate the two honorees. We didn't. I caught Riley outside and told him what I needed.

"A civilian?" he asked.

"I think so." I described the guy to him. About five-foot-eight or nine, one hundred and thirty-five pounds, reddish hair that he wore in some sort of Afro bouffant.

"How long?"

"How long ago did we see him?"

"No. How long was his hair?"

"Only a couple of inches."

"But too long for him to be military."

"Right."

"So maybe he's a DAC." A Department of the Army Civilian.

"Right. Or maybe he's not affiliated with the military at all."

"Then what would he be doing up in the Division area?"

"I don't know. That's what I want to ask him."

The few civilians who ventured to South Korea on business stayed mainly in Seoul or the other large cities. They seldom ventured toward the DMZ. Especially since the North Korean Commando raid on the presidential palace a few years ago and the taking of the USS Pueblo crew. And tourism to the Republic of Korea was almost nonexistent. Too many people around the world still remembered the newspaper photos that depicted the death and suffering during the Korean War and the millions of refugees. Nobody thought of the ROK as a fabulous vacation spot.

Riley thought it over. "I'll check with Smitty over at data processing. And there's another possibility."

"What's that?"

"I'll get you a list of deserters."

"We still have deserters at Eighth Army?"

"Not many, but a few."

The reason there were few deserters, if any, from the 8th United States Army was not because of an excess of loyalty but because of border checks. There was only one international airport, at Kimpo near Seoul, and everyone going out or coming in was checked and rechecked by the paranoid Korean officialdom. You couldn't just go and buy a ticket to fly back to the States. Before you boarded a plane, you'd have to prove who you were and what you'd been doing in Korea. And the one seaborne international departure port at Pusan was watched just as carefully. Since Korea is a peninsula, you can leave by sea or by air, but leaving by land is even more restricted. If you traveled north, you would run into the Demilitarized Zone bordering Communist North Korea. There were 700,000 Communist soldiers on the northern side, 450,000 ROK Army soldiers on the southern side, and tens of thousands of land mines in between. Try walking across that.

So if you deserted from 8th Army, you were stuck in Korea.

"So you'll check for me?"

Riley promised he would. Then he thrust his right thumb over his shoulder. "The provost marshal wants to see you two. *Now.*"

I turned to Ernie. "I told you not to mouth off during the ceremony."

"It's not about that."

"What is it, then?"

"You'll find out." Riley stormed off.

We found Colonel Brace outside the conference room, still

conferring with the DPCA. When they were finished, he turned to us, crooked his finger, and said, "You two, follow me."

Ernie and I followed him down a long, carpeted hallway. Ernie chomped on his gum as if he didn't have a care in the world. Me, I was bothered by the crooked finger. In Korea, it's an insult to beckon someone like that. The polite way is the wave downward with your flat palm. I told myself that Colonel Brace didn't know the Korean custom, that I was becoming too immersed in Korean culture and that I should forget it. Still, it bothered me. We stepped into a small office. Lieutenant Mendelson, the young woman who'd read the award citation, rose from behind a small mahogany desk.

"You've met?" Colonel Brace asked us.

"Once," I said. It was when she'd come through the office as part of a JAG conference with the colonel.

Ernie didn't answer, just stared at her, chomping his gum.

"You'll be working with her," Colonel Brace told us, "on a case that's about to go to court-martial. I'll let her brief you."

He started to walk out of the room.

"Sir," I said, "I thought we're assigned to the case up at Sonyu-ri, working with Inspector Gil."

He stopped and turned and studied me and then Ernie.

"Yes," he said, "you still are. As it happens, the case Lieutenant Mendelson is working on happened right up in the same area. You'll be assigned to both at the same time."

A murder case *and* something else? Ernie's face twisted, probably in reaction to our time being wasted by being called back to Seoul in the first place, but I spoke before he could open his mouth. "We'll need an advance on our expense account, sir."

"Yes, of course, see Riley."

He burst out of the room as if happy to get away from us.

Ernie frowned. "Why didn't you ask for an increase?"

"Didn't think of it."

Ernie gazed down the hallway wistfully. "That's why he was in such a hurry to un-ass the area. Thinks he's getting over on us."

Lieutenant Mendelson coughed.

Ernie turned, as if noticing her for the first time. "Something wrong with your throat?"

"No," she said, "I'm fine."

"You a smoker?"

"No."

"That's good," Ernie said, sitting on a padded vinyl chair. "I hate smokers. Their mouths smell like ashtrays." He steepled his fingers in front of his nose and studied her. "What is it you want us to do?"

"Agent Sueño," she said, motioning with her hand. "Sit down." When I hesitated, she said, "Please."

Nice of her. So I did.

Lieutenant Mendelson explained the case and the information she wanted us to gather. I'd heard about the incident, but not in any detail. It sounded ugly and sordid. A black soldier in Charley Battery, 2nd of the 17th Field Artillery, had shot a white senior NCO—the chief of Firing Battery, commonly referred to as the "chief of smoke." The wound had been serious but not life threatening, and the victim had been transferred to the 121st Evacuation Hospital in Seoul. The accused perp was a young soldier by the name of Clifton Threats, rank of private first class. He was being charged with attempted murder and violation of the Civil Rights Act, since the murder was seen to be racially motivated.

"I thought that case was wrapped up," Ernie said, "witnesses and everything."

"It should be," Lieutenant Mendelson said, "but the officer appointed to defend him is claiming self-defense because the chief of smoke had been discriminating against Threets and assaulting him on a regular basis."

"In the Second Division?" Ernie said, raising his eyebrows. "I'm shocked."

Lieutenant Mendelson studied him, still trying to figure him out. Her eyes sparkled as she did so. Regaining control, she fell back on her paperwork. "Here's the report," she said, shoving it across the desk. "Read it and ask some questions while you're up there, about this alleged harassment."

I picked it up. "Has the Division provost marshal been informed?"

"Yes. And since it's coming down from the Eighth Army head shed, you'll have full access to all Division facilities. Colonel Brace is looking out for you. That way, you can work on the other case without being harassed by Division."

Ernie snorted a laugh. "That'll be the day," he said.

"What do you mean?"

"When he's 'looking out for us.'"

"Well, he is." She seemed shocked by our attitude. But she was young, a new officer, and thus far in her military career she probably had always been treated well. Most often, newly minted lieutenants had no inkling of the abuse that enlisted men could sometimes be subjected to. I saw no point in going there.

"Anything else, Lieutenant?" I asked.

"No, that will be all." Then she smiled. "And please call me Peggy."

I nodded. "Peggy it is," I said.

Ernie saluted her with two fingers.

She started to raise her hand to return the salute but then thought better of it.

Outside, I tried to hand the report to Ernie. "Don't palm that off on me," he said.

"The colonel's trying to help us," I said.

"Fat chance."

"You're too cynical."

"No, I'm not. There's something behind this."

"Maybe."

"No maybe about it."

"Should we ask Riley?"

"Forget it," Ernie said. "If Riley knows anything, which he probably doesn't, he'll be in on it too."

"Anyway," I said, "we have to get back to Division."

While at the CID office I'd made a call to Mr. Kill's office in downtown Seoul. He wasn't in, but a message had been relayed that he wanted to meet us at the Munsan police station at noon.

"We can make it if we hurry."

"We'll make it," Ernie told me. "But first we have to talk to Strange, get him to do some research for us."

Ernie unlocked the padlock of his jeep and I climbed into the passenger seat. "Strange? Why Strange?"

"Colonel Brace is helping us work with the KNPs on a case that could prove embarrassing to Eighth Army. Smoothing the skids for us up at Division." He shook his head. "That's just not how things work. Something's wrong."

"What makes you think Strange can find out anything?"

"He's a pervert. He knows everybody in Eighth Army and everybody knows him. Besides, he's in charge of Classified Documents. All he has to do is lift up the cover sheet and peek."

A pervert in charge of secrets. It made perfect sense when you thought about it.

We went to find Strange.

The Munsan police station was an impressive building for such a small town. Like other Korean National Police stations, it was constructed of sturdy cement block and the flag of the Republic of Korea—a red and blue yin-yang symbol centered on a background of pure white—fluttered from a pole on the roof. What differentiated it was the square footage out back. It was two or three times larger than most police stations, probably because of its proximity to the Freedom Bridge and, a few miles beyond that, the truce village of Panmunjom, where representatives from the two opposing governments in the Korean War and their respective allies met regularly for talks. Along the DMZ in recent years, North Korean commandos had machine-gunned American GIs standing in chow lines and even blown up a barracks on an American compound. The South Koreans suffered even greater casualties, with over a hundred dead in one particularly bad year. In this area, crisis could erupt at any moment, making a large police presence necessary.

Ernie and I pushed through the metal-reinforced front door.

A young cop in a khaki uniform rose to his feet and shouted a formal greeting. Behind a low railing, Ernie and I stood for a moment. The room smelled of fermented cabbage and cheap Korean tobacco. A sad-looking elderly couple sat on a bench, looking as if they'd been waiting there since they were young. A slightly older police officer, a lieutenant, emerged from a back office and, as if he was expecting us, motioned for us to follow. As we marched down a cement hallway, he said in halting English, "Inspector Gil soon be here." He ushered us into a small conference room with eight straight-backed chairs arrayed around a rectangular wooden table.

"Please, sit," he said.

After he left the room, I sat. Ernie paced.

Two minutes later, a young woman in KNP uniform entered holding a stainless-steel tray. On it was a metal pot of hot water and four porcelain mugs. She set the tray in front of us, and without ever looking directly at us, bowed and backed out of the room.

"She likes you," Ernie said. "I can tell."

The tray held a few Lipton tea bags and a small jar of Folgers freeze-dried coffee. The water was steaming. I poured myself a cup and used a tin spoon to stir in the coffee. Ernie followed suit, stirring some sugar into his.

We sipped and waited, but not for long. Before I finished my coffee, Inspector Gil Kwon-up, Mr. Kill, barged into the room.

"I found him," he said.

"Found who?"

"Come, I'll show you."

We set our mugs down and followed Mr. Kill out of the room. Outside, he motioned to his right. "It's not far. We can walk."

We passed wood-planked storefronts with *hangul* writing that said things like GRAIN STORAGE and AGRICULTURAL IMPLE-MENTS and SEASONAL LOANS. On the other side of town, I knew, were about a million eateries and *makkoli* houses, purveyors of rice wine, catering to the needs of the thousands of ROK soldiers stationed in the military compounds dotting the hills along the Imjin River. There were even a few *kisaeng* houses for the officers. But we were in the more utilitarian part of town.

A half-mile on, Mr. Kill turned left into a narrow pedestrian pathway. It was muddy and just wide enough for us to walk single file, occasionally dodging old women with huge bundles of laundry balanced atop their heads. Inspector Gil pulled a sheet of paper out of his jacket pocket. He showed it to me: *113 bonji, 47 ho*. An address. The walls on either side of the walkway were made of brick and cement block and occasionally wood. Every few feet, rotted panels in recessed gates were slashed with numbers in various styles of handwriting and various shades of paint. The Korean address system makes sense. *Bonji* is the neighborhood and *ho* is the number, but sometimes the sequence is off due to the constant tearing down and building up of new residences. We found number 46 and number 48, but no 47 *ho*. Mr. Kill asked a middle-aged woman stepping carefully through the mud if she could direct him to number 47. She pointed toward a narrow alley. It was there, in the darkness, about twelve feet in.

Mr. Kill stepped up to the gate and pounded on grease-stained planks. Nothing happened. He pounded again. Finally, from within, a woman's voice said, *"Nugu-seiyo?"* Who is it?

"Kyongchal," Mr. Kill answered. Police.

Urgent whispering. Cautious footsteps. Finally, the gate creaked open. Mr. Kill ducked inside. Ernie and I followed.

The courtyard was much like the pathway outside, composed of moist dirt. But there was an iron pump in the center surrounded by a circle of rocks. Beyond that was a low porch fronting a row of oil-papered sliding doors. In front of an open door sat a man in a khaki uniform, just reaching down to slip on a highly polished pair of black combat boots. As we walked across the courtyard, he looked up at us. I recognized him. Kim. The Korean contract gate guard who we'd seen in front of Camp Pelham working with the MP known as Specialist Four Austin.

Mr. Kill greeted him politely, bowing slightly. Then he pulled out his badge and told him in Korean that we had a few questions. The man nodded. I noticed he had bags under his eyes and he looked tired; the kind of fatigue that comes not from losing a night's sleep, but from four or five decades spent clinging to the lowest rungs on the economic ladder in a country ravaged by a brutal, endemic poverty. The woman who I assumed to be his wife scurried about her business, splashing water into a pail and sloshing it on the cement floor of the walk-in *byonso*.

Mr. Kill spoke in rapid Korean, getting to the point without any nonsense or preamble. I followed most of it. The gate guard nodded occasionally, shook his head at other times, and finally spoke in a slow, gravelly voice. Ernie waited near the gate, hands in his pockets.

When we were done, Mr. Kill thanked the man, turned, and started to step toward the gate.

As he did so, the gate guard spoke again. *"Chotto matte."*

Mr. Kill stopped and turned. It was Japanese, but even I knew what it meant. Wait a moment. Until 1945, while Korea had been colonized, Japanese had been the official language of the country. Older people had learned it in school when they were young. These days—and even then—it was the hated language of occupation. In my months and years here in Korea, I couldn't remember ever having heard it spoken. Even Mr. Kill seemed surprised.

Gate guard Kim continued to speak in Japanese to Mr. Kill. He knew from our first encounter that I could speak Korean and didn't want me to understand. Mr. Kill frowned as he listened. Finally, the gate guard stopped talking, and without acknowledging him further, Mr. Kill turned and ducked through the small opening in the gate.

Ernie glanced at me, raising one eyebrow. He knew something strange had happened. We followed Kill outside to the muddy lane.

When we reached the main road, Mr. Kill slowed enough for me to catch up.

"Did you understand," he asked me, "the Korean part?"

"Most of it."

It had been a routine set of denials. The gate guard said he didn't know who the woman in the red dress was, he didn't know where she'd come from or how she'd gotten there, and when she asked the American MP for help he'd told her to get lost. He claimed the woman spoke to the MP in broken English but she hadn't spoken to him at all.

"But then," I said, "gate guard Kim spoke Japanese to you."

"Yes." Mr. Kill's mouth was lined with anger.

"What did he say?" I ventured.

"He said that the woman claimed that someone was after her."

"An American?"

"She didn't say. She was hysterical. Not giving much coherent information, just glancing back over her shoulder and begging the American MP for help."

"That was it?"

"Then he went on, using Japanese, a language I don't like listening to very much. He said that it didn't matter what these whores did for their foreigners. If they ended up dead, it was better for us, because then Korea would be purified."

"He said that?"

"Yes. And he said he applauded the man who killed her. He only regretted that her body had been left in the Sonyu River."

"Why?"

"According to him, she defiled the water."

Ernie and I slurped our noodles, using both a flat spoon and chopsticks. Mr. Kill had already finished his bowl and leaned back contentedly, staring at the sea of short black haircuts surrounding us.

We were in a busy chophouse with picnic-like tables and movable two- or three-man benches. The place was packed with Korean soldiers in dark-green fatigues, all of them with their hats pulled off because they were indoors and most of them shouting and gesticulating at one another, laughing and enjoying their food and the raucous company. The place was as noisy as a Cape Canaveral launch pad.

There were no menus, only large hand-printed signs papered to the wall: *bibimbap, mae-un tang, naengmyeon,* and *dubu jjigae baekban,* amongst other delights. Sturdy waitresses wearing long cotton aprons and with their hair tied severely in white bandannas plowed through the crowd with huge, round trays laden with steaming metal bowls and plastic plates of cabbage and turnip kimchi. No elegant china in this place. When the boys blocked their way or got too grabby, fat female elbows jabbed callused knuckles and muscled ribs.

Mr. Kill pulled a sheet of paper out of his pocket, smoothed it on the rough wooden surface, and started to talk. He almost had to shout to be heard, which is why I think he chose this place, so no one could eavesdrop. I finished my noodles and shoved the bowl aside. Ernie did the same.

Bearing a huge brass pot, one of the waitresses leaned over our table and sloshed warm barley tea into thick porcelain cups. Mr. Kill barely jerked the paper away in time. Like the goddess of all floods, the waitress ignored his discomfort and, as fast as she'd come, she was gone.

"This is what was in her sleeve," Kill told us.

"The woman in the red dress?" Ernie asked.

"Yes," Mr. Kill replied. "Precisely. In traditional Korean dresses, there are interior pockets hidden inside the long sleeves. Remember that snippet of paper we found?"

I nodded.

"It had calligraphy on it," Mr. Kill continued. "I thought I recognized it at first, but I wanted to be sure, so we had it analyzed."

He slid the paper toward me. It was three lines of neatly printed *hangul*.

"Of course what she had was just a portion of this poem. The first five words, to be exact, written in ink, we think with a horsehair brush. But I recognized it from the beginning. It's the first five words of a work done in the ancient *sijo* style, probably the most famous poem in the Korean language.

"Hwang Ji-ni," I said.

Mr. Kill sat back, eyes popping wide. "You know it?"

"I know of it. I read the poem in English translation once in one of my textbooks."

"You would," Ernie said, disgusted. "Read, read, read. That's all you ever do." He grabbed a mug of tea and slurped loudly. "Okay," he went on, "so she liked poetry. So what?"

Mr. Kill ignored him. "The poem was hand copied, not with a pencil or a ballpoint pen but with a traditional writing implement. We found a single strand of hair clinging to the paper. It turned out to be horsehair."

"Horsehair?" Ernie glanced at me, then at Mr. Kill.

"That's the traditional way to make Chinese writing brushes," I told him. "Nobody makes 'em that way anymore. The few companies that do make old-fashioned writing brushes use synthetic materials."

"Maybe it's too hard to catch the horse," Ernie said.

"Except for one place that still makes them in the traditional manner," Mr. Kill said. "Red China."

"So she's a Commie spy?" Ernie asked.

"No. I doubt that. All imports from Communist countries are banned here in the Republic of Korea. Still, there are a few things people covet. Chinese ink, the inkstone, the horsehair brush—these are examples. Those who follow the ancient art of calligraphy believe that the synthetic substitutes are unworthy of their erudition."

"So some are smuggled in?" Ernie said.

"Precisely. Mostly from Hong Kong or Japan."

"They allow the import of goods from Red China?"

"Yes. Unfortunately."

"So this gal liked poetry," Ernie said, "and she used a contraband brush to write it down. So what?"

"Not your typical GI business girl," I said.

Ernie thought about that. "No. Most of them don't get past the sixth grade. But maybe she didn't write it. Maybe somebody else did."

"Maybe."

We sat in silence for a moment. Apparently, chow time was over, because the Korean soldiers rose from their benches in groups and started to depart. Many of them shot us curious glances as they passed, but they were polite. I didn't hear one soldier use the phrase *kocheingi*. Big nose.

Then I thought of something. "What about the paper?" I asked.

Mr. Kill smiled broadly. "I thought you'd never ask. Yes, that's an important clue. The paper the poetry was written on is imported also, handmade from the bark of the mulberry tree. Not manufactured here in Korea or anywhere else that I know of, other than Red China."

"If they're such dedicated Communists and modern and stuff," Ernie asked, "why do they still make these things?"

"Foreign exchange," Mr. Kill replied. "There's a huge demand in Singapore, Taiwan, Japan, and other countries with enclaves of Chinese culture."

"So they're anxious to make a buck." Ernie nodded. "But as far as we know, that red dress and the paper in the sleeve didn't even belong to the dead woman. Maybe she just grabbed them and ran, not knowing about the poetry or the mulberry leaves or any of that crap."

"Maybe," Kill said. "Probably even, since she had been in such a rush. But still, it tells us something. Whoever she's associating with had gone to a lot of trouble and a lot of expense to buy contraband Chinese writing implements."

"You can track those," I said.

Mr. Kill nodded. "We're working on it now."

"Doesn't sound like a GI," Ernie said.

"No, it doesn't," Mr. Kill answered. "But then what was this young woman doing way up here near the DMZ, running through a GI village right outside of an American compound, speaking broken English, pleading with an American MP to save her life?"

The question hung in the air. None of us had any answers.

A different MP and a different Korean contract guard manned the front gate of Camp Pelham. I didn't ask about gate guard Kim because I figured he'd been reassigned to either one of the back gates or, worse, perimeter patrol. The MP stared at our badges stoically and then called the Camp Pelham MP station. After a few mumbled words, he waved us through the gate. Apparently, the 8th Army provost marshal's directive to cooperate was working, at least so far.

We'd been here before, to the battalion headquarters, but we bypassed that single-story complex and kept walking down the narrow blacktop road. Green Quonset huts lined either side of the road, interspersed with whitewashed signs sporting black stenciled lettering: BATTALION AMMO POINT; ALPHA BATTERY, 2/17TH FA; BRAVO BATTERY; and finally CHARLEY BATTERY, 2ND

OF THE 17TH FIELD ARTILLERY. Without knocking, we pushed through the double swinging doors of the orderly room.

A first sergeant was waiting for us. He didn't stand up. "You're here about Threets," he said, pulling a half-smoked stogie out of his mouth.

"We're here about the shooting," I said.

"Yeah. Same same. You'll want to talk to the CO and the executive officer. They're both out. Don't know when they'll be back." He had a smug smile on his face, as if we'd just been checkmated.

"What makes you think we want to talk to them?" Ernie asked.

The first sergeant's eyes narrowed. He was a husky man, muscle bulging out of a neatly pressed but faded fatigue blouse. His name tag said Bolton. "Because they're in charge," he said in a low, menacing tone, daring us to contradict him.

"I know who we want to talk to," Ernie replied, "and it ain't no freaking officers."

First Sergeant Bolton stood, placing the remnants of his cigar gently into a glass ashtray. "No one talks to the men until the CO says so."

"Bull," Ernie replied. He turned and together we walked out of the orderly room. Off to the left was a small billeting area, probably for the NCOs. In front of us, across the narrow street, were two large Quonset huts linked together by a cement-block building with steam rising from aluminum vents. Two enlisted barracks with a latrine wedged in the middle. The same setup we'd seen in camp after camp throughout the Korean peninsula.

We walked across the street. Neither First Sergeant Bolton nor anyone else bothered to follow us.

On the door of the barracks, a rectangular sign hung from a

single remaining nail. I had to twist my head to read it: OFF LIMITS EXCEPT TO AUTHORIZED PERSONNEL. Ernie pushed through into the Quonset hut. The lights were dim in here. A couple of GIs sat near a window, cleaning their M16 rifles.

"Where is everybody?" Ernie asked.

One of them shrugged. The other GI spoke up. "At the motor pool, mostly," he said.

In the back, past the exit to the latrine, stood a line of wall lockers, as if the Quonset had been partitioned. Low mumbles escaped from behind the line of grey lockers. Ernie walked past a row of bunks. At the end, on the far side of the lockers, a group of GIs in fatigue uniform lurked in the darkness. Some of them standing, two sitting. All of them were soul brothers, black soldiers. Ernie used a hand signal to let me know he'd take over from here.

"What's happening?" he asked, ignoring the fact that no one answered. He walked past the row of wall lockers and took a seat on one of the square foot lockers at the end of a bunk, pulling something from his front pocket as he did so. Then he was mumbling, using the same tone the GIs had been using. They stared at him, hostile at first, and then I saw curiosity overtake their stares. Ernie kept talking, holding something between his fingers, fiddling with it. One of the GIs smiled. Another mumbled back.

When I left, Ernie was still mumbling. I thought I knew what he was doing, and if I was right, I didn't want to know any more about it. I hurried out of the building. First Sergeant Bolton was waiting for me in the company street, arms crossed, felt cap pulled low across his forehead.

"I thought I told you not to talk to our troops."

I was worried about what Ernie was doing in the barracks, so I decided to stall. Instead of telling him to drop dead, I pulled out my badge and patiently explained to him that, when on a case, the Criminal Investigation Division doesn't require the permission of superior officers to speak to potential witnesses.

"None of these guys witnessed *nothing*," he said.

"They were on the range, weren't they?"

"Yeah, but it happened so fast. Threats swiveled, fired his rifle, and the chief of smoke went down. These guys didn't see *nothing*."

"But *you* saw something," I said.

Bolton's face flushed red. "I didn't see *nothing*."

With that, he stormed past me into the barracks. The two GIs I'd seen earlier were still cleaning their weapons. In back, behind the row of wall lockers, Ernie and the black GIs had disappeared. Apparently, in a puff of smoke.

The MP barracks sat off by itself, on the far side of a circle of reinforced gun emplacements. The bunks were lined up in a similar fashion, but the wall lockers were evenly spaced. No partitions here. A couple of MPs were asleep, with pillows pulled over their heads, probably night-shift workers. Others were flopping around in white boxer shorts and rubber sandals, heading back and forth to the latrine. They looked at me curiously.

"Groverly," I said to one of them. He glanced upstairs, toward the front of the huge Quonset hut. I hurried up the wooden stairway, figuring I didn't have much time. Groverly was awake, sitting on the edge of his bunk, dressed in a crisp pair of fatigues, lacing up a pair of spit-shined jump boots. I recognized him from his rank insignia, buck sergeant, and his embroidered name tag.

"Swing shift?" I asked.

Slowly, he looked up at me.

"You're the CID guy?"

"That's me." I smiled.

"You're not supposed to be talking to me."

"That's a matter of opinion."

"It's a matter of orders."

"The orders don't override a murder investigation." I stared at his eyes as I spoke. They were green, his face was long, soft, almost girlish, but there was a steel to his countenance, and I understood why this guy was an MP in a combat unit. He was tough. He'd be able to hold his own. I spoke quickly, knowing I might only have a few seconds to convince him to cooperate.

"She was murdered," I said, "probably held down face-first in the freezing water and the mud. She didn't have a chance. The worst part is she saw it coming. She knew somebody was after her and she knew they were about to catch her. After talking to you she ran to the ville, to the nightclubs, asking mama-sans for help. Nobody wanted anything to do with her. She was trouble, she was a crazy woman. Then a woman heard her in one of the alleys heading toward the Sonyu River. He must've caught up with her there. They argued, she struggled, then she was gone." I reached into my coat pocket and pulled out the black-and-white photograph Mr. Kill had provided. "This is how she ended up."

I handed the photo to him. Gingerly, he took it in his hands and studied it.

After a pause, he said, "This is her?"

"She looks different," I said, "from when you talked to her?"

Sergeant Groverly nodded. "Different," he said.

"No one's blaming you," I said. "You had no jurisdiction over her. It was a Korean matter. In fact, gate guard Kim says you told her to go talk to the KNPs. You even pointed her in the right direction."

Groverly nodded. "I did."

Now he was staring at the floor. Then he looked back up at me and finally started talking. "There was nothing I could do," he said. "I couldn't leave my post and there was no point in even talking to the watch commander. We don't deploy MP assets for Korean civilians. It just isn't done. Never. It's a matter of jurisdiction. If we did, the KNPs would have a fit."

I nodded. He kept talking.

"She was so desperate. It was clear that someone was right on her tail." He paused and stared at the glossy tip of his jump boot. "I figured it was her pimp or her boyfriend or something like that. He'd knock her around, maybe. I figured she'd be okay . . ."

His voice trailed off.

"Where had she come from?" I asked. "Which direction?"

"I don't know," he said. "Suddenly she was just there."

"What else did you notice?"

"She was on foot, and stepping carefully." He gazed at me as if it were the strangest thing in the world. "She didn't have any shoes."

"What else did she say, Groverly?"

He shook his head, as if to clear it. "That's it. She said it in English. 'Help me.' And then something in Korean to Kim. '*Saram sorry oh,*' or something like that."

"*Saram sollyo,*" I said.

"Yeah, that's it."

It means help. Literally, save a person.

I stood silent for a moment, waiting for him to add something more. He didn't. He leaned forward, elbows on his knees, slowly shaking his head. Finally, I thanked him and walked away. He still hadn't finished lacing up his boot.

"The Black Star Club," Ernie told me as we exited the main gate of Camp Pelham.

I waited until we were off compound to say it: "What the hell's the matter with you?"

"What do you mean?" he said, innocent and red-faced.

"Your eyeballs are as big as platters."

"Oh, that. Yeah," he said, "some good shit."

"You brought reefer up here?"

"Yeah, shared it with the brothers."

"First Sergeant Bolton was looking for you."

"The brothers knew that. We went to a good place, out behind the motor pool."

An exasperated sigh escaped my lungs. "You know the Division doesn't play. They'll lock us up and drop the key in the Imjin River if they catch us with that shit. Do you have any more?"

"No," Ernie said, "all gone."

"You're sure?"

He glanced at me. "You don't trust me?"

"Sure, I do," I said.

But not when it came to drugs. I didn't say that part. Ernie had spent two tours in Vietnam, volunteering to go back for the second. He always said it was a "sweet one" and there'd never be another war like it. On his first tour, young boys sold hash to the GIs, dirt cheap. On his second tour, all the hash was gone, replaced by pure China White. Also cheap. Ernie had picked up the habit there, but I had to admire him, he'd kicked the jones completely here in Korea. Of course, there was no heroin to be had in Korea, not by anyone. The South Korean government checked every bag of every traveler coming in or out of the country, and possession of heroin was punishable by life in prison. The sentence for trafficking was death. And they'd carried out that sentence more than once, standing the erstwhile drug kingpin up against the wall and executing him by firing squad. The 2nd Infantry Division and 8th Army in general were also tough on drug possession. But when it came to marijuana, the Americans might take a hard line but the Koreans were surprisingly more tolerant. After all, it was a natural plant, grown by local farmers, and although it was technically illegal, the KNPs wouldn't prosecute a poor farmer for making a few extra bucks by selling weed to American GIs. Koreans weren't interested in the stuff, with the exception of a few business girls who'd picked up the practice from their clients. Still, Ernie worried me, but as long as he promised he didn't have any more, I had to trust him.

"You showed them the picture?"

Mr. Kill had provided us each with a three-by-five-inch glossy of the corpse in the Sonyu River.

"Showed 'em," Ernie said. "They never saw her before."

"How about Threets?"

"Him, they knew well and they gave me an earful."

"They didn't look like a very talkative bunch."

"You just have to get them started," he said. "Besides, I brought an icebreaker."

"Where's The Black Star?" I asked.

"Up that crack," he said, pointing toward a narrow pedestrian lane just past Miss Cho's Brassware Emporium. For the first time I noticed that there was a small neon sign with a finger pointing optimistically into the darkness.

"There's a club up there?"

"Yeah, for them."

"They don't hang out with the white GIs?"

"Did you see any black GIs when we ran the ville?"

I hadn't thought of it, but he was right. In the village of Sonyu-ri, all I'd seen were white GIs, a few Hispanics, and dozens of Korean business girls.

"So if the brothers told you all they know about Threets, why are we going to The Black Star?"

"The Ville Rat," Ernie replied, grinning now.

"The who?"

"The Ville Rat. While we were talking about Threets, I asked them about the skinny white guy with the red Afro. The one who stopped us on our way out of Sonyu-ri last time and led us on that merry chase. When I described him, their eyes lit up. After some coaxing, they told me about him."

"They knew him?"

"Of course they knew him. He thinks he's a soul brother himself. Come on, I'll show you."

The proprietress of The Black Star Nightclub was a grumpy old woman with streaks of grey hair that fell past her ears. As she talked, she kept brushing unruly strands from her eyes, trying at the same time to keep a cheap Turtle Boat cigarette lit.

"I don't know Ville Rat," she told us.

"White guy," Ernie told her, holding his hands to the side of his head. "Red hair. Sticks out like a soul brother."

"I don't know," she said stubbornly.

I showed her my badge.

"*Ajjima*," I said, using the honorific form of address for an older woman. "We don't want to bother you, we just want to know about the Ville Rat. But if you don't want to talk to us, you can talk to this gentleman."

I pulled out Inspector Gil Kwon-up's calling card and showed it to her. She took one look at the emblem of the Korean National Police and started shaking her head.

"I don't wanna talk him."

"Okay," Ernie said. He walked around behind the bar. "Then you talk to me." He rattled the chain that locked the metal cooler. "Open it."

The old woman frowned, took a long drag on her cigarette, and snuffed it out on a metal ashtray. "Okay, okay," she said. "Anyway he black market. Sell me this shit."

"Who?" I asked.

"Ville Rat," she said impatiently.

She pulled a ring of keys out from a pocket in her skirt and opened the cooler. Inside were the usual brown bottles of OB beer, but stacked neatly beside them was a row of ice-cold sixteen-ounce cans. She pulled one out and handed it to Ernie. "Soul brother like," she said.

It was a Stateside product, malt liquor, a brand known as Colt 45. It had a higher alcoholic content than regular beer. I'd tasted it before and hadn't liked it much since it also had a fermented tartness that, as far as I was concerned, ruined the flavor of the hops and barley.

Ernie held it up to the light to see if there were any customs labels on it. There weren't. "Where does the Ville Rat get this stuff from?"

The old woman shrugged. "How I know?"

"What else does he bring?"

She glanced at the liquor bottles behind the bar. There were three or four brands of imported cognac. Ernie lifted them up to the light and all of them had ROK customs labels on them. But the bottles looked ancient, scratched and chipped, probably refilled a thousand times. "Cognac?" Ernie asked.

The old woman shrugged again. "Maybe brandy."

She refilled the expensive bottles with cheaper booze. Standard practice. After a few snootfulls most GIs couldn't tell the difference, if they ever could in the first place.

"Who else does he sell to?" Ernie asked.

"Me, I'm the only one."

"The only one in country?"

"The only one in Sonyu-ri. Maybe he go 'nother village, sell to 'nother club have soul brother."

She pronounced the word "village" like "ville-age-ee" and the word "soul" like the capital city of the country, "sew-*ul*."

"How often do you see him?"

She shrugged again. "Maybe once a month."

"At mid-month payday or end-of-month payday?"

"Maybe end-of-month."

"Does he live here in Sonyu-ri?"

"No. Not live here."

"Where does he live?"

"I don't know. Maybe far away."

"Like where?"

"How I know?"

"Does he have a girlfriend here?"

"Any Black Star girl like him."

"They do? Why?"

"Because he smart. Not stupid, like GI. He make money."

"GIs make money," I said.

"*Skoshi* money," she said. Little money. "All the time Cheap Charley."

"The Ville Rat is not a Cheap Charley?"

"No. He spend money, buy girls *tambei*." Cigarettes. "*Satang* sometimes." Candy. "Any GI like Ville Rat too."

"So he's spreading it around," I said. She didn't understand what I meant by that, so I said, "Who does he stay with when he visits The Black Star Club?"

"I don't know. Before curfew, he all the time go." She waved her hand toward an unknown distance.

A skinny little boy ran into the club. Breathless, he spoke to the proprietress.

"*Ajjima*," he said. "*Migun wa-yo*." Aunt, American soldiers are coming.

"*Otton migun?*" What kind of American soldiers?

"*Honbyong*," the boy said. MPs.

That's all I needed to hear. We thanked the woman and departed, in a hurry.

-6-

Ernie and I scurried through a narrow pedestrian lane, hopping over mud puddles, dodging ancient cobwebs that swung from rafters like low-hanging vines.

"You think they're after us?" Ernie asked.

"Probably," I replied. "We're up here on the Threets case, and according to the memo from Eighth Army, the Threets case *only*."

"That's what we're doing," Ernie said indignantly.

"Maybe," I replied. "Either way, it's best if we un-ass the area."

The pedestrian lane let out onto a two-lane blacktop that I recognized. It ran north toward more small farming communities and, beyond that, the winding flow of the Imjin River. South only a couple hundred yards, it intersected with the road that ran in front of Camp Pelham and through the village of Sonyu-ri. We trotted across the street and when we hit the intersection we turned left. About fifty yards on stood the entrance to *meikju changgo*, the Non-Appropriated Fund transshipping point. We waved to the gate guards whom we'd already plied with packs of

Kent cigarettes, and trotted to Ernie's jeep. He started the engine and said, "Are we done up here?"

"For the time being," I said.

He backed out, spinning gravel as he did so.

Ernie's left foot worked the clutch as his right hand fondled the crystal skull that topped the four-on-the-floor gear shift. He loved this jeep and had put a lot of work into it. Well, not work, exactly. What he did was, at every end-of-month payday, he gave a gift of one quart of Johnny Walker Black to the head honcho dispatcher at the 21st Transportation Car Company, or "21 T Car," the main motor pool for 8th Army headquarters. As a result of this highly prized gift, what Ernie received was his personal jeep that was always dispatched to him and *him* only, topped off with gasoline, with maintenance thrown in and new tires every six months. In addition, Ernie popped for the tuck-and-roll black leather upholstery that puffed up proudly in the backseat.

"Never know when some dolly might want to crawl back there with me," Ernie'd told me.

We sped out of the front gate of *meikju changgo* and turned right, heading for Sonyu-ri. The MPs approaching The Black Star Club had been on foot, and when we'd passed the intersection minutes ago there'd been no activity. So when we saw two MP jeeps lurking behind a brick wall on the near side of the Camp Pelham main gate, Ernie and I were both taken by surprise. As we passed, the MPs started their engines, turned on their overhead emergency lights, and gave chase.

"Aren't they ever going to stop messing with us?" Ernie asked.

"This is Division," I replied.

As if that explained everything, Ernie stepped on the gas. It was mid-afternoon, so the denizens of the Sonyu-ri nightlife were up and about and the roads teemed with pedestrians. Ernie swerved past kimchi cabs parked on the side of the road, avoiding an old man pushing a cart filled with *yontan* charcoal and rushing past scantily clad business girls carrying pans filled with soap and shampoo on their way to the public bathhouse. We must've been doing forty by the time we passed the front gate of RC-4. A half-mile later, we sped past the spot, off to our left, where the corpse of the woman in red had been found. We raced past the Country Health Clinic, still leaving the MP jeeps in the dust, when five hundred yards ahead a three-quarter-ton truck nosed out onto the road.

"*Damn.*" Ernie swerved to his left, but the truck kept coming. To avoid it, he swerved back to his right, but the driver of the military vehicle seemed to have anticipated Ernie's move and quickly backed up. Ernie slammed on the brakes. Behind us, the two MP jeeps kept coming. Ernie glanced back, shifted the jeep into reverse, but it was too late. The MP jeeps nudged up to our rear bumper and cut off all means of escape. Armed MPs hopped out of the rear of the three-quarter-ton truck.

A half-dozen MPs surrounded us. Slowly, Ernie and I clambered out of the jeep.

"You're interfering with a freaking investigation!" Ernie shouted.

Ignoring him, the MPs closed in. One of them I recognized: Specialist Austin, the gate guard who hadn't given us the time of day. The ranking man appeared to be a buck sergeant. Four of them pulled their batons and the other two stepped toward us.

"Assume the position," the buck sergeant said.

Ernie replied with his usual brilliant retort: "Get bent."

The four MPs hopped forward. I grabbed one of them, shoved him away, and Ernie popped another in the jaw. After that, confusion reigned, and after much jostling, Ernie and I ended up in the backseat of an MP jeep, hands cuffed behind our backs. An MP driver started the engine and, after another MP hopped in the passenger seat, he sped back toward Camp Pelham, Ernie and I bouncing in the backseat. But much to my surprise, when we reached Camp Pelham, the driver kept going past the main gate, continuing east, toward the hills that rose inland from the Western Corridor.

"You guys are *fucked*," Ernie shouted at the driver. "We had authorization to be up here!"

He kept at it, screaming at the top of his lungs, calling the two MPs three kinds of asshole when finally the one riding shotgun cracked. "You *had* authorization," he shouted back, "until you interviewed Groverly!"

Ernie looked surprised and turned to me. I grimaced and then shrugged. Either Groverly had admitted that he'd talked to me or someone in the MP barracks had spotted us talking. Either way, Division was apparently using that as an excuse to take us into custody and ship us back south. At least, that's what I thought was happening, especially when we turned right at one of the country roads and wound our way through hills and cabbage fields that led to the city of Popwon-ni. I figured we'd keep moving south from there, running parallel to the MSR on a road that would eventually reach the mountains just north of Seoul. But I was wrong. Four or five miles on, we turned into the back gate of Camp Howze.

"Why are we going here?" I asked.

The 2nd Infantry Division MP headquarters was at Camp Casey in the Eastern Corridor. The Western Corridor and the Eastern Corridor were both traditional invasion routes that stretched from China, through Manchuria, through North Korea, and finally ended at the capital city of Seoul. In ancient times they'd been used by Chinese legions, Manchurian raiders, and Mongol hordes. During the early 20th Century, the Japanese Imperial Army had used them to go north toward Siberia. Most recently, they were guarded by the GIs of the US 2nd Infantry Division. We were still deep in Division territory, more than ten miles north of the outskirts of Seoul.

Neither MP answered. But I believed there was a certain smug satisfaction in their silence, a satisfaction that grew as we wound through the rows of olive-drab Quonset huts perched on the hilly ridges that comprised Camp Howze. It seemed like an awkward place for a military compound, surrounded by hills, until you realized that those same hills would probably provide excellent protection from North Korean artillery.

We stopped at the back door of one of the larger Quonset huts. The three-quarter-ton truck pulled up behind us, and MPs hopped out and took up positions with nightsticks drawn. Like a couple of Brahma bulls, Ernie and I were pulled out of the jeep and herded through a door that said: NO ADMITTANCE. AUTHOR-IZED PERSONNEL ONLY.

Amongst the US Army's favorite directives.

I expected an ass chewing. None came. Ernie and I sat in an inter-rogation room that was locked from the outside. Our handcuffs had been removed, but we hadn't been provided chow, and from the growing darkness outside the painted window I could tell that night had fallen.

Impatient, Ernie rose and pounded on the door. No one answered. He kept pounding. Finally, he shouted, "*Goddamn it!* I have to take a leak."

Five minutes later, the door creaked open. Before Ernie could pounce, a metal bucket was shoved in and the door slammed shut. Ernie carried the bucket to the far corner of the room and took his leak. Later, I took mine.

We were dozing on a wooden bench and I wasn't sure how many hours we'd been cooling our heels when there was a quick knock on the door and it swung open. My eyes opened at the same time. A man walked into the room; he wore baggy fatigues. He stopped in front of us and jammed both fists into his narrow hips.

"What the *hell* is wrong with you two?" It was Staff Sergeant Riley.

"Up yours," Ernie replied, lazily rubbing his eyes.

"I had to drive all the way up to Camp Howze to bail your sorry asses out!"

"Bail?" I said.

"They made me sign a chit. Taking responsibility for you two lowlifes and guaranteeing you'd un-ass the Division area."

"What about the Threets investigation?"

"Finished," Riley said. "Done. Kaput."

"It ain't finished," Ernie said, growling.

"It's finished up here," Riley said. "Come on."

We followed him out into the hallway.

The MPs wouldn't give us Ernie's jeep back, not until we were out of the Division area. Instead, two of their MPs drove it, their headlights tailing me and Ernie and Riley in Riley's green army sedan. Just past the last Division checkpoint, we pulled over onto the side of the dark road. The two MPs hopped out of Ernie's jeep and walked over to the floodlight illuminating the checkpoint. Soon they were bullshitting with the checkpoint guards, exchanging cigarettes, apparently waiting for transportation back.

Riley drove south in his sedan. Ernie and I jumped in his jeep and followed. Speeding off, Ernie leaned out of his side of the door, held his arm high, and flipped the Division MPs the bird.

"It's past midnight," I told him. "They can't see what you're doing."

Ernie shrugged. "It's the thought that counts."

The compound known as ASCOM, the Army Support Command, sits about fifteen kilometers west of Seoul, just outside the city of Bupyong, not too far from the shores of the Yellow Sea. Ernie and I left early and drove on a two-lane elevated highway that wound through fallow rice paddies and past clusters of straw-thatched farmhouses. Metal chimneys spewed ribbons of charcoal smoke into the blue sky. At the ASCOM main gate, an MP checked our dispatch and rusty wheels squeaked as a Korean gate guard rolled the barbed-wire fence open. We drove through onto a small compound composed mostly of tin Quonset huts, which looked like all the other US military compounds in the country except that it was interspersed with massive concrete buildings that had been constructed before World War II by the Japanese Imperial Army, supposedly for ammunition storage.

One of those huge storage bunkers was surrounded by another

chain-link fence with a small administration building out front. The sign at the entranceway said: WELCOME TO THE 8TH UNITED STATES ARMY STOCKADE. AUTHORIZED PERSONNEL ONLY.

At the front desk, we showed our badges to a bored clerk. A couple of phone calls were made and then, after about ten minutes, an MP with a steel helmet and a plastic faceguard motioned to us with his truncheon. We followed. A long hallway led into the heart of the concrete bunker and, once inside, the world changed. Sounds were amplified. Metal clanging on metal and the sharp shouts of commands echoed down whitewashed corridors. We followed the MP through one of those corridors, turned right, and finally reached a door marked PRISONER CONFERENCE ROOM. He pulled out a ring of keys, unlocked the door and waved us in.

"I'll be right outside the door," he said. "Have a seat. The prisoner will be brought in shortly."

Ernie and I pulled straight-backed chairs out from beneath a counter and sat down. The partition reached from floor to ceiling and the windows were made of thick plastic with a metal mesh to speak through.

"Where are the telephones?" Ernie asked.

"What?"

"In the movies," he said, "the prisoner sits on one side and his visitor sits on the other, talking through telephones."

I studied the little metal duct.

"I guess Eighth Army couldn't afford them," I said.

Ernie peered through the thin wire. "You can spread germs through this thing."

Five minutes later, a burly MP, similarly masked with a metal helmet and a plastic visor, escorted in the prisoner. He wore army fatigues, but without rank insignia or a belt to hold up his baggy pants. Instead, he clutched them with his right hand, which was handcuffed to his left. His name tag said Threets. Peering at us, he remained standing until the guard pointed at the chair with his nightstick. Immediately, Threets sat down. The guard backed out of the room and shut the door behind him.

Ernie glanced at me. I think I knew what he wanted to say. Threets looked like a child. The flesh of his face was soft and without whiskers, and even though he was rail-thin, baby fat rounded his cheeks. He wore Army-issue horn-rimmed glasses and his hair was tufted out a little too long for Army regulation.

"Hey, buddy," Ernie said. "How's it going?"

Threets didn't answer. Mostly, he stared at his hands in his lap, but occasionally his eyes popped up to study us. Ernie introduced us and then said, "Monk up at Charley Battery says hello."

Threets's eyes lit up. "Monk?"

"Yeah. We smoked some reefer together. He says he wants to testify on your behalf, but so far they won't let him."

Threets glanced back down. "I don't do no reefer."

"Yeah, I know," Ernie said. "They told me." He paused, glancing at me to see if I wanted to say anything, but this was his show. Ernie cleared his throat and stared again. "So Monk said it was an accident. You didn't mean to shoot nobody."

Threets kept his eyes down. In reply, he raised and then lowered his narrow shoulders. This wasn't good. The unwillingness to answer, in the military mind, meant agreement.

Ernie didn't push it. "They say Smoke was riding you."

"Smoke" meant Sergeant First Class Vincent P. Orgwell, formally the chief of Firing Battery.

When Threets didn't answer, Ernie said, "You're a gunner. Young for a gunner. But Monk and the other guys tell me that you can work the numbers in your head. Lay the gun faster than any other gunner in the battery. The chief of smoke knew that. He knew you were good."

Ernie paused. Still Threets said nothing.

"Maybe that's why he rode you," Ernie said. "Because you're young and you're smart." Ernie let the silence hang. Finally, he said. "And because you're black."

Threets's mouth tightened. Still, he didn't speak. When he finally did say something, it was almost a whisper. Both of us leaned forward to hear what he said. He repeated it, louder this time.

"He didn't ride me because I'm black," he said.

Ernie waited again, longer than he had before. For some reason it hung in the air, the feeling that what Threets was about to say was something that neither Ernie nor I really wanted to hear. It was intuition, I suppose, although I don't really believe in those things. Somehow, mysteriously, both Ernie and I sensed that what was coming wouldn't be good.

"It wasn't because I was black," he said. "It was because he wanted to train me."

"To be a better gunner?" Ernie ventured.

For the first time Threets showed some emotion. Violently, he shook his head and in an exasperated voice he said, "*No*. Nobody understands."

"Understands what?" Ernie asked.

"Nobody understands what Smoke really *is*." For the first time Threets looked up at us, in turn, staring us both in the eye. "He told me to report to him, after work, but to tell no one. 'For extra training,' he said. I met him in the training room. It was empty, just him and me, and then he . . ."

Suddenly, Threets lost his nerve and stared at the ground.

"Then he what?" Ernie asked.

This seemed to enrage Threets. "What are you, stupid? Don't you get it?" He stood up. The helmeted MP burst into the room. As he grabbed Threets by the arm, Threets twisted away and screamed at us. "Don't you get it? Smoke is a *fag*. He's a goddamn *fag!*"

The MP pulled Threets away.

This was not good news.

Homosexuality was a crime in the US Military, and 8th Army brass didn't like dealing with it. It was too touchy. Nobody wanted to be assigned to a "homo investigation"; nobody wanted to type up the formal accusation, and field-grade officers didn't like to be appointed to the boards of inquiry or, worse yet, the courts-martial that had to prosecute such a case. Still, it was our sworn duty and it had to be done. And it would explain why Threets turned his weapon on the Chief of Smoke. He was being coerced by a senior noncommissioned officer, a man older and more experienced than him, into doing things that he didn't want to do.

As far as 8th Army was concerned, the Threets case was a simple prosecution for armed assault. It was about to get uglier.

On the trip back from ASCOM we didn't talk much. When we returned to the Yongsan Compound, Ernie entered through the back gate to South Post. After winding through some tree-lined lanes, he parked the jeep in the lot across the street from the "One-Two-One Evac," the 121st Evacuation Hospital.

At the front desk, a female medic told us where we could find SFC Vince Orgwell. We clattered down long tile-floored hallways. As we did so, Ernie's head kept swiveling, checking out the nurses and the medical aides clad in their tight white jumpsuits. Finally, we reached a ward with a half-dozen beds on either side. SFC Vincent P. Orgwell was the third on the right.

"Smoke," Ernie said. Orgwell opened his eyes. Seeing us, he pushed himself farther up on the raised bed, pulling the white sheet higher as he did so.

"Who are you?" he asked.

We flashed our badges. This time I did the talking. I asked him to describe what had happened on the firing range. He did. Everything he said matched what was in the initial MP report. He'd been the safety officer on the left side of the range. Initially, he'd pointed the green disc of his signal paddle at the fire control tower, indicating that the six firing points on his side of the range were all clear. But then he'd seen that PFC Threets was not pointing his weapon up and down range, so he'd immediately signaled with the red side of the paddle.

"I remember the voice coming over the loudspeaker," Orgwell told us. "'Cease Fire! The range is not clear. Repeat, the firing range is not clear!'" He mimicked it with the authoritative voice of a fire control officer.

"What was Threets doing?" I asked.

"He was climbing out of the foxhole," Orgwell said. "I went over to see what the hell was wrong with him and, without warning, he turned and fired."

I glanced down at his leg.

Orgwell leaned forward and touched the cast. "Won't lose my

knee," he said. "The docs here have done a hell of a job, although they say I won't be doing any squat thrusts any time soon."

He was referring to one of the exercises in the army's "daily dozen" calisthenics drill.

"Are you putting in for disability retirement?"

"Don't want it," he said. "All I want is to return to Charley Battery."

"Hope you make it," I said.

"Thanks."

I paused. "Do you have any idea why Threets did this to you?"

Orgwell shook his head. "Fed up with the army, I suppose."

He thought about it a moment and then he continued.

"He was like most of these kids, didn't take it seriously. Also, you know how some of these blacks keep bad-mouthing the 'man.' Claiming every time their pass is pulled it's racist." He studied me as he said it, wondering if I was a full-blooded member of the club. Apparently, he decided I was. "Just an excuse to not pull their weight," Orgwell said. When neither Ernie nor I reacted, he added, "in my opinion."

"Threets says there's another reason he shot you," I said.

"Yeah?" Orgwell was suspicious now. "What was that?"

"You know," Ernie said.

Orgwell swiveled his head. "I know?"

"Yeah," Ernie said. "You know damn well."

Orgwell pulled the sheet up closer to his neck. "I don't know what you're talking about."

"Threets says you made a pass at him," Ernie said.

"A pass?"

"You tried to enter into a homosexual relationship with him," I explained.

Orgwell's face flushed red. He began to sputter. "You must be out of your mind!" When we didn't respond, his face grew more contorted, and then he'd thrown the sheet back and he was sitting up, the brace surrounding his wound strapped tightly against his leg. "You lie!" he shouted and then lunged at Ernie.

Ernie stepped back and Orgwell tried to grab him, but his leg gave out and he tumbled to the tile floor in a heap, screaming in pain as he did so. An orderly entered the ward and started to pull him upright. Orgwell continued to sputter until a nurse hurried in and helped the orderly get him back into bed. Once he was settled, she turned to us and pointed with her forefinger for us to leave. As we walked out of the ward, Orgwell was still swearing.

"He said, *she* said," Riley told us. Then he corrected himself. "Or in this case, he said and the other *he* said. Either way, you can't prove nothing."

"Not up to us to prove it one way or the other," Ernie said. "It'll be up to the court-martial to decide."

"Threets better not demand a court-martial," Riley said. "He'd better settle and take the time they give him. If he forces Eighth Army to go to trial and if he throws this homo stuff at him, they'll put him away until he's as old as . . ."

Riley paused, groping for the right comparison.

"As old as one of your girlfriends," Ernie interjected.

"Right," Riley said, and then he caught himself. "What do you mean by that crack?"

Ernie shrugged and continued reading the sports page of *Stars and Stripes*.

I was seated at a field desk near the coffee urn typing up our report. Ernie liked for me to do them, since he had no patience for paperwork. I liked paperwork. Sitting at the typewriter relaxed me and spelling everything out gave me a chance to put it all in perspective. Make sense of what was essentially unending chaos, like the case of the frozen lady in the red dress. By typing out our report, it was made clear to me where we had to go next. We had to go after the one lead we had. We had to find the Ville Rat.

I considered this to be a revelation. The masterstroke of a great detective. Or at least I did until Ernie stepped in front of the coffee urn, poured steaming java into a thick mug, and said, "Strange wants to talk to us."

"Finally?"

"Yeah."

"He found something out?"

"Apparently. He says it's all hush-hush."

"Where do we meet him?"

"Where else? The Snatch Burr."

Which is what Strange called the 8th Army snack bar.

"At lunch?"

"Yeah." Which is when we usually met him, in the middle of a crowd, where we'd be less conspicuous and less likely to be overheard.

"In the meantime," I said, "we have to find the Ville Rat."

"Why do you say that?"

"He knows something. More than he's telling."

Ernie nodded. "So where do we start?"

I thought about it. Then I said, "We start with the Colt 45."

■ ■ ■

The Central Locker Fund was very possibly the neatest military warehouse I'd ever seen. The vast cement floor was swept immaculately clean, and the wooden shelves lining the walls and running in three long rows down the middle aisles were made of pine-smelling wood and shining nails. A purring forklift carried pallets laden with neatly stacked cardboard cases of Carling Black Label toward the small mountains of beer in the back. Toward the front, Korean workmen rolled flat metal carts laden with cases of imported scotch and vodka to the rows of shelves closer to the main office.

"Clear the booze out of here," Ernie said, "and you'd have space for a C-130." A military air transport.

Light shone behind a glass enclosure. We entered a short hallway and followed it to a double-doored entranceway. Inside was another vast warehouse, about half as big as the other, this one filled with rows of desks interrupted by grey hedge rows of Army-issue filing cabinets, all of it populated by industrious-looking Korean workers hunched over stacks of onionskin invoices or hauling manila folders from one wire in-basket to another or talking animatedly on heavy, black military phones.

"It ain't easy keeping Eighth Army half loaded," Ernie said.

He was right about the consumption. Not only did the Central Locker Fund have over 50,000 soldiers, sailors, and airmen to provide beer and liquor for, but they also had about 20,000 dependents and Department of the Army Civilians (DACs) to worry about. And that might've been just the tip of the proverbial iceberg. Ernie and I both knew that a lot of the beer and booze that the Central Locker Fund provided, if not most of it, ended up on the Korean black market. Imported liquor was extremely popular in Korea, but the Korean government, in order to protect its own fledgling industries, imposed high customs duties on all imported goods, especially luxury items. The US military shipped everything over for free, with no customs duties. As a result, a GI—or more likely his Korean wife—could sell a bottle of imported scotch on the Korean black market for three or four times what they paid for it.

A Korean woman wearing a white blouse and black skirt stood in front of us, both hands placed primly in front of her, fingers pointing downward. She bowed and asked if she could help. I flashed my badge and told her who we wanted to speak to. She bowed again and led us toward a glass-enclosed office against the far wall.

Inside, at a desk larger than those in the main work area, a figure sat in what appeared to be solemn meditation. A dapper man, he wore a suit and had brushed-back brown hair greying at the temples. Rick Mills was somewhat of a legend in 8th Army. It was said that he'd been a mess sergeant in the Korean War who'd been put in charge of setting up the Class VI stores—the branch of the post exchange that sold liquor and beer—from one end of the Korean peninsula to the other. He'd done such a good job and his work was appreciated by so many high-ranking officers that when he retired from the military he'd been given the same job, running the Central Locker Fund, as a Department of the Army Civilian. He'd held the job ever since, for more than twenty years. In military life this was common. You build relationships while on active duty and then parlay them into a lifetime job. Rick Mills had become an institution at 8th Army. Some said he was into illicit activities and more than once a zealous provost marshal had tried to bust him, but Rick Mills had always come through any investigation unscathed. Most recently, in the audit performed by our colleagues, Burrows and Slabem, Rick Mills and the 8th Army Central Locker Fund had been shown to be efficiently run and in full compliance with all pertinent regulations.

Maybe.

He stood as we approached. I flashed my badge and explained why we were here. Rick Mills studied us briefly, shook our hands, and then asked us to have a seat. Unbidden, the same Korean lady who'd ushered us in appeared expectantly at the door.

"Coffee," Rick Mills asked, "or something else to drink?"

"A case of scotch would be nice," Ernie said.

I overrode him. "No, nothing, thank you."

Rick Mills turned to the lady. "Thank you, Miss Jo, nothing today." She bowed and backed out of the room. He turned to us.

"It's about malt liquor," I explained.

His eyes widened.

"How much of it do you import?" I asked.

Rick Mills seemed surprised by the question. "Malt liquor? Why, none."

"None?" Ernie asked.

Rick Mills turned to him. "Yes. We don't get much call for it."

"But the black troops," Ernie replied. "Colt 45. And what's that other one?" He snapped his fingers.

"Jazz City Ale?" Rick Mills said.

"Yes. The green death."

"That's what they call it."

"So why don't you ship it over if the black troops like it?"

Rick Mills looked down at the desk blotter in front of him,

as if searching for an answer. I noticed that behind him, neatly arranged on a polished mahogany shelf, were a series of framed photographs. One showed a much younger Rick Mills in uniform, standing with a group of fellow GIs in front of a jeep. All were smiling and laughing. The rest of the photos were more formal, with Rick Mills standing with one general or another, receiving a plaque or some kind of award. There were close to a dozen of them. Providing booze to the troops can be a rewarding career.

"It's been decided," Mills said, "that the alcohol content in malt liquor is too high. For the health and welfare of the troops, we don't order it."

"The alcohol content in liquor is even higher," Ernie said. Mills didn't answer. Ernie went on. "It's because the black troops like it," he said. "They like the fact that it gives them a quick kick and they don't have the bloated feeling they get from beer. It's a ghetto thing. You don't want them drinking the same shit they drank back on the block."

Mills looked up at Ernie. "It's not me."

"The command," Ernie said.

Mills shrugged.

"And for the same reason," Ernie said, "you don't order cheap wine, like T-Bird or Bali Hai. Only the expensive stuff, for the officers."

"Trade-offs are made," Mills said. "We can't order everything."

Finally, Ernie shut his mouth. I was glad he did. No sense blaming Mills for the priorities that 8th Army demanded. In the military, it was the highest-ranking officers who made the decisions that affected the rest of us in every aspect of our lives. Invariably, they made them according to their own likes and dislikes. The likes and dislikes of the black troops, as far as I could tell, were not even considered.

Ernie leaned back in his chair. It was my turn.

"If a person wanted to get ahold of malt liquor," I asked, "how would he do it?"

Mills slid his fingertips across the smooth white paper of the blotter.

"What type of malt liquor?"

"Does it matter?"

"No. Not really. If you ordered it directly, you'd not only pay a small fortune in transport costs, but also be hit hard by Korean customs duties." He was silent for a moment and then he said, "The merchant marine, in the Port of Inchon or the Port of Pusan. It wouldn't be easy, but occasionally a Korean guard at the port can be bribed to look the other way. You could bring in a shipment that way."

"It would still be expensive. The payoffs would be almost as big as the customs duties."

Mills shrugged again. "I imagine."

"Any other way?" Ernie asked.

Mills seemed to have gotten fed up. He stared at Ernie steadily. "Are you implying something?"

"If anyone knows how to import alcoholic beverages into Korea, it would be you."

"Our record is clean," Mills told him. "Nothing through here without it being logged in and logged out."

Miss Jo entered Mills's office. Her face was slightly flushed but still she placed her hands in front of her again and bowed. She apologized profusely and said, "There's been an accident."

Mills rose to his feet and bolted out the door. We followed. On the way to the warehouse I noticed the signs that said: ANCHON CHEIL. Safety first.

The reek of booze hit us like a fist. One of the forklifts at the huge main entrance to the warehouse had apparently collided with a green army pickup. The front end of the truck had been dented and the forklift was wedged against the fender at an almost forty-five-degree angle. Cases of liquor had crashed to the floor, flooding the smooth cement slab with a small tsunami of spirits.

"Gin," Ernie said. "Beefeater."

Leave it to Agent Ernie Bascom to notice the important details.

A Korean man stood next to the forklift clutching a blue cloth. I checked his wound. Bleeding, but not arterial. Two other workmen approached and led him to another vehicle. Rick Mills conferred with them and they sped off, escorting the wounded forklift driver to the local dispensary.

A tall GI in starched fatigues paced next to the pickup truck, back and forth, sliding his green cap across a bald skull. He was about six-foot-one, thin, with the belt of his uniform cinched tightly around a narrow waist. His eyes were large and blue and moist and his name tag simply said Demoray. His rank insignia indicated that he was a master sergeant, one step below the highest enlisted rank.

"I told Han not to take those corners so tight." He was speaking mostly to himself but occasionally he glanced over at Rick Mills, who was glaring at him. "He comes barreling out of the warehouse just as I'm turning in and I didn't see him, and I sure as hell didn't have time to stop."

Then he looked at Ernie and then at me. He pointed a long, bony finger.

"It's your fault. If you hadn't been here, I never would've needed to come over. Didn't we just finish one freaking CID inspection?"

"That's enough, Demoray," Mills said. "Get this mess cleaned up. And then get over to the dispensary and check on Mr. Han. I want a full report by noon."

Demoray stared at him for a moment, moist blue eyes blaring indignation. He rubbed his head again, tilting back his cap. Then he turned, throwing his arms up in the air in exasperation, shaking his head, and stalked away.

Mills turned to us. "He's a good man, usually. Just very emotional."

"And he drives too fast," I said.

Mills nodded sadly.

Ernie poked through the broken bottles. "Why was he so worried about us?"

"He's very protective of the operation here."

"That's a good thing."

Mills sighed. "It can be."

"Had any *strange* lately?"

We were at the 8th Army snack bar. Men and women in uniform jostled with Department of the Army Civilians and balanced trays of food from the serving line, wedging themselves into booths and tables that filled the massive Quonset hut. I'd bought myself a mug of coffee, Ernie was having tea, and the man we knew as Strange, a sergeant first class in the US Army, sipped on a straw that stuck out of a plastic cup.

"Before we get to that, Strange," Ernie said, "what've you got for us?"

"The name's Harvey."

"Right, Harvey. I forgot."

Strange was a pervert. Ernie and I weren't. At least, we didn't think we were. And the only reason we associated with Strange was because he was the NCO in charge of the Classified Documents section at 8th Army Headquarters. A pervert who had access to the most sensitive military secrets. In addition to that, he was a gossip. He thrived on other people's stories; he knew almost everyone at the 8th Army head shed and he eavesdropped on every conversation he could. And he was discreet. Most of the time people hardly knew he was there. Like the proverbial fly on the wall. As a result, he was an invaluable source of information for Ernie and me. The catch was that in exchange for his secrets, Ernie had to tell him about the *strange* he'd gotten recently. That is, new sexual conquests. I doubted that Strange had ever had a sexual conquest in his life, but he sure liked hearing about them.

Strange looked sharp. His thinning brown hair was combed straight back and he wore sunglasses even though the only light in the snack bar was from the overhead fluorescent bulbs. A plastic cigarette holder dangled from his lips, with no cigarette in it.

"I'm trying to quit," he'd tell anyone who asked, although I don't think anyone had ever actually seen him smoke. Oddly, he swiped imaginary ashes from the neatly pressed sleeves of his starched khakis. Strange glanced around the room, making sure we weren't being watched. Then he leaned forward. "The Gunslinger," he whispered.

"The what?" Ernie asked.

"Not so loud. The Gunslinger. That's what this is all about."

"What's all about?" Ernie asked.

"This case you're working on."

"Which one?"

Strange seemed exasperated. He blew air into his straw, making the soda at the bottom bubble. "The one about the dolly up north. The one you found in the river."

"Who's the Gunslinger?" Ernie asked.

Strange grimaced. "Don't you know nothing?" He glanced around the room again. "The Gunslinger is the two-star general who runs the Second freaking Infantry Division. Real name's Kokol. *Army Digest* even ran an article on him. Changing the whole culture of the Division. Gung-ho rallies, karate classes, the whole works."

"Yeah," Ernie said. "So?"

"You still don't get it, do you?"

"Get what?"

"Eighth Army's got a case of the big ass. Division is getting all the publicity. The honchos here in Seoul don't get squat."

"So they're hoping the murder, and the Threets case, will bring him down a notch."

"Exactly." Strange grinned. It was a difficult thing to watch. Greasy lips formed into a bowl-shaped gash. Somehow, out of that mess, he continued to talk. "The honchos are out to get him, and to do that they're using *you*."

Ernie sipped on his tea. "So the honchos are jealous of each other. So what? They're always jealous of each other."

"Not like this."

"What do you mean?"

"If they get rid of Kokol, they're thinking of sending your boss, Colonel Brace, up there as Division XO." Executive Officer.

I set my coffee down. "He'd get a star?"

"That's right." Strange's smile seemed to have reached his ears. "Brigadier general, a shiny silver star on his shoulder, handed to him on a plate."

"So that's why the Division MPs have been messing with us," I said.

Strange smiled even more broadly, enjoying his superior knowledge. "You're like two white mice scurrying between tomcats."

Ernie didn't like the analogy. "What do you know about Colt 45?"

Strange's smile drooped. "The weapon?"

"No, the malt liquor."

"Rotten shit."

"I'm not asking for your culinary opinion. If someone wanted to buy some and sell it down in the ville, where would they get it?"

"How in the hell would I know?"

"So find out." Ernie started to stand. Like a shot, Strange reached out and clutched the back of his hand.

"Hey, what about our deal?"

"No stories today, Strange."

"The name's Harvey."

"Okay, Harvey. Telling us that one general's jealous of another doesn't tell us nothing. We need some real dope, not bullshit." He pointed his forefinger at Strange's nose. "Find out how to get ahold of some Colt 45. Who could do that? How? Then you'll get a story."

Strange grimaced, and then the grimace turned to anger. Reluctantly he loosened his grip on Ernie's hand. As we left, he blew more bubbles into his cup, louder this time. Outside, Ernie rubbed his hand where Strange had touched him.

"Christ," he said. "The Eighth Army honchos are using us against the general in charge of the Second Infantry Division?"

"Yeah," I said. "Who woulda thunk it?"

"Anybody who knew them."

At the 8th Army JAG office, Second Lieutenant Peggy Mendelson was not pleased. She slid my report across the desk.

"Are you sure you want to submit *this*?" she asked.

"I already have," I answered.

"Hearsay, that's all it is. And accusations made by the accused. Who's going to believe Threets? He'd say anything to get out of being sent to Leavenworth."

"If you want corroboration," Ernie said, "we'll get you corroboration."

"*No.*" Lieutenant Mendelson said it too fast. Then she composed herself. "We're not going to start an investigation into alleged homosexual activity by an experienced NCO based on the word of a soldier accused of aggravated assault."

"Why not?" Ernie asked. He was slouched in the grey vinyl chair across from Peggy Mendelson's desk, enjoying her discomfort.

She slid a carved glass paperweight from one side of her desk to the other. "The command is interested in the shooting and only the shooting. It was a flagrant case of assault, reflecting poorly on unit cohesion and esprit de corps."

"Piss-poor leadership," Ernie said.

Peggy swiveled her head. "Exactly."

I'd seen it before. Too often. The command trying to mold a criminal case into something that made an ethical or legal point they wanted to make. Something they could contain. But crime is sloppy, usually tragic, and often bloody, and people's motivations for doing what they do can be beyond the control, or even the understanding, of the honchos of the 8th United States Army.

"So the 'gunslinger' isn't properly controlling his troops," Ernie said.

"Lack of training," Lieutenant Mendelson said. It was a reflexive statement, one the army uses to explain virtually any failing.

"Will the 'gunslinger' be asked to testify at the Threets court-martial?"

Lieutenant Mendelson looked sharply at Ernie. "That hasn't been decided yet."

"But you're not going to go with the homo defense?"

"Not my call."

"Whose call is it?"

"The officer assigned as his defense counsel."

"Who's that?"

"We don't know yet. The first one resigned."

"Why?"

"He has deployment orders. No time to properly prepare his defense."

"So who's been appointed to take his place?"

"That hasn't been decided yet."

"With less than a week to go before the trial starts, don't you think you ought to assign someone?"

"That's our job, not yours."

Ernie grinned, pulled out a pack of ginseng gum and offered her a stick. She declined.

"What about our report?" I asked.

"You refuse to change it?"

"No reason to change it," I said. "It's based on face-to-face interviews."

"Hearsay."

"Unless it's corroborated, yes."

She slid the report into a folder.

"Okay. It's your butts on the line."

"I love it when you talk like that," Ernie said. She glared at him.

I dialed and listened to the phone ring once, twice, three times. On the fourth ring someone picked up and, in an exasperated tone, said, "BOQ." Bachelor Officer Quarters.

It was a woman's voice, so I knew I had the correct number.

"Hello?" she said.

I kept my silence. She listened. "Okay," she said finally. "No heavy breathing, so you must be the mystery man."

She waited for me to reply, but again I said nothing. She sighed and the phone clattered to the wooden table.

"Prevault!" she shouted, her voice echoing down the hall. "It's *him* again."

Footsteps pounded into the distance and a few seconds later, lighter footsteps returned. The phone was lifted up and then a hushed voice came over the line, muffled, as if she'd covered the receiver with her hand.

"George, is that you?"

"It's me," I said.

Captain Leah Prevault was a psychiatrist at the 121st Evacuation Hospital; she and I had worked together on a previous case. We'd also gotten to know one another pretty well and one thing had led to another. But our relationship had to be kept secret because, even though as a CID agent my rank was classified, I was still an enlisted man and pretty much everyone on Yongsan Compound knew it. Captain Prevault, on the other hand, was a commissioned officer. Under the provisions of the Uniform Code of Military Justice, we were prohibited from fraternization—for the maintenance of good order and discipline, supposedly. Violation of this directive could make either one of us—or both—subject to court-martial. Which is why I didn't identify myself the few times I called her at the BOQ.

"Where are you?" she asked.

"Have you interrogated Orgwell yet?"

"We don't call them 'interrogations.'"

"But you asked him about the case?"

"No. I let him talk."

"That must've been tricky, getting him to open up."

"We have our ways."

I imagined her wearing her bathrobe, a white towel wrapped around her hair, holding the phone with both hands and leaning against the wall in the center of the BOQ hallway.

"I have a favor to ask," I told her. She waited. I explained what Threats had said at the 8th Army Stockade in ASCOM.

When I finished, she said, "They'll claim he's lying."

"I know. Can you meet with him?"

"I'll need a referral."

"They have a doctor down there in ASCOM, don't they?"

"I suppose."

"Contact him. Tell him someone told you that Threats needs help."

"Does he?"

"A lot of it."

"But mainly you're just trying to evaluate his credibility."

"Yes," I replied.

She sighed. "I'll see what I can do."

"When can we meet?" I asked.

She told me.

The Kit Kat Club sat in the maze of narrow pedestrian lanes that comprised the district in Seoul known as Samgakji. Literally, the

Three-Horned District. It derived its name from a famous three-way intersection centered at the Samgakji traffic circle. Roads ran from there north to the Seoul Train Station, south to the Han River Bridge, and east to 8th Army headquarters—and, beyond that, to the village of Itaewon.

It was a short walk out of the western gate of 8th Army's Yongsan Compound to the red-light district of Samgakji. However, it was a walk that white GIs seldom took. The village of Samgakji was frequented almost exclusively by black soldiers. White soldiers frequented Itaewon, a mile away on the other side of the compound. Nobody enforced this segregation, it had just developed over the years, but for some reason it was an unwritten rule that was seldom broken.

Except for tonight.

Ernie and I pushed through the front swinging doors of the Kit Kat Club.

Marvin Gaye wailed through the withered speakers of a jukebox. It was early, so there were only about a dozen GIs in the place, some of them shooting pool, others standing near the bar, laughing about something. But the laughter stopped when Ernie and I walked in.

We weren't in uniform. We were wearing our running-the-ville outfits: sneakers, blue jeans, sports shirts with collars, and blue nylon jackets with fire-breathing dragons embroidered on the back. Beneath the writhing reptile, Ernie's jacket said: *I've served my time in hell.* Somewhat of an overstatement, unless he was talking about his two tours in Vietnam. Mine said simply: *Korea: 1970 –1974.*

Most of the black GIs wore slacks and colorful shirts,

occasionally with a beret or fedora tilted rakishly to the sides of their heads. None of them wore blue jeans.

Ernie was all out of reefer but he approached the GIs at the bar and offered them sticks of ginseng gum. There were no takers. While he bantered with them, I ducked behind the bar and flashed my badge to the barmaid. Her hair was tightly curled into a bouffant Afro, and as I started opening the beer coolers, her mouth dropped open. I was sliding up the first one, illuminating the contents with my flashlight, when she found her voice.

"Whatsamatta you?" she said.

"Inspection," I replied, an English word most Korean workers in GI bars understood. Not only were inspections a big part of their GI customers' lives, but they were also a favorite means of control utilized by Korean government authorities. Not so much to make sure that the bars complied with safety and health regulations, but rather as a means of coercing payoffs.

"No can do," she said. When I didn't stop, she repeated, "Mamasan say no can do."

She scurried into the back room.

I found them in the last cooler, hidden in a cardboard box that said Samyang Ramyon: a dozen sixteen-ounce cans of Colt 45.

An older woman appeared behind me.

"Whatsamatta you?" she said. A favorite expression around here. But her voice was more gravelly, scraped raw by years of booze and tobacco smoke.

I showed her my badge.

"This," I said, holding up one of the cans. "Where you get?"

"Present-uh," she said quickly. "Some GI present-uh to me."

"It was a gift?"

She nodded quickly.

"And where did the GI get it?" I asked.

"PX," she said. "He buy PX."

She was lying and I was about to call her on it when something heavy slammed onto the bar. A sledge hammer. That's what I thought at first. But then I turned and looked. An angry black GI held a pool cue aloft, threatening to use it again.

"You don't *mess* with the Kit Kat Club. You *arra*? You don't mess with Mama and you don't mess with the brothers."

He was a burly-looking character with a broad face and angry eyes. The rest of the GIs in the bar were slowly approaching at his rear to back him up.

I held up my hands in surrender, palms facing forward.

"All right," I said. "Just a health and welfare inspection." I came out from behind the bar and Ernie joined me. We pushed our way through the small crowd, staying on the opposite side of the pool table from the guy with the pool cue, and were about halfway to the door when one of the GIs said, "Health and welfare inspection, my *ass*."

An eight ball slammed against the door in front of us.

We hurried outside, but before we exited Ernie turned and waved and gave the patrons of the Kit Kat Club a slight bow.

Out on the street, Ernie said, "Nice fellows."

"A little territorial," I replied.

The next bar was called the Aces High Club. It was smaller but had piped-in jazz and a longer bar with a few booths along the wall. Three or four older business girls sat in the booths, smoking and gossiping, but interrupted their talk long enough to gape at us as we walked in. The bartender was a young man wearing a white shirt, black bow tie, and black vest. Ernie ordered an OB. I surprised the bartender when I said, "Colt 45."

"No have," he said.

"Why not?" I asked. "I thought everybody have."

"Most tick have."

"When?"

"Tomorrow we get, maybe."

The black market in Korea is so widespread that no one bothers to deny its existence.

I settled for an OB and waited for one of the business girls to approach. Within five minutes, two of them did. Ernie horsed around with them, getting them laughing, and when they asked us to buy them drinks, I mentioned the lack of Colt 45. The girls looked concerned, anxious that I wasn't pleased. For a moment they chatted between themselves in rapid Korean. I followed most of it and picked out the words *"maeul ui jwi."*

Then one of them turned to me and said, "Tomorrow have."

"What time?"

That stumped her. "Tomorrow daytime, anybody bring Colt 45. Tomorrow night you come Aces High, have."

I decided not to press them, not right now. I didn't want to spook whoever was bringing the Colt 45 tomorrow.

Ernie and I finished our drinks, thanked the girls, and left them mumbling that we hadn't bought them a drink. I told them we'd see them tomorrow. I don't think either of them believed it. Of course, neither did I.

■ ■ ■

Prior to the Civil Rights Movement, the US Army ignored segregation and prejudice within its ranks, pretending it didn't exist. Now, because of mandates by Congress, Equal Employment Opportunity training had been established, but the effects of race riots only a few years ago and what the black GIs saw as the bias of the predominantly white officer corps meant that nerves were still rubbed raw. As such, most of the black GIs treasured their time off compound, where they could get on down with the Korean girls and commiserate with their brothers. And they weren't real happy when white GIs burst through their porous little bubble and stepped into their world.

Ernie and I tried three more clubs, keeping a low profile, not wanting to piss off the black GIs any more than we had to. At each club, I mentioned the name *maeul ui jwi*.

"What's it mean?" Ernie asked.

"A rat of the village."

"The Ville Rat," Ernie replied.

"Right."

We managed to locate two bar owners, three waitresses, and two business girls who gave me a description of him: skinny, curly red puffed-out hair, a wispy mustache. His clothing was strictly nonregulation: slacks and leather boots and brightly colored shirts with starbursts and swirls.

"Migun?" I asked. Is he an American soldier?

The response was unanimous: *He was, but he's not now.* Bit by bit I gathered that the Ville Rat made his money by selling malt liquor and imported cognac to the bars in Samgakji and elsewhere. He traveled from GI village to GI village, selling his wares, showing up on a set schedule to replenish supplies. He was white but he sold to the bars that catered to black GIs. Most of the bars charged 1,500 *won* for a can of Colt 45, three bucks, which was a hell of a lot. So not many GIs bought it. But there were a few who did. Maybe because it reminded them of home. Maybe because they wanted a little more kick than beer offered without having to drink so much that they'd put on weight.

I tried to find out what the bar owners paid the Ville Rat for each can, but they were evasive. Black marketeering was widespread but still a crime. I figured they probably paid a thousand for it. The Ville Rat would want twice what he paid for it, standard remuneration on the black market. So maybe he paid a dollar for it, sold it to the bar owner for two and they in turn sold it to their customer for the equivalent of three US dollars, or 1,500 *won*.

I wasn't sure of any of this, but the economics made sense. Nobody sold what they purchased out of the military PXs or commissaries without receiving at least twice what they paid for it, and sometimes more. The catch was that the Ville Rat wasn't buying the Colt 45 out of the PX or the Class VI store because 8th Army's Central Locker Fund didn't carry it.

Ernie and I strolled down the main drag of Samgakji. Groups of GIs standing near the front of nightclubs stopped talking as we approached and glared at us. Clicking loudly on his ginseng gum, Ernie raised a hand in greeting, as if they were old friends. No one returned the gesture.

"So where does the Ville Rat buy the Colt 45 and the cognac?" Ernie asked.

"If he's not in the army anymore," I said, "he doesn't have a ration card, so he can't buy the cognac out of the Class Six."

"And the Colt 45?"

"He can't buy that anywhere," I said. "There's no demand for it amongst Koreans, so no one imports it."

"Do we know that for sure?"

"Okay," I admitted. "Maybe we don't. But we do know about the customs duties and the transportation costs. You buy a can of Colt 45 from a wholesaler in the States, you pay maybe fifty cents for it. Then you have it shipped overseas and then you pay the customs duties."

Ernie whistled.

"Right. By then it costs you at least two bucks. Maybe more."

"And two bucks, a thousand *won*, is what he's selling the Colt 45 to the bar owners for."

"Right. He'd lose money on the deal."

Ernie thought about that. "So maybe he's like Johnny Appleseed, just spreading joy around the world."

A brown bottle hurtled out of the sky, missed my head by a few inches, and crashed to the pavement. I ducked. Ernie turned and ran toward the dark alley where it had come from. He halted when he looked down the narrow pedestrian lane and saw no one there. Across the street, a pack of black GIs stood in front of a juke joint. Music blared out of the bar in a sinuous, thumping rhythm. A single bulb illuminated their faces—all of them sweaty, flushed, lined with glee, greatly enjoying our anxiety.

Fists clenched, Ernie glared back at them.

I grabbed his elbow and pulled him away.

"Shit heads," he said. That seemed to make him feel better.

When we hit the road that led back to the compound, a blue KNP sedan blocked our way. A dapper Korean man in an overcoat stood next to the vehicle. The dim yellow bulb of the street lamp illuminated his face: Mr. Kill.

He motioned for us to get in. We did. He sat up front, next to his driver and full-time assistant, Officer Oh. As usual she wore the official KNP female uniform: low-cut black oxfords, navy blue skirt, neatly pressed baby-blue blouse, and a pillbox cap with an upturned brim pinned to her braided hair.

"How'd you find us?" Ernie asked.

Inspector Gil Kwon-up, chief homicide inspector of the Korean National Police, shrugged.

"We have our ways."

Ways like police stations strategically placed throughout the entire metropolis of Seoul and foot patrols branching out from there.

"*Why'd* you find us?" I asked.

"There's something I want to show you," he said

Officer Oh drove toward the main drag that headed from Samgakji circle toward the Seoul Train Station, stepped on the gas, and plowed into heavy nighttime traffic.

Ernie leaned forward, gazing avidly past her left ear, excited by something. Maybe the traffic. Maybe the chase. More likely, her. There's nothing he likes better, he once told me, than a woman who's a fascist.

A *kisaeng* house is an institution in Seoul that virtually all men of any means participated in, at least occasionally. Of course the *kisaeng* houses for the rich and famous are elaborate edifices behind stone walls with accoutrements so luxurious that people like me and Ernie can only imagine what they might be like. But there are lower-level *kisaeng* houses, more like converted homes, where women in traditional Korean gowns, the *chima-jeogori*, dance and sing and pluck tunes on the *kayagum* zither. Where kimchi and soju and marinated beef and various delights from the sea are served and hardworking businessmen take off their jackets and loosen their ties and sit cross-legged on cushions on a warm floor and allow the gorgeous female *kisaeng* to rub their brows with warm towels and massage their backs and giggle musically every time they tell a weak joke.

That was the type of place Ernie and I had been to a couple of times, and it was the type of place Mr. Kill took us to this time. Stoically, Officer Oh waited outside in the sedan. Bright red Chinese characters shone from a white background on the neon sign. Mr. Kill glanced at me, raising one eyebrow. I read it.

"*Myong Un,*" I said. "Bright Cloud."

Kill cracked a begrudging smile. "Very good," he said.

At the entranceway, at least a dozen pairs of men's shoes sat beneath the raised wooden floor. A heavily made-up middle-aged woman in an embroidered silk gown bowed to us and spoke in rapid Korean to Mr. Kill. We slipped off our shoes, stepped up on the polished surface, and followed her as she floated down the long hallway. She turned right, then left, and finally stopped and slid open an oil-papered door, motioning us in and bowing as she did so.

Ernie and I followed Mr. Kill into the room. He slipped off his overcoat and hung it on a coatrack. We did the same with our nylon jackets. Ernie arranged his so the fire-breathing dragon snarled at anyone who might approach. Then we sat on flat cushions on the floor around a low rectangular table. Mother-of-pearl white cranes flapped their wings against a black background, attempting to lift themselves into a beckoning sky.

"So what the hell are we here for?" Ernie asked.

"To talk to a girl," Mr. Kill said.

Ernie's eyes widened. "That's what everybody comes here for."

The oil-papered door slid open. The middle-aged woman entered again, this time carrying a wooden tray with three steaming cups of barley tea and a small porcelain pot for refills. She poured the cups, offered them to us with two hands, and bowed once again before backing out of the room.

I sipped on my tea. So did Ernie, gathering by Mr. Kill's silence that more answers wouldn't be forthcoming. Not, at least, until he was good and ready.

Footsteps pattered down the hallway. Tentative, light. The footsteps of a small person, almost childlike except for the deliberateness of the step. They paused in front of the door, as if they had to take a deep breath to summon courage. There was a moment of silence, and then the door slid abruptly open. A small young woman bowed very low and shuffled into the room.

Mr. Kill motioned with his open palm. *"Anjo."* Sit down.

She did.

Her face was full cheeked but not fat, and heavily made up. The *chima-jeogori* she wore was made of cotton, not the fine silk of the older woman's, and had a broad print pattern of red, green, and blue stripes, not elaborate hand embroidery. She stared at the tabletop, fingers interlaced in front of her waist. What she looked like was a rice-powdered chipmunk waiting for a falcon to swoop down and snatch her into the sky.

"Miss Kwon," Inspector Gil said gently, speaking in Korean, "do not be afraid of these two men. They are here to listen, not to hurt you."

She nodded very slightly to indicate that she had heard. In a halting voice she told her story.

She was from the province of Kyongsan-namdo and her parents had been very poor; itinerant laborers moving from farm to farm. She hadn't acquired even the nationally mandated six years of schooling, and when she reached her teens her parents were approached by a recruiter looking for young women to purchase for work in Seoul.

"Purchase?" I asked, using the Korean word.

Mr. Kill motioned for me to be quiet. "Once you started work," he said in Korean, "your employer promised to send money directly to your parents?"

She nodded.

"Did he?"

"I'm not sure."

"What happened then?"

"They took me to a *kisaeng* house in Mapo. There I was trained in how to serve men." Her face reddened as she said this. "Later, when they thought I was presentable enough, I was driven along with three other girls to Seoul."

"And one of these girls was the woman you knew as Miss Hwang?"

"Yes. That's what she called herself."

None of them, I figured, would be using their real names. In fact, Mr. Kill hadn't even used this young woman's name. Remaining anonymous made it easier for her to confess.

"And they took you where?" Kill asked.

"To a dormitory, somewhere out near Guri." Just east of Seoul. "I thought it was strange. I mean, strange that we didn't have to entertain men at night. And then I found out why."

She paused, looking down. We waited while she composed herself. I was beginning to realize what a brave little woman this was. She took a deep breath and started again.

"They had a van, and a driver. They would take us to various places. Office buildings after they were closed, hotel basements, even picnic areas outside the city."

"What would you do there?" Mr. Kill asked.

"We would serve the men," she said simply.

"In what way?"

For the first time, she looked up at him. "In every way."

"And Miss Hwang always went with you?"

"She was one of us."

"How well did you get to know her?"

"Not very. They kept us separated during the day. They had work for us to do. Mending old dresses. Washing. Ironing. Trying to make old rags look like new." She shook her head at the memory. "We tried to look like *kisaeng*, but we weren't *kisaeng*. We were the lowest of the low. Shuttled around from one place to another. I read about it in a movie magazine once. We're what the Americans call 'party girls.'"

She pronounced it in the Korean way: *pa-ti gu-ruhl*.

"How long did this go on?"

"Months. Until I escaped."

"How did you escape?"

"The van driver was lax. And the man who was supposed to accompany him was sick. We were stuck in traffic, late in the afternoon, all dressed up and on our way to another party. Right in the middle of the road, I slid open the door, jumped out, and ran."

"In your *chima-jeogori*?"

"Yes. And my rubber sandals. The driver wasn't able to leave the van, and the traffic was so heavy that he couldn't turn around. Not in time, at least."

"Where did you go?"

"I don't know. I just ran. When night fell and I realized that I was safe, I started to beg. No one would help me, but one kind woman gave me some money. With that, I caught a bus and came here, to Mukyo-dong."

"Why Mukyo-dong?"

"Because I knew there were real *kisaeng* houses here. Where the girls just served the men in the traditional way, not that other way. I thought maybe I could get a job."

"And you did?"

"Yes. I found the Bright Cloud and knocked on the door, and by that time I looked horrible, but the woman who owns this place is kind. She took me in. She fed me. She took care of me."

Tears came to her eyes.

"And you've worked here ever since?"

"Yes."

"You took a big risk by trying to escape."

"Yes."

"What would they have done to you if they caught you?"

She hugged herself and shuddered. "I'm not sure."

"The same thing they did to Miss Hwang?"

She stared at the far wall. "Yes, maybe."

Inspector Gil Kwon-up, the man known as Mr. Kill, leaned closer. "What exactly did they do to Miss Hwang?"

-8-

The elderly woman knocked and breezed into the room. Briskly, she replaced the cold pot of tea with a new one, dumped the cold tea in our cups into the old pot, and poured us steaming cups of fresh tea. I figured this was her way of letting us know that we'd been here too long. Already, male voices talked and laughed down the hall. After a few drinks, they'd be clapping their hands in rhythm and singing ancient Korean songs and, eventually, after even more cups of soju, they'd be dancing, with the girls or with each other.

Being a *kisaeng* was a legitimate occupation, like being a barmaid or a hostess in the States. As long as, that is, the girls weren't required to sleep with the customers. Apparently, the Bright Cloud was on the up-and-up.

After the oil-papered door was slid closed, Mr. Kill turned to the young woman and said, "Tell us about Miss Hwang."

She clenched her hands, staring straight ahead, and started talking.

"Of all the girls, she was the most beautiful. All the men wanted her to sit next to them. She was sweet and kind, and even though we had to do those things, sometimes the men would give her extra money. Later, the men in charge took the money away from her but they beat her less."

"Less than the other girls?"

"Yes."

"By the time you escaped," Mr. Kill said, "Miss Hwang was already gone."

"Yes. Gone." We waited while she composed herself. "One night they took us to a warehouse."

"Do you know where?"

"Not exactly . . . They kept the shades drawn on the van, but somewhere in Seoul."

"You told me before there was much traffic and even though you moved very slowly, there was no honking."

In downtown Seoul, in order to cut down on noise pollution, using a car horn is strictly prohibited. KNP traffic patrols enforce the rule with stiff fines. Hundreds of cabs and other vehicles jostle ruthlessly for position, but as odd as it might seem to the Westerner, none of them honk their horn. Try that in Manhattan.

"So you were downtown?"

"I believe so. We were led through the back door of a small warehouse. There were many boxes with printing I couldn't understand. Finally, we reached a side room. There were foreign men there."

"How many?"

"Six, maybe seven."

"What were they doing?"

"Playing cards. Not *huatu*, foreign cards."

"What did they look like?"

"Big. Ugly. Big noses." She glanced at me, suddenly shy. "Their eyes were so enormous, I was afraid to look at them."

"But you had to."

"I kept my eyes down."

"So you served them. Beer? Liquor?"

"Yes. Some of the girls were bold. They started to teach them to sing and after they had drunk much whiskey, they danced."

"With the girls?"

"Yes."

"Korean dances?"

"Yes. They taught them."

"And you?"

"I sat still, hoping they wouldn't notice me."

"Did they?"

Her face was very red now. She swallowed hard. "Yes, one of them. He took me behind the boxes."

Mr. Kill was silent for a moment. "And what happened to Miss Hwang?"

"One of the men wanted her."

"Yes?"

She realized that her meaning wasn't clear. "He wanted to keep her."

"Keep her?"

"Yes. Later the girls told me that he offered much money. Or maybe he traded for her, I'm not sure."

"Traded what?"

She shook her head violently. "Oh, I don't know. They told us nothing. All I know is that after the party, Miss Hwang left with one of the foreign men. We never saw her again."

Mr. Kill said very softly and very patiently, "Do you know what this man looked like?"

"Like a foreigner," she said.

"Yes, but . . ."

"He had a big nose and big eyes." She glanced our way. "Like them. I don't *know*. I was afraid to look."

Mr. Kill reached inside his coat pocket and pulled out a black-and-white picture. It was the official police photo of the dead woman lying beside the Sonyu River, damp dress spread around her, eyes staring lifelessly at the grey sky. He slid it across the table. "Is this Miss Hwang?"

The girl glanced at it, nodded violently, and then she was crying. Mr. Kill glanced toward me.

I took a deep breath, looked at Ernie. He shook his head. I turned back to the girl, speaking in Korean. "Do you have any idea why this foreign man singled out Miss Hwang?"

"She was pretty."

"Any other reason?"

"Her writing."

"Writing?"

"She often did that at parties. She would pull out a writing brush and paper and either write Chinese characters, for good luck or happiness, or sometimes she would sketch faces. Make people laugh."

This wasn't unusual. The *kisaeng* were expected to use one talent or another to entertain their guest. Sometimes dancing, sometimes playing a musical instrument, sometimes other things.

"Did she do this at this party?"

"Yes. I didn't see most of it." She blushed again. Apparently, while Miss Hwang was putting on her show, this young woman was otherwise occupied in another part of the warehouse.

When I had no further questions, Mr. Kill policed up the photograph and slid it back into his pocket. As we were leaving, I slipped a ten thousand *won* note, about twenty bucks, onto the table. The small *kisaeng* didn't even look at it. Her face was down, flushed red, her eyes moist.

Second Lieutenant Bob Conroy sat on a black vinyl divan in the dayroom of his BOQ, Bachelor Officer Quarters, while a couple of other young officers played pool on the table nearby. Stacks of legal documents were spread over the cigarette-burned coffee table in front of him. He looked up from his work when Ernie and I walked in.

We introduced ourselves and shook hands all around.

"When were you assigned to the Threets case?" I asked.

"Last night. After chow. Peggy Mendelson found me and handed me my orders." He pointed at a sheet of paper stuck beneath a larger stack.

"The trial's in two days," Ernie said. "Do you think you'll have time to prepare?"

Conroy stared at the paperwork wistfully. "There's a lot to absorb."

"Which is why you're working so late," Ernie said.

"Yes."

"Any chance of a continuance?" I asked.

"Peggy told me to forget it. We go to trial in two days, by order of the commanding general."

"All right then," I said. We pulled up two straight-backed chairs and sat down opposite Second Lieutenant Conroy and explained to him everything we knew about the case. He didn't seem too comfortable with the allegations of homosexual coercion.

"If you call a couple of witnesses from Charley Battery up at Camp Pelham," Ernie said, "they could corroborate Sergeant Orgwell's sexual preferences." Ernie wrote two names on a sheet of paper and handed it to Conroy. They were amongst the young black troops Ernie had smoked reefer with behind the Charley Battery motor pool.

"I'll try," Conroy said.

"If they don't let you call them, at least get it on record during the trial that you tried to call them. It might be useful in an appeal."

"So you already think Threets is going to have to appeal this thing," Conroy said glumly.

"No offense, Lieutenant," I said, "but you're inexperienced and they're giving you virtually no time to prepare a defense. That makes it clear that Eighth Army has decided to wrap this thing up as quickly as possible, and that they've already chosen a side."

"Well," he said, "Threets did shoot a superior NCO."

"Yes, but there were extenuating circumstances."

"Circumstances Eighth Army doesn't want to talk about."

Ernie thumbed through the paperwork idly. "Congratulations, L.T. You just summed up the entire case."

In the jeep on the way back to the barracks, I said to Ernie, "Where do you figure this warehouse is the little *kisaeng* was talking about?"

"The Far East Compound. Gotta be."

The only US military base in downtown Seoul was the Far East Materiel and Support Command. Most of the people who worked there were civilians, either Koreans or DACs. It was a small base geographically, but much of the logistics planning that supported the 50,000-plus US troops in Korea and their 50-plus military compounds was conducted at the Far East Materiel and Support Command. That they might have an occasional poker game wasn't surprising. That they would bring in girls wasn't too surprising either. All civilians were generously paid, drawing not only with their government paychecks but also the overseas differential and a generous housing allowance. Compared to a GI humping the line along the DMZ, they had money to burn.

"We need to pay a visit to the Far East Compound," Ernie said.

"Everything's shut down right now," I said, "and word will spread too fast if we start asking questions during regular business hours. Whoever's responsible will cover their tracks."

"If they haven't already," Ernie said. "So when?"

"Tomorrow's Friday night, the perfect time for a poker game."

Ernie tightened his grip on the steering wheel. "And the perfect time for me to bust some fat-ass civilians for gambling on compound."

By noon the next day, Ernie and I were back in Samgakji. There weren't many GIs out this time of day, and we didn't expect there to be. Most of them were either working on compound or eating chow at the big 8th Army Dining Facility—better known as the mess hall. But Samgakji was nonetheless bustling at this time of day: housewives carrying plastic baskets on their way to and from the open-air market; old women balancing bundled laundry atop their heads; business girls with dented pans propped against their hips, dressed in T-shirts and shorts, on their way to the bathhouse. In front of the Kit Kat Club, a three-wheeled flatbed truck blocked our way. Bare-chested workmen flipped back dirty canvas, revealing huge one-yard-square blocks of shimmering ice. Resting a towel on his back, one of the workmen pinched a block of ice with huge metal tongs, hoisted it onto his shoulder, and bending forward, lugged it into the Kit Kat Club. After plopping the ice into a stainless-steel sink behind the bar, the workman left and the truck drove off.

Ernie and I approached the barmaid, a young woman we hadn't seen last night. There were no other customers in the club and she was surprised to see us, but she recovered quickly when I plopped three one-thousand-*won* notes on the bar. "Colt 45," I said. "*Tugei.*" Two.

She rummaged around for a set of keys, opened one of the coolers, and pulled two sixteen-ounce cans of Colt 45 out and set them on the bar. Before she opened them, Ernie cupped his hands atop the cans. He crooked his finger, to bring her closer. While he kept her occupied, I ran around behind the bar. Peering into the beer cooler, I noticed two things: the supply of Colt 45 hadn't been replenished, and there was a strong smell of garlic I hadn't noticed before lingering inside the stainless-steel compartment. Using my flashlight, I searched for a jar full of kimchi that might explain the aroma, but I didn't find any. I straightened up and peered at the barmaid. "The Ville Rat hasn't come yet?"

"Who?" she asked.

"*Maeul ui jwi,*" I said.

"*Moolah*," she said—I don't know—slightly frightened by our behavior, and by me having the temerity to barge behind the bar.

Ernie slid the two cans back toward her and said, "*Ahn mogo.*" We don't want.

I snatched up my three thousand *won*. As we walked out, the barmaid stared after us, puzzled, but placed the two cans of Colt 45 back into the cooler.

We found places to wait that we hoped would be inconspicuous. Although it was difficult for two American GIs, both of us over six feet tall, to find a way to appear inconspicuous in a Korean neighborhood that, at least for the moment, was bereft of foreigners.

Most of the lanes in Samgakji were narrow affairs, just wide enough for one or two pedestrians to walk abreast. The main drag, the one road navigable by taxicabs or delivery trucks, cut a dogleg through the maze of wooden hooches and one- or two-story brick buildings. It was along this road that the nightclubs and the bars and the chophouses were located, and that's where we waited. Ernie at the bent knee of the dogleg, beneath an awning in front of a small, open-fronted store selling cigarettes, soft drinks, packaged noodles, wheels of puffed rice, and strings of dried cuttlefish. They also sold ginseng gum, with which he quickly reprovisioned himself.

I decided to keep moving. I was pretty lousy at making myself unnoticeable, so I wandered into and out of the various tailor shops, brassware emporiums, and photography shops that catered to American GIs frequenting Samgakji nights and weekends. Most of the shop owners were friendly to me but disappointed when they discovered I wasn't there to buy anything.

I pretended to be conducting a verbal survey on the general impact of American soldiers' presence on locals in the area. Did they feel that they and their families were safe? Did they think that law enforcement, particularly the American MPs, were doing a good enough job? To my surprise, they were more than willing to talk about it; enthusiastic, in fact. Yes, they thought that the MPs and the KNP patrols were doing an adequate job, but they also thought that some of the problems were caused by the MPs themselves. The black GIs were boisterous but generally well-behaved; it was when a patrol of white MPs came around that there seemed to be a thickening of tension. A few of the shop owners asked me why the American army didn't have more black MPs.

I didn't respond, mainly because I didn't know what to tell them. I'd wondered that too. The military claimed that to be an MP, you had to meet certain qualifications that were more stringent than in other parts of the army, and it just so happened that more white soldiers met those conditions than black ones. Maybe. My own theory was that some black soldiers were reluctant to become MPs—it was like siding with the enemy. And some white soldiers couldn't wait to become MPs—to have the authority to lord it over others. Still, most MPs, in my experience, were honest and even sometimes heroic.

Korea specializes in three-wheeled trucks. There's a small cabin up front, just wide enough for a driver and one passenger, and a long, narrow bed in back enclosed by a short wall that can be loaded with enormous mounds of agricultural produce. Already, I'd seen a few trucks heading toward the open-air market piled high with fat daikon radishes, mounds of Napa cabbage, and canvas-covered bundles of fresh garlic cloves.

I'd hit virtually every mom-and-pop retail establishment in Samgakji. It was more than an hour past lunchtime and I was hungry. I strolled down the road. Ernie was still there sitting on a wooden stool, leaning against a splintered wooden plank, his eyes half-closed and his fingers laced across his belly.

One eye popped open. "Anything?" he asked.

"Not yet. Maybe the Ville Rat's not coming today."

"Maybe he heard we were asking questions about him."

"Maybe."

Ernie stood up. "Anyway, tonight we'll find that poker game the little *kisaeng* told us about."

"Yeah," I agreed.

"So let's go get some chow. We can always stop by here tonight, see if a delivery was made."

I agreed and we started to walk down the lane back toward the compound. From behind us, I heard the low growl of an engine. Probably another produce truck, I thought, but the engine noise grew louder and started to scream. Or it might've been a woman screaming. Either way, Ernie said, "Watch out!" and, startled, I leapt toward the far side of the road.

It was the wrong choice. I turned in time to see a three-wheeled garlic truck heading right for me. People up the road were shouting and cursing and leaping out of the way. Inside the cab sat two men with dark hair who, from this distance, appeared to be Korean. The truck was piled high with garlic. Behind me in either direction, a brick wall ran for more than ten yards. The truck was too close and moving too fast for me to make it to the end. The driver was hunched over the wheel, staring right at me. He wasn't stopping. And he was already bouncing the side of his truck against the wall. Within seconds, if I didn't do something, he could crush me, leaving my blood and guts smeared against the brick like a giant squashed bug.

Ernie shouted something I didn't quite catch, then stepped out into his side of the road, about five yards closer to the truck, and waved both arms in the air. The truck jogged toward him momentarily, but Ernie leapt back into the safety of one of the pedestrian lanes and the driver swerved back in my direction. I started to run but realized I couldn't make it past the wall in time. I was vaguely aware of the roar of the engine and the shouts of bystanders and the screams of high-pitched voices, but I was also resigned to the fact that I wasn't going to make it. Either this truck was completely out of control or, more likely, this guy driving the garlic truck was out to get me. Either way, I was about to be roadkill on the side of a dirty brick wall.

Ahead, a low-hanging tile jutted from a roof. Someone had left a few wooden crates, still strewn with wilted green leaves, shoved against the brick wall. I had an idea. Building up all the strength I could muster, I charged toward the crates. The truck was only a few yards behind me now. Using my left foot, I stepped up onto them, feeling them give way and shift beneath my weight, but their support was just enough to help me leap upward toward the curved edge of the overhanging tile. I grabbed hold with both hands and ran up the side of the wall, catching a foothold on some jutting brick and pulling myself up as I did so. The truck was just below me now and crashed wildly along the edge of the brick, grinding metal and emitting a hideous screech. I kept pulling myself up, trying to arch my stomach skyward to get myself out of the way, but I couldn't pull myself high enough, and something slammed into my spine. I realized it was the top of the cab of the truck, and the shock of the impact was enough to make me lose my grip. I tumbled backward, the truck still moving forward and scraping crazily along the brick, and then the piled garlic was beneath me, but the truck kept moving forward and I was rolling toward the rear, tumbling through mounds of flaking garlic as I did so. The engine roared louder than ever, and the next thing I knew I was falling. Ernie ran past me toward the truck, but just as I glimpsed him I hit the ground with a thump, hundreds of solid little garlic bulbs cushioning my fall. I watched the rear of the truck speeding away, crushed crates careening in front of it, Ernie lunging madly after it, and then something flew through the air and cracked into my skull. I passed out.

When my eyes popped open, Ernie was grinning down at me.

"Didn't know you could climb so fast," he said.

I shook my head. "Neither did I." I tried to sit up.

Ernie placed his hand on my chest. "Lie down. The medics are on their way."

I lay back down.

"What about the truck?" I asked.

"It's gone. Don't worry, you're safe."

Suddenly, I realized I was angry. I wanted to find and prosecute the guy who tried to kill me. "Did you get the license plate number?" I asked.

"I did better than that," Ernie said. He grinned again and reached to the ground and lifted something up, twisting it to show it to me. It took a second for my eyes to focus, then I realized what it was. A dented and rusty piece of metal with numbering on it. Ernie'd done better than jot down the license plate number. He'd ripped the whole thing clean off the back of the truck.

"You guys smell like *shit*!" Riley screamed. "Get the hell out of my admin office."

"Go plow a minefield," Ernie told him.

The medics had checked me out at the scene, given me some vision tests, and asked me a few questions like who'd won the World Series last year and things like that. The specialist four in charge said he thought I was okay, but standard operating procedure said I should go to the 121 Evac Hospital. But by then I felt okay. Ernie'd helped me dust off most of the garlic leaves and I sat on a stool in the open-fronted store with a can of guava juice that the owner insisted I drink. When I tried to pay, he waved off the money.

Ernie didn't seem enthusiastic about driving me over to the 121 Evac emergency room and sitting around all day waiting for the results of a bunch of damn tests, so I told the medics that I'd go on sick call tomorrow, which seemed to satisfy them. On our walk through Samgakji my legs were a little wobbly, but I believe that was more from fear than from the lingering effect of a concussion. We climbed in Ernie's jeep and drove back to the 8th Army CID office, where we were greeted so warmly by Staff Sergeant Riley.

Miss Kim held a lace-edged handkerchief to her nose and studied me with a worried expression. *"Byongwon ei kaya-ji,"* she said. You should go to the hospital. By speaking Korean, she was purposely excluding Riley and Ernie from our conversation.

"Nei-il," I told her. Tomorrow.

She accepted my decision but still seemed worried about it.

Colonel Brace entered the admin office, something he rarely did. Riley shouted *"Ten-hut!"* and stood at rigid attention. Ernie and I were already standing.

"At ease," Colonel Brace said. Then he approached me. "You all right, Sueño?"

"Fine, sir," I replied.

He sniffed the air. "You smell like garlic."

"So Sergeant Riley was just pointing out."

"According to the MPs, you were hit by a truck full of the stuff?"

"I wasn't actually hit. I managed to get out of the way."

"Good. What were you two doing in Samgakji anyway?"

Ernie told him about our lead on a guy who had apparently witnessed murder of the woman found dead near the Sonyu River. He left out all the stuff about black marketeering. No need to confuse him.

"That's the one up by Camp Pelham?" Colonel Brace said.

Ernie nodded.

"Good. Keep working that. And this Threets thing—stay close to Lieutenant Mendelson. I don't want you two bogarting out on your own."

"We're just reporting the facts as we find them, sir."

"But we're much too close to game time to be changing our strategy now. The court-martial's the day after tomorrow. Better to concentrate on the Sonyu River murder case. Do you have any suspects?"

"Not yet, sir."

He gazed at the top of my head. "Have someone take a look at that knot, Sueño."

"Yes, sir."

He nodded, turned, and strode out of the room.

Riley sat back down behind his desk. "You heard the man. Get your butts in gear on that Sonyu River murder."

"You plowed that minefield yet?" Ernie asked him tauntingly.

Miss Kim gazed at me one last time, then hurried out into the hallway toward the ladies' room. When she came back, she held a clean towel with which she wiped the bruise on my head, then applied a couple of adhesive bandages and what the Koreans call *mycin*, antibiotic ointment. I thanked her and asked if she could call Inspector Gil's office for me. She did. I heard her talking to Officer Oh, explaining what had happened and giving her the license number off the plate that Ernie had snagged. When she was done, she made me sit down on the best chair in the office and fixed me some Black Dragon tea.

After she returned to her typing, Ernie pulled up a straight-backed chair next to me. "How much you figure this Ville Rat makes?"

I thought about it. There were just over fifty US compounds in Korea, each with a GI village outside its gates. Most had at least one bar that catered exclusively or mostly to black GIs. Some places had more than that, like Camp Casey, the 2nd Infantry Division headquarters, which had both Samgakji and Tongdu-chon. That was at least fifty bars or nightclubs that might want to order Colt 45. If the Ville Rat made 500 *won* profit, or one dollar, on each can and sold only one case per month to each bar, that was twenty-four dollars times fifty, which was over a thousand a month. And that wasn't counting the cognac. Still, maybe I was being overgenerous in my estimate.

I told Ernie, "If he hustles, five hundred US dollars a month."

"Maybe three or four times that," Ernie said.

"Maybe."

Rent for a Western-style apartment in Seoul ran the equivalent of $250 per month. If he lived in a Korean hooch, with no central heating, with an outdoor toilet and only enough electricity to support a single bulb, rent would be half that. Food was cheap in Korea, and besides, the Ville Rat was skinny. He wouldn't eat much.

"So he's making a good living," Ernie said.

"Seems like it."

"Enough to pay two garlic truck drivers to commit murder?"

"I doubt those two guys drive a garlic truck full-time."

"No. The truck was probably stolen just so they could use it to splat you against the wall."

"Why not you?"

"I'm sure they would've taken us both out if they could, but figured that killing one of us'd be enough to warn the other one off."

"Off of what?"

"The Sonyu River killing."

"Why?"

"I'm not sure," Ernie said. "Apparently, somewhere along the line, we struck a nerve."

But where, exactly? That's what we weren't sure of.

"What a waste of garlic," Ernie said.

Ernie and I occasionally frequented a joint in Itaewon that specialized in *dengsim gui*, roast flank steak. The thinly sliced meat was placed on a brazier in the center of the table and side dishes were served—cabbage kimchi and diced turnip in hot sauce and small saucer-sized plates of fresh garlic. Most people roasted a clove or two to add flavor to the meat, but Ernie emptied the plate onto the grill and popped the burnt garlic into his mouth like peanuts, washing them down with shot glasses of soju rice liquor, and before we'd finished our meal Ernie'd polished off two or three plates of garlic, much to the surprise of our waitress.

The next day, Ernie would show up at the CID detachment in his neatly pressed uniform, clean shaven, shoes polished, hair combed—looking like the squared-away soldier in a recruiting poster—but as he paraded around the office, people would start sniffing the air. "What's that smell?" someone would say. Oblivious, Ernie went about his business, caring not one whit that his pores were emitting the odor of the pungent herb he'd so gleefully consumed the night before.

Which explained his current air of bereavement. The garlic truck was a burnt-out shell.

"How do you know this is the right truck?" I asked.

Mr. Kill guided us around to the front. A singed license plate matching the one Ernie had snagged was still legible. About twenty yards away, across a beach of rough pebbles, the Han River flowed serenely. We were about two hundred yards north of the Chamsu Bridge in an area that at night would be dark and isolated. Someone had poured gasoline onto the truck, set it on fire, and hoofed it back to the main road where a confederate presumably stood by to whisk the arsonist away. In which direction? Into the heart of the city of Seoul, or south across the bridge to the Seoul-Pusan Expressway that could carry them almost anywhere in country? We had no way of knowing.

"Will you find the owner of the truck?" I asked.

"We already have," Mr. Kill told me. "A produce shipping company. One of their oldest and most reliable drivers was waylaid after picking up a load of garlic. Two toughs he'd never seen before threatened him with a knife and dropped him far in the countryside. He had to walk back to civilization, but even then he was too frightened to report the theft to the police."

"But he's talking now?"

"We convinced him."

"Do you believe his story?"

"Yes, he's a family man who'd have nothing to gain by murdering an American CID agent."

"Glad to hear it," Ernie said. "Can he identify the thieves?"

"He's with the sketch artist now. But they stuck a knife to his throat. He was too panicked to be very observant."

I knew Mr. Kill would do everything possible to glean any clues this truck might yield, but we both knew that he'd probably hit a dead end. The guys who'd tried to kill us seemed professional. It was unlikely we'd find them soon.

Mr. Kill read my thoughts. "I have another lead," he said. "Remember the calligraphy we found in Miss Hwang's sleeve?"

Miss Hwang. We knew the victim's name now. A nice name. Probably not her real name, but a nice name nevertheless.

"I remember," I said.

"We've been talking to teachers of calligraphy. Most are private and give lessons in their home, but there aren't many anymore. It's a dying art."

"One of them knew Miss Hwang?" Ernie asked.

"No. Better than that. One of them, Calligrapher Noh, gave lessons to an American."

"There must be plenty of Americans who study calligraphy," I said.

"Not many. And certainly not many who are GIs. Come, I'll let you talk to Noh."

Mr. Kill hopped into the front seat of his sedan, Officer Oh driving. Ernie and I followed in the jeep.

The road wound up one of the oldest and most crowded hills in Seoul, near Chongun-dong, just below the ramparts of the ancient stone wall built to protect the capital city during the Chosun Dynasty. The homes up here were tightly packed, hidden behind wood or brick walls, with narrow lanes just wide enough for a wooden pushcart. Officer Oh parked her sedan, blocking most of the road, and Ernie edged his jeep up tightly behind her. We climbed out and trudged up flagstone steps the last few yards. At an indentation in the stone wall, Mr. Kill stopped and pressed a button. An intercom buzzed and soon a voice said, *"Nugu-seiyo?"* Who is it?

Inspector Kill identified himself and another, louder buzz sounded as we pushed our way through the gate into a well-tended garden. On the far side of the garden, an elderly man in traditional white pantaloons and a blue silk vest waited for us on the raised porch. Inspector Kill bowed to Calligrapher Noh and the man bowed back, but his timing was off. I realized he was blind, relying on the white cane in his hand for both support and navigation. We slipped off our shoes and stepped up on the varnished wooden floor. The man, hearing our approach, turned and led us down a short hallway. At the end, he slid back an oil-papered door and we entered what appeared to be the study of a scholar from the thirteenth century. The floor was warm and covered with layers of rice paper. The old calligrapher lowered himself behind a mother-of-pearl writing desk that stood only about two feet high. Waving his cane, he motioned for us to sit opposite him on the flat seat cushions provided. Behind him were shelves stuffed with scrolls and codices and even a few bound books, all of them dusty, as if they hadn't been touched in years. He had a wispy grey beard and wrinkled eyes that, though sightless, smiled at us.

Ernie leaned toward Mr. Kill and said, "He can't see at all?"

"Some. Light and shadow. But in his youth, when he could see, he was a very famous calligrapher, so students still seek him out."

After a few pleasantries, Calligrapher Noh said in Korean, "You want to know about the American." Mr. Kill said yes and the old scholar began to talk.

It was somewhat less than a year ago that the man appeared at his front gate. He just knocked on the door and said something in English that the scholar didn't understand. Calligrapher Noh called his niece on the phone because she'd studied English in school and the American told her he wanted to become a student of calligraphy. Tuition was agreed upon, and from that day forward the American showed up every Tuesday night, spent an hour taking instruction, and left an envelope of money after each lesson. Apparently, the old scholar's niece would come over every morning, count the money, and made sure it was deposited in his bank along with the tuition from his other students.

"Did your niece," Mr. Kill asked, "or any of your other students ever see this American?"

"Never. He dealt only with me. As a student, he wasn't bad. He paid attention to technique, ink preparation, paper quality, maintenance of the writing brush, and he was obsessed with the details of stroke order and the proper grip." The old man frowned.

"But there was something about him," I said, interrupting. "Something that worried you."

"Yes. He was obsessive, which can be good, but isn't good when carried too far. When I criticized the first characters he attempted, he became angry, asked me how I could know they were wrong if I could not see them."

"How could you know?" Inspector Kill asked gently.

"From the sound of the brush on the paper, whether he was pressing too hard or too lightly, allowing too much ink to sink into the parchment, and by the amount of time he spent turning the brush at a curve or when blotting a stop."

"If he didn't trust your instruction," I asked, "why did he come to you?"

"I asked him the same thing."

"He could speak Korean?"

"No. Mostly I taught by demonstrating to him, holding his hand, making sure the grip was correct, and listening. He had potential, but after the third or fourth lesson, when I realized that he lacked the patience to become a true artist, I called my niece. She spoke to him and translated my words."

"What did he do?"

"He said nothing. Just set the phone down, sat still for a long time, and left."

"He quit?"

"Yes."

"Did he pay you for the last lesson?"

"Yes. The next day, my niece told me that he'd paid double."

"So money was no problem for him?"

"No."

"How did you know he was a soldier?"

"At the entranceway, when he took off his shoes, I heard the heavy clump of combat boots. And on his first visit, he brought me a gift."

As was customary for Korean students when they first visited a teacher. He slid it across the writing desk. A bottle of imported Hennessey cognac.

Ernie lifted and examined it. "No customs stamp," he said. "No import duty paid. Straight out of the Class Six."

"If we encounter this man," I asked the old scholar, "how will we be able to identify him?"

"Well, I can't tell you what he looks like, other than I believe he's tall and thin from the sound of his footsteps and the way he moved carefully through the house, but what most set him apart for me was his silence."

"Silence?"

"Yes. Whenever I corrected him, by guiding his hand or showing him the correct technique, he would sit very still for a long time. So long I almost wondered if he'd managed to slip away. I heard him sliding his fingers across his face or his head, and then finally, after I'd almost forgotten what we'd been doing, he would reach out and, as if nothing had happened, we'd start over."

"Silence?" I said.

"Yes, prolonged silence. The silence of a man trying very hard to control himself."

"Do you have any idea why he struggled so much to maintain control?"

"Yes. It's subtle, but I noticed an odd difference in the way he handled the inkstone and the brush."

"What do you mean?"

"When he used his left hand, his motions were fluid. His right hand, the one I guided for his brush strokes, was capable but not as capable as his left."

"How could you tell?"

"The motions were slower, more hesitant. More studied."

"So you believe this man was originally left-handed?"

"Yes. Once when he was having trouble with a stop and a slash to the right, I told him to try it with his other hand, his left." The old calligrapher clasped his narrow fingers, clutching them briefly at the memory. "This was the longest silence of all. I thought he would explode."

"So you think he was abused as a child because he was left-handed?"

The old calligrapher thought about my question. "Probably for much more than that. I thought of him as a cripple."

"A physical cripple?"

"No, physically he's quite capable. I thought of him as an emotional cripple. One of the most emotionally crippled people I've ever encountered."

A light shone in the guard shack of the main gate of the Far East District Compound. The small base had served as the headquarters for the US Army's Corps of Engineers in Korea since the end of the Korean War. It was nestled amidst high-rise buildings in downtown Seoul, only a few blocks from the massive Dongdaemun shopping district.

We'd said our goodbyes to Inspector Kill and Officer Oh and made our way here alone. Ernie drove up to the gate and a bored guard emerged from the shack. He wasn't an MP, just a GI with the rank of buck sergeant with a leather armband hanging from his left shoulder that read DUTY NCO. Stitched above the lettering was the red and white cloverleaf patch of the 8th United States Army.

Ernie showed him our dispatch.

"CID? What the hell do you guys want?"

His name tag said CAMPIONE. He was slightly overweight, his uniform was slovenly, and he could've used a shave before he started the night shift.

"What we want," Ernie said, "is none of your freaking business."

Campione's eyes narrowed. "We have a squared-away compound here," he said, "and if I remember correctly, a complete inventory was just conducted by a couple of you guys."

He was right; I recalled the purportedly award-winning audit by Agents Burrows and Slabem.

"Yeah," Ernie said. "So what?"

"So you got no business messing with the Far East Compound again."

This was too much. Ernie climbed out of the driver's seat. I stepped out of the passenger's seat and walked around to the front of the jeep.

"Who in the hell do you think you are?" Ernie said. "The freaking provost marshal of the Far East Compound?" Campione backed up half a step. Ernie leaned in closer. "Open the goddamn gate. It ain't up to you where we go and where we don't go."

"We're not part of Eighth Army," Campione protested.

"The hell you're *not*!"

"We run a tight little compound here and we don't *need* this shit."

"I don't care what you need or don't need," Ernie told him.

I stepped into the guard shack and pulled a handle that released the crossing bar. Ernie swiveled away from Campione, jumped back in the jeep, shifted it into gear, and rolled across the threshold. I jogged to the side of the jeep and jumped in. As we drove onto the compound, Campione glared at us for a moment, then hurried back into the guard shack, lifted the phone, and started dialing.

"He's calling reinforcements," I said.

"Screw them," Ernie said, still fuming. "A bunch of freaking supply clerks trying to tell us where we can and can't go."

Trees lined the road, fronting well-tended lawns. Behind them were yellow bulbs illuminating signs that labeled the stone and brick buildings: LOGISTICS PLANNING; 34TH SUPPLY AND MAIN-TENANCE BATTALION; SHIPPING AND IMPORT CONTROL; HIGHWAY AND BRIDGE CONSTRUCTION. The compound was a square about a half-mile on each side; we cruised around in the jeep, not quite sure what we were looking for.

"Cushy assignment," Ernie said. "Looks like a college campus."

We rolled past a well-lit sign that said: FAR EAST DISTRICT COMPOUND CLUB, ALL RANKS WELCOME. They weren't big enough to have their own officers' club, and besides, to the best of my knowledge, the handful of officers assigned to the Far East District Compound were quartered five miles away on Yongsan South Post and commuted here every day. They would mostly use the 8th Army officers' club. There was only one barracks on the Far East Compound, a two-story cement-block building housing about three dozen enlisted men. What must've been half of them stood on the broad cement steps in front of the club, searching the night, staring in our direction. One of them pointed.

"Looks like Campione alerted his buddies."

"Yeah, and they don't like strangers," I said.

Ernie snorted.

We continued to cruise through the compound, searching for a warehouse with a back entrance that might match what the little *kisaeng* had described. The place where a late-night poker game had been held; where several young girls had been trucked in against their will and one—a talented calligraphist who called herself Miss Hwang, her real name perhaps lost indefinitely once her corpse turned up on the banks of the Sonyu River some twenty-five miles north of here—had been purchased by an American.

"How about that?" Ernie said, pointing.

The sign out front read: CENTRAL LOCKER FUND, FAR EAST COMPOUND ANNEX.

We drove around back. There was indeed a back entrance. Ernie parked the jeep.

"How are we going to get in?" I asked.

Ernie reached in his pocket and pulled out a ring of keys.

"Where'd you get those?"

"From Strange. They're the extra set of keys kept by the Eighth Army staff duty officer."

I shone my flashlight at the thick steel ring. A metal tag was imprinted with the words FAR EAST DISTRICT COMPOUND. It was a large ring holding about three dozen keys of various shape and age. Some had cryptic numbers and letters scratched on or written in permanent marker, and others had paper tags Scotch-taped to them. I shone the flashlight steady on the lock on the back door while Ernie knelt and methodically tried each key. About halfway through the ring, the door popped open. Ernie turned the handle and shoved it forward as the heavy door creaked open.

"Class Six Heaven," Ernie said and shone his flashlight into the darkness.

Before I closed the door behind us, I peered outside at the small asphalt parking area. No movement. Beyond the walls of the compound, traffic purred, lights in tall buildings blinked on and off, and the pulsing life of the massive city of Seoul beat with the steady rhythm of a prehistoric beast; a beast ready to reach down and chomp us with its yellow fangs.

I closed the door.

"Over here," Ernie shouted.

We strolled past pyramids of cardboard cases of beer and soda, then long rows of all types of liquor—gin, vodka, scotch, bourbon, rum—arrayed neatly on ten-foot-high metal racks. After a short section of brandy and liqueur was the wine, and behind everything was an accounting office near the huge roll-up metal door that opened onto the loading dock.

I followed the sound of Ernie's voice, off to the side past the latrine and a supply cabinet for mops, brooms, and cleaning supplies. Finally I found him by a cement door with another padlock on it.

"Air-raid shelter," Ernie said. "You grab a case of booze, run downstairs with some dolly, and wait for the shooting to stop."

"Great way to survive World War Three."

It was a weak joke, but with some truth to it. Many observers thought that the Korean peninsula was a prime candidate for the starting point for World War III. After all, Korea was a country bitterly divided between the Communist north and the capitalist south, and was surrounded by three great powers: Red China, the Soviet Union, and Japan. And the most powerful country in the world, the United States, was heavily committed to the defense of South Korea, not only stationing 50,000 US troops here, but also sending squadrons of Air Force bombers on patrol out of Okinawa and Guam and keeping the US Navy's Seventh Fleet in Japan and in the waters nearby. Meanwhile, of course, we had plenty of booze and party girls—to soothe our worried brows.

Once again, I aimed my flashlight while Ernie knelt and studied the lock. He touched it, heard something rattle, and then gently pulled the hasp away from the wall.

"It's phony," he said. "Just here for show."

He grabbed the metal handle of the door and tugged. It didn't move. "Stuck," he said. He braced himself and pulled with two hands. The heavy door slowly slid open, swinging in a ponderous arc, cement scraping on cement. Ernie reached inside and fumbled along the wall until he found a switch. Below, down a short flight of steps, a weak yellow bulb switched on, glowing inside a metal mesh cage.

"Prop the door open with something," Ernie said.

I stepped toward the nearest rack, hoisted a case of triple sec from its shelf and set it on the floor up against the open door.

Clutching his flashlight, Ernie led the way.

The stairway turned back on itself. Down one more flight, Ernie found another light switch. This time, an overhead fluorescent bulb sputtered and blinked to life, exposing a large room. It was square, about ten yards on each side, and empty for the most part. Tile flooring had been swept clean. Cement walls, no windows, but what appeared to be ventilation fans overhead. On the far wall was a large steel sink, like those found in restaurant kitchens, and two faucets, one of them dripping patiently as if waiting for us.

In the unlit corners, Ernie's flashlight found large slabs of varnished lumber leaning against the wall.

"What the hell is this?"

"Dividers," I said. "Hinged. You can separate the room with

these. Maybe make a kitchen area over here, a serving area over there."

"No chairs," Ernie said.

But he was wrong about that. In a far corner, covered by a sheet, was a stack of straight-backed banquet chairs. I pulled the sheet off.

"Okay," Ernie said. "Plenty of beer and booze. Chairs. A place to make snacks in. What about a table?"

That's what was missing: a poker table. But why would anyone move one, unless they were trying to cover their tracks?

We searched. No table. But in a corner near a trash can, Ernie found shards of splintered wood. He picked up one of the pieces. Hanging from its edge, apparently glued, were a few strands of something green. Ernie fondled the material. "Felt," he said.

"Then there's more," I said.

"Outside?"

We hurried upstairs, turning off the lights and closing the doors behind us. On the far side of the asphalt lot, a row of metal drums sat atop a long wooden pallet; standard trash disposal at 8th Army. Every few days, a truck full of Korean workmen came by, hoisted the cans up and dumped the trash into the back of the truck. Primitive, but at least it provided jobs.

Using our flashlights, Ernie and I searched each of the drums. At the far end, one was full of nothing but shards and plenty of ripped green felt. Ernie pointed to one of the chunks of varnished wood.

"Corners. It was probably in the shape of an octagon. A gutter for chips, green felt on the inside."

"A poker table," I said. "But why'd they chop it up?"

"And recently, too," Ernie said. "They must pick this trash up at least twice a week."

For years I'd been seeing trash trucks winding their way through various military compounds in Korea, never paying them much mind.

"So whoever chopped up this poker table did it today. Or maybe yesterday."

"Why?" Ernie asked. "What set them off? They could've been having poker games in that room for years."

"And whoever was hosting them was making serious money."

The usual house rake was one chip out of every twenty-five. That was a fat 4 percent of every dollar bet, and in a typical high-stakes game, thousands of dollars would cross the green felt, with the house pocketing big money.

Gambling was illegal in Korea, except in the handful of casinos the government has authorized for tourists only. Private games were strictly prohibited. Korean television news is full of stories of locals being busted for illegal gambling and perp-walked in front of the klieg lights. But here on the Far East District Compound, conveniently located in the heart of downtown Seoul, the Korean National Police had no jurisdiction. The only law enforcement we'd seen so far in this little enclave of Americana was Sergeant Campione with his DUTY NCO armband.

"This might've been going on for years," Ernie said.

I stared at the shards. "So why stop now?"

Footsteps scraped on asphalt. We turned. Across the lot, approaching through the harsh rays of the overhead floodlight, a group of men approached. One of them was Campione, apparently off duty now, wearing baggy blue jeans and a sweatshirt with a drawing of a bulldog and the words NORTHERN NEW JERSEY STATE stenciled beneath the canine's drooping jowls.

There were ten men behind him, all of them looking grim. But what most caught my attention was what Campione held in his hand: a short-handled axe, its blade glistening in the harsh light.

I stared fixedly at the axe blade, but shook off my fear. When you're outnumbered and outgunned, the best strategy is to go for the bluff.

"Sergeant Campione," I said, as the men approached. "Good. I was just about to go looking for you."

I pulled my CID badge out of my pocket and held it over my head in the glare of the floodlight. Showing a confidence I didn't feel, I strode toward the men, raising my voice. "I'm Agent Sueño of the Eighth Army Criminal Investigation Division. This is my partner, Agent Bascom. I'm glad you're gathered here, because all of you are going to have to be interviewed."

The men stopped. I glanced at the axe. Campione still clutched it tightly in his grip.

"You've got no *right*," he said. "This is the Far East District Compound, not Eighth Army. You've got no right to mess with us."

I slipped my badge back into my pocket and held both hands up. "I know what you're thinking. One inspection just finished, and now another. But we're going to keep this one short and sweet. All we want to know is who was involved with the illegal gambling that was going on here. That's all. After we know that, we'll leave you alone."

The men glanced at one another, murmuring sullenly.

"What game?" Campione said. "We don't know what you're talking about."

From the darkness behind me, something large flew out of the night. It arched toward Campione and then crashed in front of his feet.

"How about this, Campione?" Ernie shouted.

Everyone stared at the chunk of wood that had just landed on asphalt. It was a corner chunk of the poker table, with a clear indentation for holding chips and what amounted to almost a square yard of green felt.

Ernie stepped forward. "You should've chopped finer," he said, gesturing toward Campione's axe.

A voice in the crowd said, "Why don't you get off our compound?"

Another voice said, "Yeah." And then a chorus joined in, cursing us and moving forward en masse. Ernie and I backed up. Somebody picked up the chunk of wood and lobbed it into the air. It landed with a thump on the hood of Ernie's jeep.

That did it.

He reached inside his jacket and pulled out a .45 automatic. He brought the charging handle back with a clang. Before I could stop him, he fired a round into the air. The men leapt back. He leveled the weapon.

"You first, Campione. Drop the axe!"

When Campione didn't respond, Ernie fired a round past his head, the lethal slug zinging into the night and exploding on the high brick wall about ten yards away. Some of the men crouched.

"Stay where you are!" Ernie shouted, but by now the discipline of the mob had broken and individual GIs were slinking off into the shadows. Soon they were running. Campione stood alone now, the axe fallen to the asphalt, holding his open palms off to the side of his head.

Ernie leveled the pistol at him.

"Ernie," I said.

"I'm tired of this shit," Ernie shouted. "First they try to run you over with a garlic truck, then they send this fat slob to come at us with a freaking *axe*. It stops *now*!"

"Ernie," I said.

He breathed deeply, sighed over the .45, and then, taking another deep breath, lowered the pistol until it pointed at the ground.

"Did you run that poker game, Campione?" I said.

"No way. None of us enlisted men are allowed in there."

I stepped toward him. "But you knew about it?"

"I didn't know about *nothing*."

"But you knew about the girls being brought in. You saw them, when they were driven through the gate." He shuffled nervously. "And somebody told you to chop up that poker table. And you did what you were told."

His face flushed red. "Okay, so we got it good here. No duty other than our regular jobs and gate guard. None of that military horseshit."

"Good enough that you were willing to chase us off," Ernie said, "with an *axe*."

Campione looked away.

"How much did you make from the poker game?" I asked.

"We didn't make *nothing*." Campione's eyes were moist, burning into mine. "Who do you think runs this compound? A sergeant E-5? No chance. The DACs run this freaking compound."

Department of the Army Civilians.

"Like who?" I asked.

"Like I don't know. There's Mister this and Mister that and they pretty much keep to themselves. We're the worker drones, you know, us and the Koreans. And at night they leave us alone except for one or two things that go on in the offices or in the Central Locker Fund warehouse, and it ain't none of our business, you understand."

"Bull," Ernie said. "You're getting your cut. That's why you tried to chase us away. You know the deal. Keep the bosses safe and they'll take care of you."

For once, he didn't have a smart-mouth answer. I motioned to Campione to get lost. He did, moving quickly for such a big man.

I told Ernie I'd drive. He didn't object. Still holding his weapon, he climbed in the passenger side. I grabbed the big chunk of splintered poker table and tossed it into the backseat. Maybe it would come in handy as evidence, or at least we could use it to put pressure on somebody. Then I slid in behind the steering wheel, started the engine, shoved it into gear, and drove slowly out of the Far East District Compound.

I dropped Ernie off at the barracks and kept the jeep, taking a drive through the dark 8th Army compound. A moonlit smattering of snow guided my way. The CID office was abandoned this time of night, with only a yellow firelight glowing over the front door. I used my key to let myself in and walked down the long hallway to the admin office. Inside, I switched on a green lamp over the wooden field table I usually used to write my reports, but this time I set the typewriter aside. From my inner pocket, I pulled out the poem Mr. Kill had given to me. It was the complete text, in both Korean and English, of a poem done in the three-line lyric *sijo* style by Hwang Ji-ni, one of the most famous *kisaeng* of the sixteenth century. A fragment of the poem had been found in the sleeve of the murdered *kisaeng* up in Sonyu-ri.

> *I will break the back of this long, midwinter night,*
> *Folding it double, cold beneath my spring quilt,*
> *That I may draw out the night, should my love return.*

Had the woman in the red *chima-jeogori* been forced to write this, or had she done so for personal reasons and kept it a secret? Had the killer forced her to write this, or had he written it himself? I wasn't sure. The poem expressed loneliness, certainly, and longing and desire. And the hope that, by the sheer force of emotion, a person could change the inexorable flow of time.

Miss Hwang hadn't been able to break the back of time; she'd met the inevitable end of her night in the frozen flow of the Sonyu River. I kept making notes, pondering the poem's beauty, recalling what it had been like when that garlic truck barreled toward me—how frightened I'd been.

The phone rang.

Startled, I went to grab it. It was the one on Miss Kim's desk.

"Hello?" I said, forgetting for a moment the proper way to answer a military phone.

"George."

It was Captain Prevault.

"How'd you find me?" I asked.

"I called the barracks, Ernie told me you weren't there. What are you doing?"

I glanced at the ancient poem. "Would you believe me if I said I was reading poetry?"

"You," she said, "I'd believe."

"Is it safe to come over?"

"It's never safe. But come over anyway."

-10-

The next morning, after leaving Captain Prevault's quarters before dawn, I returned to the barracks to catch a little more shut-eye and ended up arriving at the CID office a few minutes late. Lieutenant Mendelson left us an urgent message saying that she wanted to talk to us before the Threets court-martial tomorrow. We figured that she mostly wanted to make sure we hadn't come up with anything new, which we hadn't, so we didn't bother calling her back. Staff Sergeant Riley wanted to know where we were off to, but we figured the less the honchos knew, the better.

We drove the jeep over to the 21 T Car motor pool and gassed up. Then we backed it into the garage and Ernie convinced a Korean mechanic to check the lube order. While we waited, we entered the operations office, Ernie flashed the high sign at the dispatcher's desk, and we continued on back to the windowed cubicle of the warrant officer-in-charge, Chief Milton, who was on the phone, as was his wont.

"Okay, Colonel," he said. "Got it. Eagles plus six." He jotted something in a leather notebook in front of him and set down the phone and looked up at us.

"George," he said. "Ernie. What can I do for you?"

Chief Warrant Officer Milton ran not only the operational arm of the 21st Transportation Car Company, but also the most exclusive bookmaking operation in 8th Army. His clients included some of the highest-ranking officers in the command, and it was even rumored that the US ambassador occasionally put down a bet. Making book here in the motor pool was convenient because Milton could pay drivers to pick up cash from the losers and deliver fat envelopes to winners. We didn't bother to bust him because it wouldn't do any good. He had too many connections with the highest muckety-mucks in 8th Army. Besides, betting on football was something all red-blooded American males did. It wasn't seen as a crime. As a matter of fact, if a soldier didn't take an interest in pro football, he'd be written off as either effeminate or, worse yet, downright unpatriotic. Personally, I found the spectacle of a bunch of overpaid brutes banging into one another less than interesting. As a child, I'd played football and greatly enjoyed it. But in high school, when the adults got involved and tried to turn it into a religion, for me, it lost its charm.

We sat in chairs opposite the chief's desk. He stared at us quizzically, perhaps sensing that we weren't our usual calm, collected selves.

"I heard about the shit somebody tried to pull over in Samgakji," he said. He stared at the bandage on my head. "You okay?"

"I'm fine. We need information."

He toyed with a pencil. "How can I help you?"

"The poker game at the Far East District Compound," Ernie said. "Ever been there?"

"Nice operation. Very professional. A lot of big-shot Koreans happy to get away from the KNPs."

"Afraid they'll get busted?" I asked.

"No. Those arrests you see on TV are only for show. Usually, the KNPs are paid off and nobody's the wiser. People only get busted when they don't pay up. On compound, a high roller only has to worry about the four-percent rake. Life is easy."

"Do you join the game often?"

"No. Poker's not my thing."

"You're not much of a gambler, are you, Chief?"

"I work too hard for my money."

Running a book wasn't gambling. The odds were set by how much money was coming in on either side of a bet. Regardless of which team won or lost, the smart bookmaker always made his vig, the cut, which amounted to about 10 percent.

"The Far East game's closed down," I said.

He lifted an eyebrow. "It is?"

"Yes. We were there last night."

"Why'd they close it?"

"We're not sure yet. But we believe somebody's nervous about something more than gambling."

"Who runs the game?" Ernie asked.

The chief shrugged. "I don't want to mention any names, but for years it's been like an institution. A way for the civilians running the compound to socialize with the movers and shakers who get things done. Contractors, financiers, people like that. They like to relax like anyone else."

"But somebody's making a lot of money."

The chief shrugged again, doing his best to distance himself from whatever was happening at the Far East District Compound. "The money's parceled out," he said, "to the Korean help, to the GIs who look the other way, even for landscaping to make the compound look more beautiful. Some of it even goes to an orphanage."

"Sounds like a charity."

"For years it's been harmless."

"How about the women brought in as hostesses?"

"There used to be a couple of gals to serve the drinks and the food. Nice-looking gals."

"Did they provide other services?"

"Not that I knew of. People were there to gamble. If they wanted to get laid, they'd go to a whorehouse."

"So you hadn't heard anything about the game coming under new management?"

"No."

The phone rang. The chief raised his finger and lifted the receiver. "Motor pool," he said. After listening to a muffled voice on the other end, he covered the receiver and said, "I have to take this."

Ernie and I rose, thanked the chief, and left.

Outside, in front of the maintenance garage, Ernie asked, "Should we arrest Campione? Sweat him?"

"He's sweating now," I replied. "Besides, something tells me he might not know much. Just because he or some of his pals were taking a cut from a poker game, that doesn't mean he knows about the sale of a *kisaeng*."

"It went on right beneath his nose."

"Right. But maybe he didn't want to know. And even if he does know, he won't say anything. Not right away."

"Like only if it's part of a plea bargain, which could take a long time to set up."

"Right. We need information *now*."

The confrontation at the NAF had proven that we were on the right track, but we would lose the trail if we didn't act quickly.

"So what's our next move?"

"There's one guy out there who *wanted* to give us information. The Ville Rat."

"Great idea. But how in the hell are we going to find him?"

"We need a lead."

"There's a keen observation."

"And when it comes to information on a black marketer, there's one guy who can give it to us."

Ernie thought for a moment. Then he turned to me. "Why didn't I think of that?"

When the jeep was ready, we showed our dispatch at the 21 T Car main gate and hung a right on the MSR. At the Coulter Statue intersection, Ernie took another right and headed for Itaewon.

Haggler Lee was the most notorious black marketer in Itaewon. As huge as his warehouse was, it was hidden from view amongst the maze of two- and three-story hooches and apartment buildings in the teeming neighborhood that surrounded the main drag of nightclubs and bars in Seoul's red-light district of Itaewon. The winding pedestrian lanes were so narrow and convoluted that if you didn't know where you were going, you could easily get lost. But we knew where the warehouse was because we'd been there before. Many times. At the huge wooden double door, Ernie grabbed the heavy metal knocker and banged on teak.

It took five minutes, but a small rectangular entranceway in the much larger door creaked open. A wrinkled face peeked out.

"We're here to see Haggler Lee," Ernie said.

The old woman opened the trapdoor wider and we ducked through into a poorly lit, dungeon-like warehouse. After barring the door with a metal rod, the old woman led the way, plastic shoes scraping on cement. We passed dusty bins filled with various pieces of military clothing and then neat rows of stacked C rations. Finally, we reached a somewhat tidier area with refrigerators still in plastic sheeting and air conditioners and fans in colorful boxes emblazoned with both English and Japanese lettering. Atop a raised wooden *kang*, Haggler Lee sat in the lotus position on a flat cushion. In front of him, incense burning, the fat belly of Kumbokju, the Korean god of plenty, glowed. We kicked off our shoes and stepped up on the varnished wooden surface.

Haggler Lee's eyes popped open.

"George! Ernie! So good to see you."

He was a youngish man with a soft, baby-like face and dark hair combed straight over a round skull. Beneath his nose, a black mustache quivered. I figured him to be about forty, but he dressed like what GIs would call a papa-san. He wore the traditional white pantaloons and embroidered silk vest of a man who'd long since passed retirement. Looking older was something many Koreans strived for; they thought it gave them gravitas and respect in society, so unlike in the States, where old age was rated one step below a communicable disease.

"Sit, please," he said, motioning toward two cushions opposite him. Then he clapped his hands and a few seconds later a young woman in a flowing *chima-jeogori* appeared, carrying a stainless-steel tray. She served us tea in porcelain cups with no handles. Haggler Lee lifted his with two hands and saluted us. We all drank. "Now," he said, setting down his cup. "What can I help you with?"

"*Maeul ui jwi,*" I said.

His eyes stared at me blankly.

"*Maeul ui jwi,*" I repeated.

"Oh," he said, "you're speaking Korean. Sorry. I was expecting English."

Haggler Lee's English was excellent, although sprinkled with GI slang. His language skills had been honed by running the largest black-market operation in Itaewon. GIs, but more often their Korean wives, brought him literally tons of imported goods and foodstuffs. In return, he paid them double what they cost in the military PXs and commissaries, a boon to financially strapped military families. Then Haggler Lee took those goods and provided them wholesale to Korean retailers. As a result, he had extensive contacts amongst the purveyors of illicit items at the Korean open-air markets at both the South Gate and the East Gate in Seoul.

He said the phrase again. "*Maeul ui jwi.* The Ville Rat."

"Right," I said. "Do you know him?"

"Not personally."

"But you've heard of him?" Ernie said.

"Oh, yes. Our paths have never crossed, but certainly I've heard of him."

"What's his angle?" Ernie asked.

Silk rustled as Haggler Lee shrugged. "Special order," he said.

"Such as?"

"Apparently some black GIs like certain refreshments that aren't so popular with white GIs."

"Like malt liquor?"

"Precisely," Haggler Lee replied. Then he pursed his lips, as if sucking on a lemon. "Awful stuff," he said.

"You tried it?"

"Once. Of course, I might not be the best judge. I don't even like beer."

"You sell enough of it."

"That's business."

Ernie and I had never bothered to bust Haggler Lee for black marketeering. In order to have jurisdiction, we'd have to catch him in the act of purchasing something from an American soldier or an American dependent. Even if we did, since he's a Korean citizen, we'd have to turn his prosecution over to the KNPs. They would hold him for maybe an hour or two, fine him a few thousand *won*, and then let him go; all of which would be a futile exercise. Instead of alienating him with such a pointless charade, we used him instead for the information he could provide in more important cases. His vast business connections made him a great resource—but a resource we didn't bother to tell 8th Army or the provost marshal about.

"Our knowledge is," I said, "that the Ville Rat specializes in Colt 45 malt liquor and imported cognac, selling them to the black nightclubs since they're popular with the black GIs."

Haggler Lee nodded.

"What is he," Ernie asked, "a GI or a civilian?"

"I believe," Haggler Lee replied, "he was once a GI. His current status, I wouldn't know."

"Do you know where he was stationed?"

Haggler Lee shook his head sadly, as if bitterly disappointed that he couldn't help us. Ernie asked him something that fell more into his area of expertise.

"Where does he get his merchandise, this Colt 45?"

Haggler Lee shrugged again, more elaborately this time. "I've wondered that myself. But I don't know. They don't sell Colt 45 in the Class Six. Cognac, yes, but not malt liquor."

"He has to import it somehow," I said.

"Yes. Maybe he has a contact at the Port of Inchon or the Port of Pusan."

"Some customs official who looks the other way?"

"Maybe. And he'd need a merchant ship to haul the stuff in."

"Expensive," I said.

"Very.

"But he sells the Colt 45 for a thousand *won* a can."

"Not possible," Lee said, "if he's smuggling it in."

"So he has another source," I said.

Lee nodded. "He has to."

"Any ideas?"

Haggler Lee sipped on his tea, then set it down again. Then he raised his head and stared first into my eyes, then into Ernie's. "Look to yourselves," he said.

"Ourselves?"

"Yes. You Americans are the only ones who can bring things into Korea for free."

By free, he meant all transportation costs paid by the US

government, not by an individual. And no customs duties paid to the ROKs. That speculation left us pretty much where we started. The Central Locker Fund didn't import Colt 45, so who else would? I tried a different angle.

"How can we find the Ville Rat?"

"Be there when he makes deliveries."

"We tried that in Samgakji."

"Someone must have known you were coming. Did you advertise?"

"We were there the day prior, asking questions."

"That would do it. When you barge in asking questions about black-market items, it's reported up the line. Didn't you know that?"

We did, but we hadn't realized exactly how steadfast these reporting requirements were.

"You must be more careful." Haggler Lee polished off his tea. "Better if you know his movements in advance." We waited. He placed his laced fingers on his flat stomach and leaned back contentedly. For the information he was about to impart, we'd have to pay. "There's a shipment," he said, "of Seven Dragon wall clocks. Handmade in Red China, then shipped to Hong Kong, where a new manufacturing label is slapped on."

"So they're legal for the US military to purchase."

"Precisely." He smiled, seemingly at the beauty of it all. Fighting godless Communism was one thing, making a buck was another.

"Seven dragons," Ernie said. "That's good luck, isn't it?"

"Very. They go on sale in your main PX on Tuesday. They'll be rationed, one per customer. By the end of the day, the entire shipment will be sold out."

"And the Korean wives who buy them will bring them out here to you."

"Not all," Haggler Lee said, smiling, "but most."

"You'll pay double for them?" I asked.

"Triple. Top dollar."

"And you'll sell them for more than that."

"Handmade in China, seven dragons, long life and good fortune. What self-respecting household can afford to be without one?"

"What do you want in return?" I asked.

"Can you make sure none of my customers will be busted for black marketing on that day?"

Ernie and I were usually on the black-market detail. We were the only CID agents who had the nerve to follow black marketers into the back alleys of Itaewon and bust them in the act of actually exchanging cash for merchandise. If we didn't bust them, nobody else would.

"Depends on what we get in return," Ernie said.

"What you get," Haggler Lee said, "is the Ville Rat." He smiled more broadly. "How would you like to find him tonight?"

Ernie and I both held our breath. Finally, I ventured, "Where would that be?"

"It's Wednesday. He always makes his deliveries in Songtan-up on Wednesdays."

"You know this, how?"

Haggler Lee looked slightly offended. "What kind of businessman would I be," he said, "if I didn't keep track of the competition?"

The young woman in the silk dress breezed into the room and swept up the teapot and the cups. Ernie told Haggler Lee that if the information panned out, he had a deal.

"Pan out?" he asked.

"If the information is good," Ernie replied.

"Oh, it's good."

Then he told us which clubs the Ville Rat would deliver to first.

Songtan-up was known to the GIs as "Chico Village" for some unfathomable reason. Maybe they thought Chico Village sounded cool, but to me, *songtan* was a much more evocative name. It literally means pinewood charcoal, which was perhaps one of the main products the area produced in days gone by; *up* is merely the geographical designation meaning town.

Songtan-up presses against the main gate of Osan Air Force Base, the largest US air base in Korea. In addition to the two or three thousand airmen stationed at Osan, Songtan sees a large influx of US Marines from Okinawa who are given rest-and-recreation leave and hop on military C-130 transports that fly them from their little island in the South China Sea to the exotic vacation spot of Osan Air Force Base on the Korean peninsula. Most of the marines stay in the extensive transient barracks on base, which only sets them back about five bucks a day. The marines bring a lot of tourist dollars into the Songtan bar district—but also a lot of strife.

Our first stop was the Blue Diamond Club. It was walking distance from the front gate of Osan Air Force Base. The pedestrian exit was narrow, one GI at a time with identification and, if necessary, pass or leave orders had to be shown to the Air Force Security Police before a GI was buzzed out into the wonderful world of Songtan. From there he was greeted by vendors pushing carts, old women acting as pimps for much younger girls, and, at night, a sea of flashing neon: the Zoomies Club, the Dragon Lady Bar, the Suzy Wong Nightclub, the Airman's Hideaway, and about three dozen others at various walking distances from the big arch over the two-lane road welcoming the world to Osan Air Force Base.

Officially, the United States Air Force didn't condone segregation, certainly not on base. But off base, their control was limited. One of the first things every GI new to Songtan learned was that when you walked out the front gate, if you were black, you turned right, into the crowded neighborhood that housed most of the bars and eateries that catered to black airmen. If you were white, you continued straight down the main drag to the larger and much more numerous bars and nightclubs. In between sat the shopping district, with its sporting goods stores, tailor shops, and brassware emporiums, as well as the central open-air Songtan Market. This middle ground was frequented by everyone, but when it came to the bars and eateries, the racial division was strict. Even the visiting marines picked up on it somehow: the black marines turned right and the white marines continued straight on.

After showing our dispatch to the security patrol, Ernie and I parked the jeep just inside the main gate. Then we walked back out the pedestrian exit, flashed our IDs and, once outside, took a right down a narrow lane. About twenty yards farther on, a small neon sign read THE BLUE DIAMOND CLUB. It was a narrow room with a long bar on the right, a few tables on the left, and an excellent sound system. If the customer kept walking through the bar, he'd reach the far door of the club that led out into the next street over, which made the Blue Diamond a shortcut from one block to the next. The light was dim and there were no customers in the place when we walked in. A lone barmaid sat on a stool, reading a comic book and listening to a romantic Korean ballad on the sound system. It was not yet four in the afternoon, and she seemed surprised when she looked up and saw us. Maybe because we were early; more likely because we were white.

"I'm thirsty," Ernie told her. "But I want something strong. What kind of beer do you have?"

She listed off the usual suspects: OB, Crown, and a couple of canned beers purchased illegally off the compound: Falstaff and Carling Black Label.

"How about malt liquor?" Ernie asked.

The girl stared at him blankly.

"Colt 45," he said.

She nodded and shuffled to the next cooler over. She had to find her keys and click open the padlock and rummage around inside, but finally she came up with a sixteen-ounce can of Colt 45.

"Don't open it," Ernie said. "How many cans do you have?"

Again she stared at him blankly. Apparently, her English wasn't too good. I said, *"Kuangtong meit-kei isso?"*

She leaned into the cooler, stood back up, and held up three fingers. Three more cans.

Ernie slid the can back to her and said, *"Ahn mogo."* I don't want it.

Puzzled, the girl placed the unopened can back into the cooler and watched as we walked out the far side of the bar. We checked three more joints, all at the recommendation of Haggler Lee. Two were completely out of Colt 45 but promised to have more in the evening. One had six cans left and said they hadn't been selling well lately. I asked if most of their customers were black or white. The barmaid told me that lately most of their customers had been white, which would explain the lack of Colt 45 sales—and hopefully portend well for racial integration, but I wasn't holding my breath.

Ernie and I sat at a table in a chophouse that straddled the wedge on the main road that divided the black and the white districts of Songtan. We sat next to the front plate-glass window so we could keep an eye on the entrance to the Blue Diamond Club. I ordered *kuksu* noodles with small clams drowned on the bottom. Ernie ordered the same.

"So when do you figure the Ville Rat will show up?" Ernie asked.

"I'm not sure. But as soon as we see that one of the clubs has a new supply of Colt 45, we'll know he's in the area."

"What if he doesn't make the deliveries himself?"

"I believe he does. Remember what the old lady up in Sonyu-ri said, the one who owns the Black Star Nightclub. She said the Ville Rat was popular with the black GIs."

"But somehow he found out that we were looking for him in Samgakji and he tried to have us killed."

"Maybe it wasn't him."

"Then who would it be?"

"I don't know. But from what we've learned so far, it seems the Ville Rat is just a former GI who's making a living here . . ."

"An illegal living."

"Yeah. An illegal living, but he's not pulling down a ton of money. Is that enough to have somebody murdered?"

"You never know," Ernie said, toying with his chopsticks. "Some GIs hate the CID."

"But somebody not only paid those two guys to steal the garlic truck; they also knew how to contact professional killers, all on short notice."

"We don't know that they were professional."

"No, but they probably were. So everything points to the hit being ordered by somebody making big bucks, somebody with connections to the Korean underworld."

"They also sent Campione and the Far East District GIs after us."

"No, those guys were amateurs. They weren't out to kill any-one—they were out to frighten us, to protect their turf."

"So you think somebody bigger than the Ville Rat is watching us?"

"They're trying to. Which means that the stakes here are more than just a few cases of Colt 45."

"Like what?" Ernie asked.

"Remember what Haggler Lee said. 'Look to yourselves.' He believes that the Colt 45 is being shipped in via the US military procurement process."

"But Burrows and Slabem just audited their books." Then he went quiet, staring at the noodles hanging off the polished wooden chopsticks in his hand.

"They're brownnosers," I said. "They wouldn't have reported anything wrong if it stared them in the face."

"They received a reward for that audit. It took them over a month."

"What does Eighth Army reward people for?" I asked.

"For not making waves." He dropped his chopsticks into his bowl and leaned toward me. "You think Burrows and Slabem purposely covered something up?"

"No. I don't believe that at all. What I believe is that they didn't look too hard. They took whatever horseshit the Non-Appropriated Fund honchos handed to them and treated it as if it were a set of commandments from on high."

"So," Ernie paused, letting it sink in, "what's really happening is that somebody is ordering stuff off the books and selling it on the black market."

"Yes. Think about it. The US taxpayer covers the cost of shipping the merchandise from the US or Japan or Europe or wherever it comes from. It's brought into Korea with no customs duties or taxes, and then you sell it to the locals at whatever markup you can get away with."

"But they don't *steal* the merchandise from the government."

"No, that would be too obvious. They pay for it, then sell it for double or triple what they pay for it." I paused, too excited to eat. "And the Colt 45 might be just crumbs falling from the table."

"Crumbs the Ville Rat licks up and uses to make a living."

"Yeah."

"But why him? Why would anyone risk the integrity of a larger operation just to allow some lowlife like the Ville Rat to make a few bucks?"

"He's out of the army now, but where did he work when he was on active duty?"

"You think maybe he's got something on somebody and he used that to force them to cut him in on the action?"

"Maybe."

"But if we find evidence, the whole thing will fall apart. Which is why they sent the garlic truck after us."

"And what about him? If we're in danger, wouldn't he be too?"

"Maybe whoever's running this operation never saw the need to use violence before. But now they see the Ville Rat as a loose cannon. If they're willing to murder a CID agent, they'd certainly be willing to snuff out a nobody like the Ville Rat."

"Do you think he knows that?"

"He should, if he's smart. He must've heard about Samgakji. Gossip spreads through the GI villages faster than smallpox."

Ernie shoved his bowl away.

"Let's get out there and find him."

I slurped down the last of my noodles, stood up, and followed Ernie out the door.

We checked the Blue Diamond and all the other bars we'd visited before, but even though the night shift had come on and GI customers were starting to filter in, none of them had yet increased their inventory of Colt 45. One of the barmaids admitted to us that the guy who usually brought it was supposed to have come in earlier but hadn't shown. I asked her to describe him to us, claiming we wanted to buy a whole case from him, and she relented. Skinny white guy, always wore loud shirts, reddish hair, teased and puffed out so he looked like a soul brother.

Ernie and I stood in the shadows beneath the awning of Kim's Sporting Goods, enjoying the cool evening breeze, watching both white and black GIs stream out of the front gate of Osan Air Force Base. Down both lanes, off to the right and straight on, neon flashed an inviting promise: fun, drinks, women.

"Maybe he's dead," Ernie said. "Maybe we're too late. Maybe after they burned the garlic truck, the two assassins went after him."

"Maybe."

"So then what do we do?"

I sighed. "We write it all down, everything we've learned, and then we ask permission from the provost marshal to reopen the NAF audit."

"Are you nuts? They'd have to admit that they gave awards to the wrong guys."

"So maybe we should do the inventory on our own."

"If we knew what we were looking for, that would make sense. But there must be a mountain of documents at the Comptroller's Office, and other places. It would take us weeks of checking and rechecking and comparing purchase orders to inventories to shipping documents and delivery invoices."

"Maybe."

"What do you mean maybe?"

"Maybe we could figure out a way to do it faster than that."

"How?"

"I don't know. I have to think about it."

At the front gate, some of the GIs were carrying out cases of beer or soda or large bags of commissary or PX purchases. They were probably going to their hooch or their *yobo's* place, and they didn't want to walk. For them, a line of Hyundai cabs had queued up at a taxi stand. But the number of GIs willing to pop for the fare were few and far between. Most of them walked. One of the cabs pulled away without a customer, which was unusual after waiting so long. Maybe he was tired of this shit and decided to go home. But the night was young . . . All these thoughts drifted idly through my mind as I thought about how a scam to import Colt 45 without it showing up in the regular inventory would work. How many people would be involved? Who would have to be paid off? How high would it go? It was certainly not worth the few bucks the Ville Rat was pulling down.

And then the cab's engine roared and its headlights blinked on and the blinding light was speeding straight for us. Ernie shouted, "Hey!" and shoved my shoulder, and just before the speeding cab reached us, something dark flew out of the night. Whatever it was, it was heavy and compact; it twirled and then slammed into the speeding windshield of the cab. On impact, the cab jogged to the right just enough so I had time to dive blindly to my left, landing headfirst in a bin of soccer balls. Tires screeched and the wall behind me shuddered and the car's glass exploded into a thousand shards. I covered my head.

After the near miss with the garlic truck, Ernie visited Staff Sergeant Palinki, the military police armorer, and demanded more ammo for his .45.

"How about you, buddy?" Palinki asked me. "You need a weapon too?"

I declined. I figured one gun was enough for what we needed to do.

Palinki was a huge man—Samoan, from Hawaii. He'd told me he hadn't originally wanted to join the army, but he'd been drafted. He admitted freely that his entire extended family accompanied him to the induction center and they'd all cried like babies when he'd been taken away. His family thought they'd never see him again, and they almost hadn't. He'd been trained in infantry tactics and sent to Vietnam, but emerged with only minor shrapnel wounds. When he returned to Hawaii, much of his extended family had moved on. The young ones were going off to college; others were landing tourist hotel or government jobs and moving into tract homes around the island.

"I had money in my pocket and stripes on my arm," Palinki said. "I was somebody, but if I get out of the army, I go back to being nobody again."

So he re-upped for six. Now, after more than eight years in the army, he was heavily invested. "Twelve more years," he said smiling, "and I'm walking. Back to the big island with a monthly retirement check and full medical." Then he smiled even more broadly, showing a gold-capped tooth. "And full dental."

Palinki was a lifer, like me. We were loyal to the army, for the most part, and patriotic, true-blue Americans, but the first rule when you're a lifer is to watch out for your brisket. If you piss off the wrong people, the army will screw you over and not even look back. Sometimes, like in Vietnam, they can even get you killed. Usually, though, they don't, at least not on the streets of Chico Village.

This time, though, they almost had.

Before I could shove the soccer balls out of the way and sit back up, I heard Ernie cursing and firing his weapon—one shot, two— into the Songtan night.

Then he ran after the cab. Down the road, tires screeched, an engine roared, and hoarse GIs shouted and cursed. Ernie fired again. By now I was out of the bin and standing unsteadily, surrounded by broken metal tubing and splintered wood. I took a step forward, and something heavy banged against my foot. I reached down and spotted a cylindrical object. I lifted it and turned it toward the light. Colt 45. A full can, warm to the touch, unopened. I heard the gunfire again, and then it stopped. I dropped the can, grabbed my throbbing head, and staggered toward the sound.

Like the sudden emersion of trapdoor spiders, Korean business girls in hot pants and miniskirts poured out of the bars and nightclubs lining the main drag. Everyone's attention was turned toward flashing blue and green and yellow lights rotating down the road. A KNP roadblock. I surged forward with the crowd and spotted Ernie, standing next to three KNPs and what looked like the same taxicab that had tried to kill me. It was parked at an angle in front of two blue KNP sedans, and two Korean men were on their knees next to the cab with their hands shackled behind their backs. One of the KNPs had his fist on the back of the head of one of the kneeling men; he was leaning over, talking at him, and the suspect kept his head bowed, nodding occasionally.

Ernie stood next to a man I recognized: Mr. Kill. He saw me and his gaze filled with concern.

"Are you hurt?" he asked.

"I don't think so," I said. "Somebody threw something at the cab. It hit the windshield and gave me enough time to get out of the way." I paused. "What are you doing here?"

He smiled. "We visited your friend, Haggler Lee, after you talked to him. He agreed that you might need some backup."

I glanced at the two kneeling Korean men. "Who are they?"

"Not sure, but we'll find out soon enough."

Ernie said, "They're lucky I didn't pop them with one of the rounds I fired."

Mr. Kill smiled. "That certainly put them into a panic."

I told them about the can of Colt 45 that someone had thrown.

"The Ville Rat," Ernie said. "Gotta be. He must be in the area."

Quickly, I explained to Mr. Kill who the Ville Rat was and told him what he looked like.

"I'll send a patrol in," Mr. Kill said.

"No." I held out my hand. "It's better if Ernie and I approach him."

Mr. Kill studied me. Then he said, "If you think it's best."

"Yes, we want his cooperation," I said, "if we can get it."

Ernie and I hurried back to the black section of Songtan.

The Blue Diamond Bar was packed. The music was so loud it blared out into the roadway as GIs jostled one another wall to wall. Inside, I could make out a half-dozen bar maids, sweating and serving drinks as fast as their hands could move. Most of the GIs were marines. I could tell by the T-shirts and headgear they wore, marked by unit insignia, and by the Japanese words—such as *musame* and *taaksan* and *skoshi*—they bantered about. Also, most of the men were in much better physical condition than your average Osan airman. Not that the zoomies didn't work hard, but most of their jobs were highly technical and often sedentary.

Ernie and I pushed our way through the crowd. The greeting we received wasn't particularly unfriendly, but it wasn't friendly either. Most of the black marines eyed us suspiciously. Like one black GI had told me long ago, when you're off duty and you finally have a chance to relax with other black GIs, you don't particularly want to deal with any white motherfuckers, not if you don't have to. We searched along the far wall with the small tables and finally Ernie elbowed me.

"There he is."

Like a red flame in a dark night, the Ville Rat's afro flashed red, orange, and yellow, depending on how the rotating strobe lights happened to hit his hairdo. He sat with three other GIs, all of them black, and they were smoking and laughing and chugging down sixteen-ounce cans of Colt 45. As we approached, he looked up at us.

At first there was fear in his green eyes. But then his black friends turned, noticing where his gaze fell, and uniformly they frowned. This seemed to give the Ville Rat courage. I pulled out my badge, showed it to the GIs at the table, and said, "We need to talk to you, outside." Two of the black GIs stood, ready to object. "Not you," I said, "only him."

They glanced at the Ville Rat. He motioned for them to sit down.

"We'll talk," he said, "but we'll talk here." His voice was high and reedy, but it had a cadence to it, like a laid-back musician who spent a lot of time playing saxophone riffs.

"Outside," Ernie said.

"Here," the Ville Rat repeated.

By now, more GIs in the crowd had noticed our presence and a small group of curious parties coalesced around us. Ernie glanced back and forth, grinned, and said, "On second thought, this is as good a place as any."

I grabbed an empty stool and sat opposite the Ville Rat. Ernie stood behind me, still grinning. He pulled out a pack of ginseng gum and offered some around. No takers.

"You threw a can at the cab," I said.

The Ville Rat lifted his cigarette from the ashtray and puffed. The smoke only crawled part of the way down his throat before he blew it out.

"Didn't want to see anybody killed," he said.

"So who's trying to kill me?"

"The same guys who are going to kill *me*."

"As in who?"

"Dangerous people," he replied. "People with connections."

"And they want to kill you because you can finger them."

"Some of them."

"What's your name?"

"Rat. That's what the GIs call me."

"Affectionately, I hope."

"I'm a popular guy."

"You tried to tell us something up in Sonyu-ri. You said it wasn't right, what they did to that girl."

"It wasn't right."

"You knew her?"

"I'd seen her."

"So who killed her?"

The Ville Rat puffed on his cigarette again. "The same guy who's supplying me."

"Through the Class Six?"

He nodded.

"But off the books."

He nodded again.

"You used to work for them," I said, "when you were in the army."

"It was different then," he said, setting down his cigarette and leaning toward me. "Nobody was getting hurt. Just some extra supplies ordered into the country. It had been going on for years before I got here. Harmless, they told me. A fund was set up to ease the way of the US Forces in Korea, to make the politicians happy; provide money for projects on compound that couldn't be done through normal appropriations. Things like tennis courts at the officers' club. A new air conditioner for the Defense Youth Activities Center. Things like that."

"They even helped orphans," I said.

"They did. They really did. Jackets during the winter, toys at Christmas; at one of them, they even paid to have a new well dug."

"Who was in charge?"

"People high up. Way up."

"Generals?"

The Ville Rat frowned. "Not them, they come and go. Civilians. They're the ones who stay here. They're the ones with the contacts in the ROK government."

"Department of the Army Civilians," I said. "DACs?"

He nodded.

"Civilians like Rick Mills?"

"I don't know. I never saw him involved directly."

"But he runs the Central Locker Fund," I said. "He had to know."

The Ville Rat didn't contradict me. I continued.

"But now the operation is threatened, so they're willing to kill me and they're willing to kill you. Your supply chain has been cut."

He spread his thin fingers.

"So give me their names. We'll bust this thing wide open."

"It won't do any good. They're too high up. If they have to, they'll sic the Korean government on you."

I thought of Mr. Kill. Did he have the power to protect us? Probably not.

"So if you didn't want to help, why did you contact us up north? Why did you throw that can of malt liquor at the taxicab?"

"I want to stop him."

"Stop who?"

"Stop the guy who's caused all this trouble. The guy who screwed everything up. The guy who murdered Miss Hwang."

"We can do that," I told him. "All I need is a name."

He acted as if he hadn't heard me. "The worst part is, he has a new girl."

"A new girl like Miss Hwang?"

"Yes. His own servant. His own *kisaeng*."

"She's in danger too, then."

"I'll say."

I grabbed his hand. "You need to give me a name."

"They'll kill me."

"You have to tell me. There are lives at stake. Yours, mine, this young woman who's being forced into being someone's private *kisaeng*. If you won't talk here," I said, "then you're leaving me no choice. I'll take you in."

Roughly, I jerked him toward me and reached for the handcuffs clipped to the back of my belt. Without warning, the Ville Rat jerked back violently. I kept my grip, but maybe because of the pounding I'd taken lately, I suddenly became dizzy. Ernie grabbed me and reached across the table for the Ville Rat. But by then the other GIs were on their feet, shoving Ernie and forcing me backward. I pushed back.

That did it.

Somebody threw a punch and then somebody else shoved and a table fell over and bottles crashed to the ground, and then Ernie was against the wall, reaching for his .45. He pulled it out and shot one round into the ceiling. The Ville Rat reeled backward into the crowd. I lunged for him, but missed and then was held back by a half-dozen hands.

A whistle shrilled at the front door. Barmaids screamed and helmeted Korean National Police pushed their way into the bar, formed into a phalanx, using heavy black batons to shove the enraged marines out of the way.

Punches rained down on me. I crouched and grabbed a knocked-over cocktail table and used it as a shield. The crowd rushed toward the back door and soon the KNPs held the central ground in the club. Ernie was still waving his .45 in the air, but the GIs were gone now, making their way out of the Blue Diamond as fast as they could move.

And the Ville Rat was gone with them.

I motioned for Ernie to put away his pistol. Wide-eyed, he stared around the empty barroom. When he realized we were safe, he switched the safety on and tucked the .45 back into his shoulder holster.

"Where's the Ville Rat?" he asked.

I pointed toward the back door. We followed the retreating crowd and with a patrol of KNPs spent the next hour searching for him. No luck. The Ville Rat had lived up to his name. Like a clever rodent, he'd disappeared.

Early the next morning, I left a note on Staff Sergeant Riley's desk for him to check with his contacts at 8th Army Personnel and find out the names and ranks of all GIs assigned to the Central Locker Fund in the last few years. I left him a physical description of the Ville Rat. Then Ernie and I, both in green dress uniforms, marched over to the JAG office.

Lieutenant Margaret Mendelson seemed relieved to see us. "*There* you are. I've been trying to get in touch with you. Have you got anything new on the Threets court-martial? Anything more about Sergeant Orgwell?"

"Not a thing," Ernie said smiling.

"Good. You screwed things up enough as it is."

My mind flew back to Private Threets's accusations of sexual assault by Sergeant Orgwell, which could well have been his motive for the shooting on the firing range. Not a good motive and certainly not a justification, but at least a mitigating factor that might become important when it came time for sentencing. None of which the army wanted to hear. The 8th Army honchos' attitude was clear. A low-ranking enlisted man shot a senior NCO in broad daylight in front of his entire unit. The answer was simple. Throw him in the federal pen and toss away the key. Don't muddy the waters with accusations of homosexuality and sexual assault. That just embarrasses everybody.

"Get over to the courthouse," Lieutenant Mendelson told us. "Bob Conroy is waiting for you." Threets's less-than-veteran defense counsel. Before we left, she added, "And don't talk to anybody."

Which was good advice, and advice that we would've followed if we hadn't been stopped ten yards in front of the courthouse entrance by none other than Major General Frederick R. Kokol, the commander of the 2nd Infantry Division, the man known to journalists everywhere as the Gunslinger.

He stood with his hands on narrow hips, hawk nose pointed at us, pearl-handled revolvers grip-forward, hanging from either side of his web belt. He wore fatigues—not the dress green uniform that everyone else wore to court-martial—but he was the Gunslinger and he didn't have to follow the usual rules of military decorum. The fatigues were starched and cut in front with a razor-like crease. His white-laced jump boots gleamed with ebony polish.

"*You*," he said, pointing at us like Uncle Sam in a recruiting poster. "You're the two who started this shit."

Ernie and I both saluted. He didn't return the salute, so we dropped our hands. A worried-looking captain stood behind him, apparently his aide. Behind him stood a senior NCO, probably his bodyguard and driver, less worried, smirking and enjoying the show.

"So what have you got to say for yourselves?" the Gunslinger asked.

"We didn't *start* anything, sir," Ernie told him, keeping his voice calm and, for once, reasonable. "The shooting at the firing range is what started it."

"But you made it worse. Now the men in the unit are upset because, according to you, a poor black man is being attacked by a white man. My soldiers who used to see nothing but the color green are now seeing themselves as black and white. *You*," he said, pointing again, "you're dividing my division!"

I'd heard enough. "It was divided before we got there," I said.

The Gunslinger turned his withering gaze toward me. "No, it wasn't! We were *one!* One body, one team, one infantry division ready to kick some North Korean ass. Now, because of you, people are laughing at the Second Division. Saying we're full of homos. Saying we don't treat our black soldiers right."

"Maybe you don't, sir."

"The *hell* I don't."

"Have you been out in Sonyu-ri lately?" I asked. "Have you visited the Black Star Nightclub? Seen how the black soldiers don't want to socialize with the white soldiers? Seen how they feel they have to stick together to protect one another? Have you seen any of that, sir?"

He stepped toward me, face burning red. "Who in the hell do you think you are? What's your name? Sween-o? What the fuck kind of a name is that?"

"Sueño," Ernie said, pronouncing it correctly, the *ñ* like the *ny* in canyon.

The general swiveled on him. "*You?* You're standing up for him? You're in on it too, trying to make the division look bad. Trying to drag our name through the mud."

"We gathered testimony," Ernie said, "the testimony of *your* soldiers."

The Gunslinger's aide stepped forward and whispered something in the general's ear. He nodded, seeming to come out of a reverie. He turned back to us and once again shook a bony finger.

"The court-martial's starting. You'd better not tell any lies up there on the stand."

With that, he swiveled and hurried into the courtroom. The aide didn't look at us, but the senior NCO turned back and grinned.

"Hope you enjoyed the show," Ernie said.

"Oh, I did."

He grinned even more broadly.

Inside the courtroom, Second Lieutenant Robert Conroy fidgeted on a straight-backed wooden chair, looking like a third grader waiting for class to start. Ernie and I sat directly behind him in the gallery and he turned around, relieved to see us. "Did you find anything else?"

"No, sir," Ernie replied, "can't say that we have. Did you subpoena Threets's buddies?"

"They wouldn't let me."

"Who?"

"Eighth Army JAG."

"You could've done it if you wanted to."

"They told me it would just make things worse for Threets."

"Bull," Ernie said.

Two MPs escorted in the accused, Private First Class Clifton Threets. He wore a wrinkled khaki uniform; nobody'd bothered to fetch his Class A uniform from Division. Hands shackled in front, Threets glanced at us sullenly and then, guided by the MPs, plopped down in a chair next to Lieutenant Conroy. The MPs retreated, one taking his place by the front entrance and the other near the rear. The accused and counsel conferred for a while, and then Conroy rose and stepped toward us. "Threets says his buddies will be here."

"They can't," I said. "Not on a duty day and not unless they're on approved pass."

"I know that," Conroy said, "but he insists they'll be here."

Ernie grinned and pulled out a stick of ginseng gum. "This I gotta see."

To our left, the Gunslinger, his aide, and the accompanying senior NCO sat grimly behind Lieutenant Mendelson at the prosecution desk. A clerk I recognized from the JAG office entered through the back door behind the dais and shouted, "Attention in the Court!" Everyone stood, including General Kokol.

Three officers walked in: one JAG colonel and two lieutenant colonels. One of the lieutenant colonels wore signal brass, the other infantry. The three men marched behind polished oak, turned, and abruptly took their seats. Everyone else sat too. Then the presiding officer banged his gavel.

"Is the prosecution ready to proceed?"

"Ready, Your Honor," Lieutenant Mendelson replied.

She stepped forward to present her case. It was precise and devastating. There was little doubt that during the biannual range qualification for Charley Battery, 2nd of the 17th Field Artillery Battalion, Private First Class Clifton Threets had, in fact, turned his weapon on Sergeant First Class Vincent P. Orgwell and shot him through the thigh. A ballistics technician testified as to the caliber of the rifle assigned to Threets, photographs of Orgwell's wounds were shown, and Orgwell himself pointed out Threets as the man who had shot him. Most devastating were the written affidavits of a half-dozen fellow soldiers of Charley Battery who claimed they had seen Threets turn his weapon, aim at Orgwell, and fire.

Two hours later, when the prosecution rested, the court called a half-hour break. Ernie and I hustled back to the CID office.

"Where the hell you guys been?" Riley said.

"In court," I replied.

"Where you belong," he growled. "How many years they going to put you away for?"

I ignored him and checked my messages. Nothing from Mr. Kill. "Did you talk to personnel?" I asked.

"Yeah." He tossed a sheaf of paperwork at me. "There's your man. Worked for the Central Locker Fund two years ago. Specialist

Five. Got out after four years active duty, chose an in-country discharge."

"He didn't go back to the States?" Ernie asked.

"That's what in-country discharge means," Riley replied.

I studied the folder. A black-and-white photo was attached to it. Ernie glanced at it.

"That's the Ville Rat alright."

It was unmistakably him. Except that instead of an Afro, he had a short haircut that didn't accentuate the bright color of his hair. But it was the same narrow face, the same pointed chin, and a grim set to his mouth, as if he'd been observing something of which he didn't completely approve. His name tag said Penwold. The personnel folder gave his first name as Orrin and his middle initial as W.

"Orrin W. Penwold," Ernie said. "No wonder he calls himself Rat."

He'd been a supply clerk who got lucky. First, he'd been transferred from Fort Hood, Texas, to Korea, skipping Vietnam, which was a good thing in and of itself, and then he'd hit the jackpot. Apparently there'd been an opening at the Central Locker Fund at about the same time he arrived and he'd been assigned to fill it. Despite acting like he didn't give a damn, Riley had taken it upon himself to request the TO&E, or the Table of Operations and Equipment, from personnel. Every unit and operating section in the army had one. It spelled out what type of personnel and equipment was authorized and budgeted for. The Central Locker Fund was authorized only one active-duty NCO. Everyone else who worked there, like the boss, Rick Mills, was either a Department of the Army Civilian or a local Korean hire. Being a GI in an all-civilian unit meant that you'd be the gopher, the guy all the shit jobs fell to, but it also meant that you didn't have to put up with a lot of military baloney, like extra training and duty on the weekends. In other words, the Central Locker Fund was a prime assignment.

"Who has the job now?" Ernie asked.

"The guy we saw when we were out there, Master Sergeant Demoray."

"Must be nice," Ernie said, "to roll out of shit and fall into clover."

"I need one more thing," I told Riley.

"What?" he barked.

I leaned across his desk and said it softly. "On the QT. Can you get me Rick Mills's address?"

"Out on the economy?"

"Yeah. CPO must have it." The Civilian Personnel Office.

I knew he was about to ask what I needed it for, but then he thought better of it and tightened his narrow lips. "You'll owe me," he said.

Last night, moonlight streamed in from an open window. Leah Prevault—also known as Captain Prevault—lay snuggled in my arms. She sighed and raised herself to tell me what she'd learned.

"Sergeant Orgwell is in an advanced state of denial," she said. "Clearly, he lives a double life and hates himself for it. I want you to stay away from him." She placed two soft fingers on my lips. "To protect himself, he could even resort to violence."

"And Threats?" I asked.

"Also dangerous. Because of the trauma and humiliation he experienced, he could explode in rage."

"So you believe he's telling the truth?"

"I believe he experienced a deep and personal trauma. Whether it was because of Sergeant Orgwell or someone else, I can't be sure."

"You could've called me. Left a message with Miss Kim."

"She seems like a nice woman."

"She is."

"But I wanted to tell you myself."

"I'm glad you did. I want to see you again."

She rose from the bed and stepped toward me. "Name the time and place," she said.

After the recess, Second Lieutenant Conroy walked forward like a kid about to deliver an oral report in front of the class. He swallowed hard and then started to talk.

"Let the record show," he said, "that we will offer testimony that the defendant Private First Class Clinton Threets of Charley Battery of the Second of the Seventeenth Field Artillery Battalion was subject to harassment and homosexual assault that resulted in severe mental stress and . . ."

The presiding officer banged his gavel.

"Lieutenant Conroy, you were informed during the pre-trial proceedings that these unfounded allegations were not going to be allowed into my courtroom."

"Yes, sir, but . . ."

"Not buts about it. I'm not going to allow this trial to be used to smear the reputation of an outstanding senior NCO with a long-standing record of excellent job performance. Now, if you plan to get into training or discipline issues, then that could be considered." In the stands, the Gunslinger squirmed. "But only if you're planning on presenting the court with concrete evidence."

"Yes, sir." Lieutenant Conroy's head drooped and he walked back to the defense table. He glanced at Ernie and me desperately, knowing that he couldn't call us to the stand to testify about Threets's allegations of assault or Sergeant Orgwell's violent reaction to those allegations. There was no doubt that Threets had shot Orgwell; Lieutenant Mendelson's prosecution case had established that beyond a reasonable doubt, so without mitigating circumstances, the defense case was pretty much blown to smithereens. There was only one thing left for Conroy to do.

"If it please the court," he said, "I call the accused, Private First Class Clifton Threets, to the stand."

"So ordered," the presiding judge said.

Threets rose from his chair and, still in shackles, shuffled forward. Quickly, he was read the oath by the clerk of court, said "I do," and took his seat on the witness stand.

The whole questioning process was painful. Conroy was nervous and Threets's voice was hollow and barely audible. One kept longing for a grown-up to take over. Still, the two young men did manage to present the pertinent testimony. Threets had just started to tell of how he was called into the day room by SFC Orgwell when Lieutenant Mendelson sprang to her feet to object.

"Your Honor," she said, "this is the very hearsay evidence that you said you would not allow into your courtroom."

The judge thought about it. "I won't allow it as hearsay evidence. But as direct testimony from the accused, I will allow it. He has a right to testify in his own defense. However, the court will consider the self-serving nature of such testimony."

Which was sort of like saying to Threets, you can tell us your side of the story, but don't expect us to believe you.

Ernie sneered. "The judge is just afraid of getting overturned on appeal."

Threets continued his testimony.

In the day room, Threets was being given solo counseling and had been told what an outstanding soldier he was when SFC Orgwell started to touch him.

The crowd murmured in indignation. Threets lowered his head. When the murmuring subsided, Lieutenant Conroy prodded him to continue.

When Threets objected to Sergeant Orgwell's advances, there was a brief shouting match. They wrestled for a while, but eventually Threets shoved Orgwell away and escaped from the room. Later, it played on his mind. Who was this senior NCO to try to take advantage of him like that? What if Orgwell told Threets's buddies? What if he tried it again? What if word got out and people thought Threets had gone along with it?

"Would you say," Lieutenant Conroy asked, "that you held a grudge against Sergeant Orgwell?"

"Yes," Threets replied. "It plays on my mind, all day, all night. Pretty soon, that's all I can think about."

"And then you went to the range?"

"He was there." Involuntarily, Threets glanced at the wounded SFC Orgwell seated in the stands. "And he smiled at me."

"What did you think when he smiled at you?"

"I couldn't take it. He act like him and me, we got a secret. We *don't*. I couldn't take it."

"What did you do?"

"I shot him." Threets shook his head. "I shouldn't have done it, but I did." Threets sat up straighter and stared right at Orgwell. "I'm sorry," he said, "but you shoulda left me alone."

Using an aluminum crutch, Orgwell stood up. "He's lying!" he yelled. "I never touched him! I never invited him into the day room! He shot me because I'm white and he's black!"

The presiding officer pounded his gavel and shouted, "Order!"

Someone next to Orgwell stood and grabbed his shoulders and tried to calm him down. When Orgwell sat back down, the presiding officer asked Lieutenant Conroy if he had any further questions of the witness. When he said he didn't, Conroy took his seat and the prosecutor, Lieutenant Peggy Mendelson, approached Threets.

"Private Threets," she asked, "how long have you been in the army?"

Hanging his head, Threets mumbled something.

"What? Speak up for the court, please."

Threets sat up straighter and said. "Two years, almost."

"And during that two years, did your training include any information about the chain of command?"

Threets nodded.

Peggy Mendelson sighed and addressed the court. "Sir, would you please instruct the accused that he needs to answer the questions verbally, not with head nodding."

The presiding officer did. Lieutenant Mendelson asked the question again, and Threets acknowledged that he had received training concerning the chain of command.

"And Private Threets, who is your immediate supervisor?"

"Sergeant Rohmer."

"And who's he?"

"My gun crew chief."

"Did you inform Sergeant Rohmer about the incident with Sergeant Orgwell?"

Threets shook his head negatively.

"Out loud, please," Lieutenant Mendelson said.

"No," Threets responded.

"And in your chain of command, who is above Sergeant Rohmer?"

"First Sergeant Bolton."

"And did you inform First Sergeant Bolton about your disagreement with Sergeant Orgwell?"

Again Threets said he hadn't.

Lieutenant Mendelson continued on like this, asking Threets about his battery commanding officer and the battalion CO and so on, until finally she said, "So you never attempted to resolve your problem by using the chain of command, did you, Private Threets?"

"No," he replied.

"Why not?"

"Because I don't trust them."

"Why not?"

"Because they don't listen to us."

"They don't listen to you, meaning lower-ranking soldiers?"

"No. I mean they don't listen to us black soldiers. They don't give a damn about us."

"Objection!"

Everyone in the court started at the strong command voice, and all heads swiveled. General Kokol, the Gunslinger, was red faced and on his feet. "That's not *true*! The chain of command *works*. I see to it personally that it works and I make damn sure that our black soldiers are treated fairly."

The presiding officer banged his gavel, then pointed it like a weapon at the Gunslinger. "General Kokol, with all due respect to your rank, you are to please refrain from interrupting these proceedings."

The Gunslinger shook a bony finger at Threets. "But he's *lying*!"

Ernie elbowed me. I turned to see three black soldiers standing in the entranceway. Two of them I recognized. The same guys Ernie had talked to and shared a reefer with behind the Charley Battery motor pool up at Camp Pelham.

"Who you calling a *liar*?" one of them shouted. His name tag said Burlington and his rank was corporal. He stepped into the room and his two buddies followed. "My man Threets be *innocent*!" he shouted. "That guy," he continued, pointing at Orgwell, "laid hands on him. He laid hands on the brother!"

By now everyone was shouting. The Gunslinger stepped toward them, ordering the three young men out of the courtroom. Involuntarily, his left hand reached for the hilt of one of his pearl-handled revolvers. The black GIs surged forward, bypassing the old general, reaching Threets and greeting him with fists tapping on fists. The Gunslinger's aide tried to pull him back, away from the men. The presiding judge kept banging on his gavel, shouting at the MPs to clear the courtroom, and finally they reacted—not approaching the skinny old man with the revolvers, but the three young black men surrounding Threets. When the first MP grabbed the closest man, he resisted. Punches were thrown, and by now the Gunslinger had pushed his aide away and actually pulled one of the pistols out and waved it in the air. The MPs unsheathed their batons and started swinging. The black soldiers fought back.

Ernie and I were still seated, Ernie grinning ear to ear.

"We have to stop this," I said.

"Can't I enjoy it for just a little longer?"

"The Gunslinger's about to shoot somebody."

"Wouldn't that be a hoot?"

We rose to our feet, but at the same moment, a squad of MP reinforcements bulled their way into the room. Batons swung everywhere, men shouted, and the Gunslinger fired a round into the air. I stepped toward him and held his wrist, making sure his pearl-handled revolver kept pointing at the ceiling.

"Let go of me, dammit!" he shouted.

"When you put the gun away," I said.

Reluctantly, he lowered his hand and shoved the pistol back in its holster. "I'll get you, Sween-o."

The MPs left him alone as he and his aide stalked out the main entrance. The three Division soldiers who'd come to support Threets were handcuffed and thrown into the back of a three-quarter-ton truck. Threets was thrown in with them, along with Lieutenant Conroy.

"He's the defense counsel," I told one of the MPs.

He shrugged. "Colonel's orders."

The presiding judge glared at us, apparently wondering if he should have us arrested too. Fortunately, he didn't give the order.

-12-

Back in the CID office, Riley said, "What in the hell did you guys *do*?"

"We didn't do nothing," Ernie told him.

"But there was a riot at the courtroom and shots were fired. You must've had *something* to do with it."

"Just innocent bystanders," Ernie told him. He stalked to the overheated coffee urn and poured himself a cup of burnt ink.

I asked Riley, "Where's the NAF inventory report?"

"The one Burrows and Slabem did?"

"Yes," I said, "the one they won an award for."

"Why do you want to know?"

"Not your business," I replied. "Where is it?"

"Already filed," he said.

"In the records room?"

"Where else?"

I stalked out of the admin office and down the hallway. At a room marked RECORDS, I entered and switched on the light. It took a few minutes of searching, but eventually I pulled out the report and plopped the thick document down on a grey table. I sat down and pulled out my notebook and a pen. It was dry, all written in officialese with plenty of graphs and charts and dozens of pages of addendums, but despite these drawbacks, it made for interesting reading.

Someone rapped on the door. Without waiting, Ernie entered.

"What the hell you doing in here?"

I told him.

"And?"

"And nothing. But some of these charts raise questions."

"Like what?"

"Just a few possible discrepancies. Let's go talk to somebody."

"Where?"

"The Eighth Army Comptroller's Office."

Ernie groaned.

"Don't worry," I told him, "it should be fun."

The head of the Non-Appropriated Fund section of the 8th Army Comptroller's Office was a Department of the Army Civilian by the imposing name of Wilbur M. Robinson Sr. He was a round-faced man with wispy hair combed straight back and an old-fashioned, neatly trimmed mustache beneath a red-veined nose. Every letter of his name was etched into a yard-wide hand-carved nameplate that covered the front edge of his mahogany desk.

"Yes?" he said, glancing irritably up at us over steel-rimmed glasses.

I flashed my badge. Ernie chomped on his gum, studying all the awards and photographs plastered to the walls. Some of them showed a youngish Mr. Robinson shaking hands and grinning with various American generals who could now be found in the indices of history books.

"Who let you in?" he asked.

"We did," Ernie replied, jamming his thumb into his chest.

"Who do you think you are?"

"CID agents," I replied, "investigating a criminal case."

"That doesn't mean you can just barge in here."

"Sure it does," Ernie replied, taking a seat in one of the leather-upholstered chairs.

Mr. Robinson reached for the black telephone on the edge of his desk. Before he could lift it, I said, "The Central Locker Fund." He stared up at me and let go of the phone. I slid one of Burrows and Slabem's charts in front of him. "Notice anything odd about that?" I asked.

He glanced at it but quickly looked back up at me.

"What are you getting at?"

"Expenditures versus receipt of inventory," I said. "They don't match. Haven't for years."

"Ridiculous."

I pointed at one of the lines. "The prices here are approximately three percent higher than expected," I said. "Have been for years."

"Prices fluctuate," he said. "You can't tell anything from a simple-minded chart."

"Simple-minded like the guys who conducted the inventory?" Ernie said.

Robinson turned and studied him. Then he turned back to me. "You're not here on official business, are you?"

"Official as the day is long," I said.

"But nobody in your chain of command chopped off on this."

Chopped off. The slang of an old Asia hand, meaning gave the stamp of approval.

"Answer the question, Robinson," Ernie said. "Why are the Central Locker Fund expenditures higher than the receipt of inventory?"

Robinson stood. He wore what appeared to be an expensive grey suit, probably handcrafted by a British tailor in Hong Kong. DACs could afford regular rest-and-recreation jaunts to Hong Kong or Tokyo. GIs couldn't.

"This interview is over," he said.

"No, it's not," Ernie replied.

Robinson lifted the phone again, and this time he dialed. A few seconds later, he said, "Fred, I've got a couple of your boys over here."

He was speaking, I believed, to Major General Frederick S. Nettles, acting Chief of Staff of the 8th United States Army.

I motioned to Ernie, and discreetly, and expeditiously, we left the room.

"What the hell did that accomplish?" Ernie asked me once we were out in the hallway.

"Built a fire under their butts," I said.

"Maybe one that will spread to us."

"Maybe. Or maybe it'll flush out a few snakes."

Before we left, we wandered down a hallway that led to the Non-Appropriated Fund Records Repository. Bored Korean clerks sat at desks with piles of pink and yellow onionskin in their in-baskets. We walked past them and entered the huge Quonset hut where the records were actually kept. Rows of metal stanchions supported wooden shelves that were labeled with dates and the type of merchandise being recorded. On the shelves, labeled cardboard boxes stuffed with records were piled almost to the ceiling. We wandered around the long rows, craning our necks skyward.

"Burrows and Slabem inventoried all this?" Ernie asked.

"Unlikely," I replied.

When we returned to the CID office, Miss Kim approached me. *"Kuenchanna-yo, Geogie?"* she asked. Are you okay?

I told her I was fine. She handed me a written phone message. It was from Inspector Gil Kwon-up. Mr. Kill. The time had been about twenty minutes ago. He wanted to meet us and said he would pick us up in front of Gate 5 in an hour. I showed the message to Ernie, who sipped on the coffee, grimaced, and set it down.

Forty minutes later, we were standing tall outside of Yongsan Compound Gate Number 5. A blue KNP sedan pulled up, Officer Oh at the wheel, Mr. Kill sitting in front in the passenger seat. The back door popped open. Ernie and I climbed in.

"Bad news," Inspector Kill said.

Officer Oh stepped on the gas and sped into traffic.

"What now?" Ernie asked.

"It's about the little *kisaeng* we talked to."

"The one at the Bright Cloud?" I asked.

"Yes. She's been taken."

"Taken by who?" Ernie asked.

"The traffickers she escaped from. They found her."

We pulled in back of the whitewashed building that housed the Dongbu Police Station. *Dongbu* means Eastern District. We were ten kilometers east of downtown Seoul, just south of Walker Hill and north of the Han River.

On the drive over, Inspector Kill briefed us on what they'd learned from the two men who'd been arrested in Songtan for trying to kill us with a taxicab. The men were hardened members of a crime syndicate and they hadn't admitted to much. But the KNPs did believe that they were the same two who had stolen the garlic truck and tried to run us down the same way in Samgakji.

"They're not very good drivers," Ernie said.

"Why do you say that?" Kill asked.

"Because if they were good drivers, George and I would be dead."

He nodded. "I supervised the interrogation myself. But there are layers in these organizations, and one can probe only so deeply into them. What these two men know is limited. What they're willing to admit to is even less."

"But you came up with something," I said.

"I came up with a hunch. A general notion that someone is very unhappy. What do you say, that someone is unhappy because the boat has been stoned?"

"Huh?" Ernie said.

I thought about it for a moment. "Rocked," I said, "not stoned. Someone is rocking the boat."

"Yes," Mr. Kill said, snapping his fingers. "That's what I meant. Someone higher in the organization is very unhappy because someone lower is rocking the boat."

"As in, leaving Miss Hwang's body by the banks of the Sonyu River," Ernie said.

"Yes. And unhappy because that event could lead to other revelations."

I recapped for him what we knew about the sale of malt liquor in the GI villages and about the man we were calling the Ville Rat.

"You have his name?"

"Yes." I gave it to him, along with his date of separation from the army. Mr. Kill jotted it down. From now on, the KNPs would be on the lookout for him.

"When a criminal operation is running well," Mr. Kill said, slipping his notebook back into his jacket, "my experience has been that it is almost always tripped up by either greed or the foolishness of those operating it."

"Or by passion," I said.

"Yes, passion," he agreed.

"A passion like calligraphy."

"Yes. Calligraphy and beautiful women."

Officer Oh shuffled in her seat, but tightened her grip on the steering wheel and continued to guide us expertly through the mid-afternoon Seoul traffic.

■ ■ ■

The interrogation room of the Dongbu Police Station was packed with khaki-clad cops. In the center were three Korean men, all of them kneeling, all of them with their hands cuffed behind their backs. Perspiration dripped from their foreheads, creating puddles that soaked their knees. Inspector Kill cleared the room until there was only me, him, and Ernie standing next to the three criminals. Gruffly, he told them to repeat their testimony. The one with the least amount of blood dripping from his mouth spoke. His Korean was guttural and full of slang, but I understood the gist of what he said. The little *kisaeng* had been hunted down and recovered as an example to the other girls that escape was futile. She'd been punished, and then she'd been sold to the same foreigner who'd purchased Miss Hwang, the one who was almost undoubtedly responsible for her violent death near the Sonyu River.

"Why," I asked, "had she been sold to this man?"

"As punishment," the criminal said.

"Punishment because he's a foreigner?" I asked.

"No. Punishment because of what he does to the girls."

"And what is that?"

"No one's sure but, so far, they've all ended up dead."

"All?"

"Yes, there were others."

"How many?"

"I don't know." Mr. Kill kicked him. "Seven, maybe eight," the man said.

"And why weren't their bodies found?"

"Usually, he disposes of them carefully. The one in Sonyu-ri was smart. She sensed what was coming and tried to run away."

What he said was true—Miss Hwang had been smart. Very smart. But not smart enough to survive.

Mr. Kill pressured him for the name of the foreigner, for a description, but no matter how rough the interrogation got, the three men claimed they hadn't seen him. The transaction was conducted by an intermediary. We tried to find out who that was, but the men were apparently lifelong criminals who wanted to continue to live. They wouldn't spill.

Finally, Mr. Kill had them taken from the room.

"They don't know who the foreigner is."

"No," Mr. Kill agreed. "They're merely thugs. When negotiations are conducted, they are not around."

Ernie chomped on his ginseng gum; upset, I believed, by the rough KNP interrogation but unwilling to admit it. "What are you going to do with those guys?" he asked.

"They'll be charged."

"With human trafficking?"

"Probably not."

The Korean government wasn't happy with admitting what happened to some of the impoverished women of their country. Mr. Kill was obviously uncomfortable with where the conversation was going, but oblivious, Ernie pressed on.

"So what will they be charged with?"

"Assault, probably."

"On who?"

"On a police officer."

"They assaulted a police officer?"

Mr. Kill held out his fist. "They bruised our knuckles, didn't they?"

■ ■ ■

On the drive back to Yongsan Compound, we discussed who the foreigner could be.

"Not the Ville Rat," I said. "He never would've exposed himself to us if he was involved."

"Or thrown that can of Colt 45 at the taxi," Ernie added.

"But he did mention another man to you," Inspector Kill said.

"I mentioned him, actually. He seems a likely suspect. He runs the Central Locker Fund, so he must know about the extra smuggling that is being done off the books, and he's been here in Korea since the fifties."

"Long enough to become interested in calligraphy," Mr. Kill added.

"Yes. And *kisaeng*."

"It doesn't take long to become interested in *kisaeng*," Ernie said.

Officer Oh drove silently, although it seemed to me that the muscles in the back of her neck were tense. Maybe it was the careening traffic. She honked her horn and swerved around a pivoting taxicab.

"Whoever's been profiting from this Central Locker Fund scam," I said, "must've made tons of money. Enough to buy whatever he wants."

"Including women," Mr. Kill said.

"Yes, including women."

Officer Oh slammed on the brakes. We all jerked forward. The brake lights of a taxicab glowed red just millimeters in front of our front bumper. Officer Oh turned to Inspector Kill sheepishly and said, *"Mianhamnida."* I'm sorry.

I noticed she didn't apologize to me or Ernie.

■ ■ ■

Ernie and I knew we were facing a mountain of trouble. The audit of all 8th Army Non-Appropriated Funds, including the Central Locker Fund, had been closed without serious anomalies. The Department of the Army Civilians who ran the funds, including Mr. Wilbur M. Robinson Sr., were firmly entrenched in their jobs, some of them having been here for decades. They had money, contacts in the private sector, and influence with both 8th Army and the Korean government. Rick Mills himself, it was said, lived in a mansion in an old part of Seoul; a part of the city that hadn't been totally destroyed by the Korean War.

We needed inside information. Ernie called Strange. He met us just after evening chow at the 8th Army snack bar.

"Don't ask me if I've had any strange lately," Ernie said, pointing his finger at Strange's nose. "I'm in no mood for it."

We were both feeling the stress, not only of the Threets court-martial fiasco but also of the vested interests we were about to go up against. We were close to something and it wasn't going to be pretty. On the other hand, we had to move fast, very fast, because the life of the little *kisaeng* was hanging in the balance. She'd been a sweet child, harmless, and I suppose Ernie and I were both affected by the thought of what some men were capable of doing to the innocent. We'd seen evidence of that on the banks of the Sonyu River.

I brought a tray with two cups of coffee and one mug of hot chocolate, with two marshmallows, the way Strange liked it. As he pulled the steaming concoction close, Strange smirked, enjoying being the center of attention and maybe enjoying our desperation even more.

As he slurped the first marshmallow down his gullet, I leaned toward him. "What do you know about Rick Mills?"

"Mr. Brainiac. Survived the soap-opera politics of Eighth Army all these years. Still sitting pretty."

"He's rich?"

"Like King Midas. Retired from the army as master sergeant fifteen years ago, now he's a GS-freaking-fourteen, pulling down big bucks. Just after the war, he and his Korean wife bought a mansion on half a hillside and paid soybeans for it. Now it's worth a fortune. Smart *yobo*. She built on the extra land and rents out apartments."

"Is he crooked?"

"Everybody says so."

"What do you think?"

"I think he doesn't have to be. Not for the money. But for the politics of it, that's different."

"To keep his position as honcho of the Central Locker Fund, he probably has to play ball with things he's not too happy with."

"Could be."

"And his wife," Ernie asked, "does she live in that mansion with him?"

"She used to."

"What do you mean?"

"She died, about three years ago." He slurped down the second marshmallow.

"How'd she die?"

"Ugly scene," Strange said. "Fell off one of the stone parapets. Cracked her skull."

"Parapets," Ernie said. "Like in a castle."

"Yeah, like where he lives."

"Did the KNPs investigate?"

"Of course. Called it an accident. Too much champagne."

My experience was that most Korean women, and Koreans in general, didn't like champagne, or any kind of wine. When they drank alcohol, it was usually whiskey, since it had social cachet and because it reminded them of harsh Korean liquors like soju. When something had a fruity taste, they expected it to be sweet, not bubbly and sour.

"So what does he do now," I asked, "now that his wife is gone?"

"Hides out in his castle. Maybe takes some dollies up there."

"Do you know anybody who's been there?"

"All of the honchos have been there. Before his wife died, he loved to throw parties."

"But not now."

"Not now."

"What else do you know about Rick Mills?" I asked.

"He's a smart guy. They say he loves poetry."

"What kind of poetry?"

Behind his opaque glasses, Strange's eyes seemed to widen. "The kind that rhymes."

"You mean like old-fashioned poetry?"

"What do you mean, 'old-fashioned'?"

"Skip it," I said. "Does he have any other hobbies?"

"He gets a haircut every night."

"Every night?" Ernie asked, astonished.

"Yeah, and a manicure. Not everybody in this world is a slob."

"Who you calling a slob?"

I waved Ernie back. "Strange, where does he get his hair cut?"

"The name's Harvey." He stared resentfully at Ernie.

"Right, Harvey," I said. "Is it on post?"

"Yes, at the Top Five Club."

"He's a GS-fourteen," I said. "He could go to the barbershop at the officers' club."

"I guess he's still an NCO at heart," Strange said. "Besides, there's some sweet dollies working at the Top Five Club."

"Is that where you get your hair cut?"

"I have my hair cut in private."

"By who?"

"By me." He rubbed the back of his neck. "I don't like anyone touching me."

"You just like to hear about it," Ernie said.

Strange glared at him. "Had any *strange* lately?" he asked.

From inside the foyer of the Top Five Club on Yongsan Compound North Post, we watched Rick Mills enjoy his early evening haircut and manicure. He lay back like a pampered potentate while the Korean male barber and his attractive female assistant attended his hair, his shave, and the shape and length of his fingernails. When he finished, the barber flicked the white coverlet and helped him put on his coat. Both the barber and his assistant bowed and Rick Mills handed them a short stack of bills which made them smile and bow even deeper. We hurried outside and waited out of sight when Rick Mills stepped out onto the broad porch and his driver swooped over to pick him up in his black Hyundai sedan. We ran to Ernie's jeep and followed at a safe distance, winding through traffic all the way across town to an elegant neighborhood in an area of Seoul known as Sodaemun-ku, the Great West Gate district.

The driver pulled up in front of a granite-walled stairway and Rick Mills got out.

On the far side of the block, Ernie parked the jeep.

Stone blocks slanted upward about twenty feet.

"It *is* like a castle," Ernie said.

We were out of the jeep now, reconnoitering. A flagstone stairway climbed two flights up to a heavy metal door embedded in a granite wall.

"We could go up and push the buzzer," Ernie said.

"And if he doesn't let us in?"

"He'd be smart."

"Right. And if he has any women trapped inside there, he definitely won't let us in."

To get behind Rick Mills's castle, we had to abandon the narrow pathway that fronted the thick retaining wall, climb back into Ernie's jeep, and drive all the way around to the far side of the hill upon which it sat. When the roads going up became too narrow, we parked the jeep. Ernie padlocked the steering wheel to the chain welded to the floor and we started walking. Korean men in suits carrying briefcases on their way home late from work, schoolchildren clad in black with heavy book bags hunched atop their shoulders, and old women with bundles balanced on their heads all passed us and stared.

"Not many *kocheingi* come up here," Ernie said. He used the Korean word for "long nose."

Finally, we reached a Buddhist shrine at the top of the hill. Inside, incense burned, illuminating with its tiny flame the metal robes of a calm-faced Buddha.

"Bow," I told Ernie.

"You bow."

In the end, neither of us bowed. Probably a mistake. Instead, we edged our way around to the back of the shrine and hoisted ourselves up onto the top of a brick wall. It was dirty, but we sat on it, staring down at the panorama below.

Off to the left, the newly built skyscrapers of Seoul blinked at us with a smattering of lights in windows. Straight ahead, across a five- or six-mile-wide valley, Namsan Mountain rose dark and imposing to the brightly lit signal tower atop. To the right, strings of light were strung like sparkling necklaces across the Han River Bridge.

"How much did Rick Mills have to pay for this view?" Ernie asked.

"Peanuts, according to Strange, when he first bought it."

"Smart guy. Back in those days, most GIs just wanted to get the hell out of Korea and make it back to Japan. Or better yet, the States."

"Rick Mills saw what Korea would become."

"It's still poor."

"Yeah, and for a lot of people, it's still hell."

We studied the mansion. It was dark and silent except for a light in the northern wing.

"That's where he must be," Ernie said. "Do you think he has servants?"

"He has to, to run a house this big."

"But does he let them go home at night or do they live in?"

"I think we're going to have to assume that with a house this big, at least some of them live in."

"But I don't see any other lights."

I searched. "Neither do I."

"So how we going to get in?"

"There doesn't appear to be an alarm system." They were rare in Korea and often didn't work. Even when they did work, they only sounded a local alarm and weren't hooked up to the KNP station.

"Or dogs," I said. Guard dogs were not popular in Korea. Not only was there limited space in most homes, but most people didn't want to go to the expense of feeding and caring for an extra mouth.

"And no foot patrols," Ernie said. That's how most wealthy people in Korea guarded their riches, with old-fashioned manpower. It was Korean custom that if someone was home and not sleeping, thieves would usually leave them alone. Crimes against property, if someone was poor and desperate, were understandable, if not completely tolerated. But physically overpowering a homeowner was considered a horrendous crime, a crime against society, and would more often than not land a perpetrator in prison for many years.

"So Rick Mills lives alone," I said, "and probably figures he can protect his home by himself."

"He probably can," Ernie said. "He was an NCO, remember, during the war."

"Okay," I said. "We wait until the lights go out, then we come back here and climb the wall."

"Using what?"

"We'll find something."

We left our perch, walked past the shrine again, and returned to the jeep. Two hours later we were back, parking the jeep in the same place, passing the shrine again, and taking our perches on the brick wall.

"Lights out," Ernie said.

"Early to bed, early to rise."

We jumped off the wall and made our way along a drainage ditch until we reached the granite back wall of Rick Mills's mansion. I handed a grappling hook to Ernie.

"How do you use this stuff?"

"The hook's padded," I told him. "Makes less noise that way. Toss it up to the top of the wall. When we have purchase, we pull ourselves up."

"Christ," Ernie said, but he didn't argue. "Where'd you get this stuff?"

"Palinki."

"He keeps it in the armory?"

"Along with a lot of other equipment. Like these." I held up a ring of picks and oddly shaped keys.

"Oh, great."

Ernie stepped back and tossed the grappling hook toward the top of the wall. His first toss was too short, but the second reached the top and slid toward the far side. When it didn't find purchase, the hook slid back down the slanted wall. We tried again and again. Finally, on the sixth try, the hook caught. Ernie pulled, testing his weight against it.

"Must be a pipe or something. I think it'll hold."

He climbed up first, not having to put all his weight on the rope because the toes of his sneakers clung to the craggy breaks in the slanted wall. For a moment he halted and I thought he was going to tumble backward, but he regained his balance, leaned forward, and continued to climb. Finally he reached the top, lay down flat, and, after checking the purchase of the grappling hook, flashed me the thumbs-up. Reassured by Ernie's success, I climbed more rapidly and joined him atop the wall in a matter of seconds.

I pulled the rope up and recoiled it on the flat stone. As I did so, we both gazed into the darkness below. The drop was about eight feet. Beyond that rose the back wall of the mansion, with a narrow walkway between. As my eyes adjusted to the darkness, I realized that the sheds nearby were probably *byonso*, outhouses. Ernie realized it too.

"He doesn't have indoor plumbing?" he whispered.

"We'll find out."

We hopped down, landing on a flagstone surface, and after waiting and not hearing anything, we walked toward the old wooden sheds. Ernie sniffed. No hideous odor. When we reached the first one, I opened the door and peeked inside. The floor had been covered with lumber, and cleaning and gardening supplies leaned against splintered walls. This *byonso* wasn't used any longer, which meant indoor plumbing had been installed. Since the end of the Korean War, it was becoming more prevalent. Especially in the homes of the rich.

We proceeded to the end of the wall, ducked down, and peered ahead. A wooden porch led up to a door. Above it, a metal pipe jutted out, twisting immediately skyward.

"The kitchen," Ernie said.

It made sense. Across a short walkway sat a brick building with a closed wooden door, probably the pantry.

We approached the back porch. I climbed up and peered in through the window. Nothing but darkness. I knelt and pulled out the burglary tools Palinki had given me. While I worked, Ernie stepped to the front of the building and peered around the corner. When he gave me the all-clear sign, I pulled my penlight from my pocket and went to work. Palinki's instruction had been thorough, but he was more experienced than I was, manipulating the delicate tools in his huge fingers like a maestro caressing the frets of a Stradivarius. I was clumsy. After ten minutes, Ernie became impatient, but just as he wandered onto the first wooden step of the porch, the back door lock clicked open. I turned the handle and shoved it slowly forward. Nothing moved. Quickly, Ernie and I stepped into darkness.

We were right. It was the kitchen. I shone the penlight on a floor covered in tile. There were two stainless-steel refrigerators, one bench-like freezer, and an industrial-sized stove with a scaffolding of gleaming copper. All the equipment was professional grade with brand names that seemed to be Swedish or Germanic. Ernie and I gazed at the huge kitchen in awe; it must've cost him a fortune to import all these things, because they clearly weren't manufactured in Korea and I doubted that the PX bothered to import them. There'd be no demand, not a legitimate one anyway.

Beyond the kitchen was a serving counter, and beyond that, double doors that led into a carpeted dining room. The table was made of gleaming mahogany and it was long enough to seat at least twenty. The walls were lined with artwork that didn't look like anything in particular other than splashes of bright color. We were probably coming close to the front entrance-way and therefore the main living room, or whatever the room would be called in a big house like this. We were impatient to find the dungeon, or at least the basement, where young women would be held against their will. That's how I imagined it. At the closed entrance door to the dining room, Ernie and I paused, listening. Still no sound. We'd been quiet, but I hoped Mills was a sound sleeper. I pushed through the door.

A light flashed in my eyes.

A voice shouted, "Freeze, motherfugger!"

I froze. And then I was staring into the unforgiving end of a double-barreled shotgun.

-13-

I should've figured it wouldn't be that easy.

Luckily, Ernie did figure. He was still out of sight, hidden in the dining room. I knew he had a .45 in a shoulder holster beneath his jacket. I kept my hands out to my sides. Softly, I said, "What do you want me to do?"

"Call your partner."

The man speaking behind the flashlight in one hand and the shotgun in the other was Rick Mills, master sergeant (retired) of the US Army and current executive director of the 8th US Army Central Locker Fund. He sat in a high-backed padded chair, wearing pajamas, slippers, and a silk smoking jacket embroidered with what looked like flying dragons.

"Easy, Mills," I said, "you're in enough trouble."

"Me?" He barked a laugh. "Looks like you two are the ones in trouble. Breaking and entering. You have a warrant?"

"We don't need search warrants in Korea."

"Not on base. But you're off base now."

He was right about that. Ernie and I had no jurisdiction in Sodaemun and no legal justification for entering his home. Our justification was hot pursuit. We had reason to believe that women were being held against their will here, raped, and even murdered. Whether it would stand up to legal scrutiny—we hadn't been worrying about that. And at the moment, I was more worried about Rick Mills's shotgun.

"Lower the barrel of the shotgun," I said. "I'm not armed."

"How about your partner?"

"We're just here to look around," I said, "not hurt anyone."

"Look for what?"

I told him.

"*Kisaeng?*" he said. "Here in *my* house?"

I told him about the murdered woman near Sonyu-ri.

"Oh, Chirst," he said. "You don't think I had something to do with that? I've been accused of every crime Eighth Army has on the books, but not that one. Your brothers at the CID have been after me for years, figuring that since I handle a bunch of liquor, I must be black marketeering. But they never found anything because I haven't done anything."

"Why should we believe that?"

"Look around. Do I need more money? Do I need to risk losing my job and my work visa? My wife bought up more shit than you can believe in the years after the Korean War. Dirt cheap. As the Korean economy grows, my wealth grows with it. Why would I want to sell illegally on the black market and risk everything? And why in the hell would I want to lock up *kisaeng* here in my house? If I want a *kisaeng*, I'll go to a frigging *kisaeng* house."

Ernie shouted, "Drop the gun, Mills!"

"You drop yours, dammit! This is *my* house."

Ernie didn't reply. I was worried he'd start firing. After all, the barrel of the shotgun was still pointed directly at me. If Mills pulled that trigger, my guts would be spilling out like a bowl of raw octopus.

"Okay, Mills," I said. "You're saying you've got nothing to hide. So prove it. Let us search the house."

He thought about that.

"You've got no right."

"No. We don't have the right. But if we search and find out we were wrong, then we'll leave you alone."

Mills pondered that. Then he said, "I want more than just being left alone."

"What do you want?"

"I want you to do something for me."

"What?"

"I want you to find the son of a bitch who's doing this to the Central Locker Fund."

"You mean ordering stuff off the books?"

Mills stiffened. "I have no direct knowledge of that."

"But you know something."

He didn't answer.

"I understand," I said. "It's been going on for years, maybe decades, the discrepancy in inventory, ordered by people with more power than you. But you didn't profit from it and you made sure that you had no fingerprints on it, so if it ever blew up, you wouldn't be caught up in it. Is that it? Do I have it right?"

He didn't answer, just sat immobile.

"I'll assume I do," I said. "But then somebody came along who wanted to expand the ordering beyond what it had been in the past. Instead of just providing expensive imported booze to the rich and powerful, maybe to Korean politicians directly, or to legitimate importers who could move the stuff in bulk, somebody threw in a few orders of something else. And they started selling it around GI villages, making a quick buck, not a fortune, but a nice pile of change. Especially if you're used to living on the paycheck of a noncommissioned officer."

Mills stared at me impassively, neither confirming nor denying.

"You remember what it was like to be a noncommissioned officer, Mills. You remember what it was like to be broke three days before payday."

Finally, he spoke. "It's been a long time."

"So, am I right? The honchos had a good thing going, running two sets of books at the Central Locker Fund, selling the booze wholesale or using it for gifts to the people at the top, pocketing some of the money but using lots of it to expand their own power. Pay off the right people, renovate the right buildings, contribute to the right charities. And then some lowlife punk comes along and endangers the entire setup. Am I right, Mills?"

Ernie dove into the room.

Startled, Mills swiveled the shotgun and fired.

I leapt face-first into the carpet. The second round of the shotgun didn't go off.

I looked up. Ernie was kneeling on the carpet, holding his .45 in front of him with both hands. "Drop it, Mills!"

Rick Mills stared at him in horror. Then he let loose of the shotgun and allowed it to slide harmlessly to the floor.

Mills insisted that we search his entire house.

"I don't want any rumors starting," he said, "that Rick Mills is holding women hostage in his mansion."

We did search, thoroughly, tapping on walls, even borrowing Mills's crowbar and pulling back paneling that seemed to have been installed in recent years. There was in fact a basement and an attic, but no dungeon. During the entire search, Mills escorted us through the house, switching on lights. Like a proud host, he pointed out heirlooms that his wife had acquired, impressing us with the appraised value of artwork and antiques.

I searched for writing brushes and other implements used in calligraphy but didn't find any. At one point, I tossed a porcelain doll to him. He caught it with his right hand.

"What's that all about?" he asked.

"Nothing. Who's that?" I pointed to a framed photograph on a linen-draped table.

Rick Mills moved toward the photo, lifted it with both hands, and stared at it longingly. "My wife," he said. He handed it to me. A stunning Korean woman with high cheekbones and piercing black eyes stared back at me. She wore what appeared to be a traditional Korean dress, but made of felt. Though the photo was black-and-white, I imagined the felt to be dark blue. She sat on an ornately carved chair, and leaning against her full skirt was a stringed musical instrument.

"The *komungo*," Mills said. "One of the first ancient Korean instruments. She studied it for years."

"How'd you meet her, Mills? You were just an NCO."

He shrugged. "People were desperate in those days, even the daughters of the landed classes. Desperate enough to hang out with a guy like me."

"You married up," Ernie said.

"Very much so," Mills replied. "She saved my life, putting a stop to all the drinking and carousing." Then he waved his hands. "And made me rich."

"How long has she been gone?"

"Almost five years now. My mourning period is almost over."

"Koreans mourn that long for a wife?" I asked.

"Not usually. But I am. See that temple out back?"

I nodded.

"I made a vow," Rick Mills said. "One I won't break."

We continued searching the house, finding nothing out of line. When we were done, Mills shook our hands. "Am I clean?" he asked.

"Clean," I said. "Unless you're keeping them off-site."

He frowned.

"You were about to tell me something, something about what it was like when you were an NCO living from paycheck to paycheck."

"It's unfair," he said.

"What's unfair?"

"It's unfair to assign an NCO to the Central Locker Fund. They see so much wealth around them and there's bound to be temptation. I'm not sure why personnel insists on assigning one to us. We could just as easily hire a Korean National."

"They want to keep their hand in," Ernie said.

"I suppose that's it. They just want to remind themselves, and maybe me, that the Central Locker Fund is, after all, a creation of the US Army."

"So that's what you wanted to tell me?" I said. "That it's unfair to assign an NCO to the Central Locker Fund."

"That's part of it."

"What's the other part?"

"Demoray," he said.

"What about him?"

"I don't trust him. He's erratic and impulsive. You saw how he blew up at that worker when you were at the Central Locker Fund."

"Not that unusual for the NCO Corps," I said.

"No. But you've never asked him a question."

"What do you mean?"

"I mean, when you ask a question, you expect an answer. That's what NCOs do, answer questions honestly and directly. Maybe a pause for a few seconds to think about it, but with him the pause can last minutes."

"What does he do during those minutes?"

"Sometimes he takes off his cap and rubs his head. Other than that, nothing. He's just completely silent. As if he's suddenly become the sphinx."

I'd heard that before. Long, unexpected silences in the middle of calligraphy lessons.

"Is he interested in Korean culture?" I asked.

"That's what they tell me, and if he wasn't so weird with the silences and explosive at other times, the Koreans would give him a lot of respect. But they don't, because they don't trust him. He's too erratic."

"What exactly do you suspect him of?"

"I'll deny it if anyone asks officially, but I've suspected him for a long time of moving stuff on the side."

"Off the books?"

"Yes. He takes long trips to the Port of Inchon. I believe he's developed a contact there."

"Someone who can get the stuff through customs."

"Yes. Easy enough as long as the inspector can at least pretend that it's military materiel."

"What's he been moving?"

"I don't know for sure."

"What do you suspect?"

Mills paused. "Malt liquor," he said.

"Colt 45?"

"Right. And California brandy. Stuff that can be substituted for cognac."

"Do you have proof?"

"I haven't looked for proof."

"You want to keep your fingerprints off it," I said.

Mills didn't answer.

"Where does Demoray live?" I asked.

"Supposedly at the Nineteenth Support Group senior NCO barracks. But I've heard he has a place off-post."

"Where?"

"I don't know exactly. Maybe somewhere in Itaewon."

■　■　■

Ernie and I drove to the Itaewon Police Station. A sleepy-looking desk officer looked up at us as we entered, surprised at first, but his face then returning to resigned resentment. I showed him Inspector Kill's calling card. It was printed in English on one side and *hangul* on the other. I told the duty officer to call him. He stared at me wide-eyed, disbelieving. I showed him my badge and told him again. He lifted the phone. After many rings somebody answered. I could hear the word *yoboseiyo.* Hello. When the duty officer started talking, I realized that he hadn't called Inspector Kill at all, but rather Captain Kim, the commander of the Itaewon Police Station.

I snatched the receiver from his hand.

"Captain Kim," I said, "we have to find someone here in Itaewon. Lives are at stake." His English was not nearly as good as Mr. Kill's, so I repeated what I'd said in Korean. He asked what I wanted him to do. "We have to go through rental records," I told him, "find a GI named Demoray who rented a home here in Itaewon."

There was a long silence. Then he asked me in English, "Do you know what time it is?"

Actually, I didn't. All I could think of since I'd stared into the barrel of Rick Mills's shotgun was death. My own death and the death of Miss Hwang on the banks of the Sonyu River and the death of the little *kisaeng.* I looked around. It was dark outside. No traffic.

"Myotsi?" I asked the duty officer. He looked at his wristwatch. *"Yoltu-shi iship oh-bun."* 12:15 A.M.

"Okay," I said into the phone. "This morning, at first light, I need a detail hitting every *bokdok-bang,* Korean real estate broker, to check their records and find the hooch rented by a GI named Demoray."

And then it dawned on me. He might've rented the place using a false name. The Korean real estate agent wouldn't care, as long as he was paid in cash.

Captain Kim didn't commit himself. He said we'd talk about it when he came in to work this morning. Suddenly, I felt foolish. We didn't have time to find Demoray the regular way, with shoe leather and traditional police work. I had to figure out a way to find him now.

Ernie and I walked up the main drag of Itaewon, now lined with dark neon: The UN Club, the Lucky Seven Club, the Seven Club, the King Club. A few yards off to our left, I knew, up Hooker Hill, was the Grand Old Opry Club, Sam's Place, and beyond that, down the steps in front of the movie theater, the 007 Club. Lonely yellow street lamps guided our way.

"He's out here somewhere," Ernie said.

"Yeah, and if you were a demented son of a bitch with plenty of money and you wanted to rent a place where you could hide women you'd purchased from human traffickers, where would you go?"

"I'd go to someplace isolated."

Itaewon was the opposite of isolated. It sat in a southern suburb of a city of eight million people. Behind the main drag of nightclubs, the hooches were jammed up like poker chips in a pile.

"So if you don't have isolation," I said, "where else can you hide?"

"I don't get you," Ernie replied.

"Think of Edgar Allen Poe. 'The Purloined Letter.'"

"You read too much," Ernie said in disgust.

"If you can't hide something away from others of its kind, you hide it in the midst of a multitude of its kind."

"So you hide abused women," Ernie said, "amongst other abused women." He thought about it. "In a whorehouse."

"Not just any whorehouse. But the worst of the worst."

We turned up Hooker Hill.

We walked through the lonely back alleys of Itaewon, searching for lights inside windows, but there weren't any. Occasionally we paused and listened. No shouts, no whimpering, just silence. Methodically we walked up and down the hills, turning toward the whorehouses we'd heard about, realizing that we didn't know where they all were, but still everything was silent.

Finally, we stopped.

"Maybe he doesn't live in Itaewon," Ernie said.

"Maybe not. In the morning we'll ask Inspector Kill to organize a task force to search for Demoray."

"What did Mills say about Sonyu-ri again?"

Before we left, I had the presence of mind to ask him about his Non-Appropriated Fund operation up north near Camp Pelham, outside of Sonyu-ri. He told me that for years some of the Korean businessmen in the area had been hosted at the *meikju changgo*, the beer warehouse near Camp Pelham, to a poker game sponsored out of the illicit funds from the Central Locker Fund.

"That was Demoray's job?"

"Yes. He transported *kisaeng* up there to serve the food and drinks."

"One of them escaped," I told him, "and was killed for her effort."

Mills shook his head, truly repentant. "It's gotten out of hand," he said. "I knew it would one day."

By the time we left, I almost felt sorry for him, but not enough to stop me from deciding to turn him in. Rick Mills had known what was going on and could've saved a life if he'd reported it.

Ernie studied the quiet Itaewon night. "Let's try one more alley. If we don't find anything, then we might as well go back to the compound."

I agreed with him. We stalked up the narrow pedestrian lanes, brick and stone walls on either side, observing the moon-lit night, listening for any sound. Nothing.

Finally, we gave up and returned to Ernie's jeep and drove slowly toward Yongsan.

"There's one last place we can try," I said.

Ernie groaned again.

"Eighth Army Billeting," I told him.

The duty NCO wasn't happy to be rousted out of his cot. He was a thin man with a heavy five o'clock shadow and a sweat-stained green T-shirt behind the dog tags chained to his neck. We flashed our badges. He rubbed his eyes.

"Somebody rob a bank?" he asked.

"Demoray, Master Sergeant," Ernie said.

The guy looked up at him and silently turned and pulled out a metal drawer from a filing cabinet that lined the back wall. He shuffled through folders and asked, "D-E-M?"

"Right," Ernie replied.

They guy stopped, pulled out a folder, and said, "Building N402, Room Five."

"Where's that?"

"On Main Post. In the row behind the JUSMAG Headquarters." Joint US Military Advisory Group.

"Thanks."

We ran back to the jeep.

As we suspected, Demoray wasn't in his room. We pounded on the door so loudly that one of the NCOs down the hall, still dressed in skivvies and a T-shirt, creaked opened his door and asked what the hell we thought we were doing.

"Do you have a key to Room Five?" I asked, flashing my badge.

"No. The maid keeps 'em around."

"Where?"

He barged past us to the small kitchen, sparingly but routinely equipped with a refrigerator and gas stove. From a cabinet above the sink, he pulled down an MJB coffee can and tossed it to us.

"You figure it out," he said, and stormed down the hallway back to his room.

The can was jammed with keys. Ernie handed them to me as I tried each one, and finally the door to Room 5 creaked open. I switched on the light.

The bunk was regulation size and tightly made up with an army blanket with the embroidered "U.S." centered neatly. There were no dirty clothes on the floor and no dust atop the wall locker; I would've thought Demoray was a fastidious guy if I didn't know that 8th Army senior NCOs paid only thirty bucks a month for laundry and maid service. I used the keys Palinki had given me to pop open the wall locker and Ernie searched under the bunk and in the foot locker, but we found nothing that could give us a hint as to Demoray's whereabouts. Only neatly pressed uniforms, highly polished footgear, and a drawer full of green army socks.

"Waste of time," Ernie said.

I didn't argue with him. There was a photo propped atop the dresser drawer. It was of a much younger Demoray, still sporting hair, wearing his Class A uniform and staring blankly into a camera. I showed it to Ernie.

"His basic training graduation photo. Why would he keep that?"

"Maybe it reminds him of a time when he was innocent."

I slipped the photo out of its frame and folded it into my jacket pocket. We left the room, closing the door and not bothering to lock it behind us.

"I hope somebody rips him off," Ernie said.

"He can afford it."

Halfway down the dark hallway, I stopped.

"What?" Ernie asked.

I shone my flashlight on a bulletin board covered with pins and squares of multicolored paper of various sizes. They were duty rosters and notes to people who might stop by and a safety announcement from the 8th Army Fire Station. In the upper left corner, a neatly printed three-by-five card had been pinned in a prominent position.

I took it down. "Look at this one," I said.

"Yeah, what about it?" Ernie replied.

"Brush strokes. Not written with a pen like the rest of these."

"What's it say?"

"It's an ad for some stereo equipment. Cheap. 'See Demoray in Room 5.'"

"Not much of a clue."

"Except for the writing."

"What do you mean?"

"Look how neat it is."

Ernie studied the card closer. "Yeah, pretty clean."

"Almost artistic," I said.

"Yeah. So what?"

"Did you see any writing brushes in his room?"

"No. Maybe we missed them."

"We didn't miss them."

"So he keeps them someplace else."

"At his hooch off-post."

"Right." Ernie thought about that. "A lot of good it does us. It doesn't tell us where his hooch is."

"No, but it does tell us something—he's our calligrapher."

After a few hours' sleep, we were back at the 8th Army CID Office.

"You're late," Riley said. "The provost marshal wants to talk to you."

"Where is he?"

"Already gone to the morning chief of staff briefing. But he's mad as hell about you two barging in on the Eighth Army Comptroller's Office like that. He wants you both standing tall, right here, when he returns."

"Can't," I told Riley.

"What the hell do you mean, *can't*?"

"We have a murder investigation to conduct. Somebody's life could be in danger." Like the little *kisaeng*. But I didn't tell him that. The less Eighth Army knew, the better. Less of an excuse for them to micromanage. Ernie and I started walking away.

"Where the hell do you two think you're going?" Riley shouted, red-faced.

"To see Mr. Kill," I told him.

He waved his forefinger at us. "Your ass will be in the wringer."

"It's been there before," Ernie said, not looking back.

When we arrived, the Itaewon Police Station was swarming with cops. Mr. Kill was already in conference with Captain Kim. After a few minutes, Mr. Kill came out and said, "No luck at the *bokdok-bang*s." The local real estate brokers who routinely dealt in the rental of apartments and small hooches.

I showed him the photograph of Demoray.

"This will help," he said. I explained that Demoray was much younger then and completely bald now. He handed the photograph of Officer Oh, who marched away with it toward the detail of cops waiting outside.

"There's one person who knows where Demoray lives—the Ville Rat. Ernie and I are going to look for him."

"He's elusive."

"We'll figure it out."

Before we left Itaewon, we stopped at Haggler Lee's. He confirmed what I suspected: on Thursday, the Ville Rat would be making his largest delivery of the week to the numerous all-black clubs outside of the 2nd Infantry Division headquarters at Camp Casey, in the city known as Tongduchon. East Bean River.

After spending an hour fighting our way north through Seoul traffic, it took another hour to reach the outskirts of Tongduchon; not because of the road conditions, but because of the long waits at the three ROK Army checkpoints. As you left Seoul and approached the Demilitarized Zone, they became more prevalent, but each time our CID emergency dispatch got us through. When we reached the sign that said WELCOME TO TONGDUCHON, Ernie found a parking spot on the edge of the bar district and we hoofed it the rest of the way.

Ernie and I'd been to the Black Cat Club before. Nobody remembered us fondly, least of all the few black GIs playing pool in the dimly lit main hall. They glared at us, as if we only had bad news to bring. When we sat at the bar, Ernie ordered a brown bottle of OB. I asked the barmaid for a Colt 45.

She popped open Ernie's bottle and then stared at me quizzically. "You white GI. Why you order Colt 45?"

"A friend of ours made a delivery. *Maeul ui jwi.*"

"Oh, he told me most tick you come."

"He told you *we* would come?"

She reached in the cooler and pulled out the Colt 45. "Yeah," she said, "two white GIs from Seoul."

"When did he bring this in?" Ernie asked, pointing at the Colt 45.

"Maybe one hour ago," she said.

"Where is he now?"

She shrugged her slender shoulders. "How I know?"

A few of the GIs were staring at us, realizing we were interrogating the barmaid. Since they were eavesdropping now, I flipped through my mental rolodex until I found a safe topic. A possible mutual acquaintance.

"Where's Brandy?" I asked.

Her eyes widened. "You know Brandy?"

"Yes. *Yeitnal chingu*," I said. Old friend. We'd met Brandy on a previous case we had up here in Tongduchon. She'd been a lot of help to us and, in return, we later helped her out of a jam she'd gotten herself into concerning a jealous GI. Anyone who looked at her would realize immediately why the GI was jealous. Brandy was one of the finest-looking women in the village.

Three GIs approached, two of them with pool cues in their hands. "*Yo!* You messing with our girlfriend? You messing with the Black Cat Club?"

"Nobody's messing with nobody," I said.

"The hell you ain't. You be asking a bunch of dumbass questions."

"Like I said, nobody's messing with anybody."

"Then why don't you take your honky-ass selves outta this place where you ain't wanted?"

Like a brown missile, a beer bottle flew past my ear. It missed me and smashed into the face of the guy talking. Ernie shot past me on my left and rammed the heavy barstool into the raised forearms of the guy who'd thrown the bottle. I leapt forward and jerked a pool cue from the hands of one of the surprised GIs and started swinging. The two guys still standing backed off. The few other customers in the bar just stared.

"Where's Brandy live?" I shouted back at the barmaid.

She fiddled with the locks behind the bar and said in Korean, "Out back. I'll show you."

The three enforcers of racial purity didn't follow.

Brandy slid back the oil-papered door and stared at us in surprise. Her hair still radiated from her head in a dark bouffant Afro, but her eyes were even wider than I remembered. Since we'd last seen her, she must've handed over more of her hard-earned money to a plastic surgeon.

"Geogie," she said. "Ernie. Long time no see, short time how you been?"

"Yeah, long time, Brandy. You still sexy."

She struck a pose with her hand on her hip and said, "Gotta be." Then her round face turned serious. "You look Ville Rat."

"Yes," I answered. "Is he still here?"

"No. He go."

"Where?"

"I don't know. But he say you gotta go someplace."

"Where's that?"

"Inchon."

"Inchon? Where in Inchon?"

"I don't know. Anyplace. He say you figure it out."

"Inchon's a big city," I said.

Brandy nodded. "No soul brothers there."

"So the Ville Rat won't be able to sell Colt 45."

She nodded again.

"So what's special about Inchon?" Ernie asked.

"How I know?" Brandy was impatient now, fiddling with a

pack of PX-purchased cigarettes. "You go find out." She waved her hand dismissively.

A group of black GIs burst out of the back of the Black Cat Club. They glared at us ominously. Three of them held pool cues and one held a blood-soaked handkerchief to his nose.

"Thanks for the info, Brandy," I said.

"Ain't no bag," she replied.

Ernie and I hustled out the back gate.

"Inchon," Ernie said.

"That's what Brandy says."

"But why would the Ville Rat want to go there? Like Brandy said, there's no black GIs stationed in Inchon."

"Hardly any GIs at all. Just that small transportation unit."

We were driving through country roads. The sky was overcast, and streams of water and mud occasionally crossed the blacktop. Ernie slowed when we passed through villages lined with brick homes thatched with straw.

"This road will get us to the Western Corridor," he said. "I take the Reunification Highway south from there, but what's the best way after that?"

"Before we hit Seoul, we turn right toward Wondang."

"More country roads," Ernie said.

"Maybe. But we'll miss the outskirts of the city. Less traffic."

Ernie sped around a cart piled with turnips. A tired horse shied away, his grey-streaked rump whipped listlessly by an old man in a broad-brimmed hat.

"How does the Ville Rat expect us to track down a single hideout in Inchon?"

"I guess he thinks we'll figure it out."

"Why's he being so secretive?"

"If everything collapses, he doesn't want to be fingered as the guy who blew the whistle on the Central Locker Fund operation."

"You mean if our investigation collapses because Eighth Army doesn't take these allegations seriously."

"It could happen."

"And the same crooks would be back in charge of the Non-Appropriated Fund."

"They're in charge now."

"But a woman's life is at stake."

"According to Mr. Kill, other women have disappeared and nobody's done anything about it."

"We didn't know."

"Somebody knew."

"And that's who the Ville Rat's afraid of."

"Right. They could turn on him next."

"Not if we catch them."

"No. But the Ville Rat's hedging his bets."

"You think he'll be here?"

"Not a chance. If we take down Demoray, the Ville Rat will want to be as far away as he can."

"Inchon is a big city. Where do we look?"

"The port," I said. "Where the booze comes in."

Ernie nodded. Made sense to him.

Like so many complexes in the Republic of Korea, the main row of warehouses along the Port of Inchon had been constructed by the Japanese. That is, during the colonial period, the warehouses were designed and built under their auspices, although I'm sure the bulk of the labor force was Korean. For over a mile, two- and three-story brick warehouses lined the wharf. All of them had at one time been occupied by the US Army. Inchon was the main port for bringing in supplies to the city of Seoul during and after the Korean War. However, in recent years, a four-lane highway had been built to the much larger Port of Pusan and the transshipment point had changed. Consequently, most of the warehouses in Inchon had been turned over to the Korean government. They in turn had parceled them out to private Korean enterprises. As such, the warehouses run by the US military were down to about a half dozen, all of them huddled on the northern end near the buildings housing the 71st Transportation Company.

Ernie and I cruised down the row of buildings.

"Demoray wouldn't want to operate too close to the military," I said.

"But he has to be near the warehouse that processes the shipments for the Non-Appropriated Fund."

On our way to Inchon, the sun had set into the Yellow Sea and small red bulbs glowed atop the double doors of the brick warehouses that stretched away for almost a mile.

"So which one?" Ernie asked.

"Can't read the signs from here," I said.

Ernie pulled up to the gateway. The Korean contact guard pretended to read our emergency dispatch, but I don't think he understood the jumble of red stamps and printing. I flashed my CID badge and told him impatiently that we only needed to park somewhere safe for a few minutes. Relieved to hear Korean, and to be given an excuse for letting us in if he needed one, he waved us through.

Ernie parked the jeep out of sight behind a wooden trash bin. He padlocked the steering wheel and, with my trusty flashlight in my pocket, we got out to walk. Mostly, we stayed in the shadows reading the signs, searching for something that indicated we'd be near either 8th Army Non-Appropriated Funds or the operations of the Central Locker Fund. But not all of the warehouses were clearly marked. The signs were old and faded, and I was beginning to believe that they hadn't been updated in quite a while.

A night watchman approached us. When he came closer, I could see in the glow of one of the red bulbs that he was Korean. I could also see that an M1 rifle was slung over his right arm. I greeted him and asked, "Where are the Eighth Army warehouses?"

We could've flashed our CID badges and probably been all right, but we didn't even need to do that. American officers had become so much a part of the daily working life of Koreans over the years that most of them never questioned our motives. He pointed toward the end of the row. I thanked him and nodded slightly, and he returned my nod and continued his rounds. Between the warehouses and the wharf was a long expanse of about twenty yards of blacktop. Canvas-covered pallets were laid out like square checkers on a board. Ernie started pulling up the canvas and checking the writing on the boxes underneath. Finally, he stopped and called me over.

"Look," he said.

I shone my flashlight on the cardboard boxes beneath the canvas.

"Falstaff," I said.

"Our favorite," Ernie replied. "Need we go further?"

"Yes," I said. We went down a row of pallets, lifting canvas, seeing all kinds of imported American beer: Pabst Blue Ribbon, Schlitz, Miller High Life. What we weren't seeing was Colt 45.

I switched off the light and studied the warehouses around us. "Anything?" I asked.

Except for the dim red bulbs, all was darkness. Behind us, the smell of the sea crept across the blacktop, picking up the scent of burnt diesel before seeping into our nostrils. Nothing moved. We listened.

"Did you hear that?"

"What?"

"It sounded like a moan."

"Where?"

"Over there. That fenced area."

A smaller building, like an administration annex for the warehouses, was separated off by itself. Surrounding it was a four-foot-high cement-block wall topped by chain-link and, above that, rusted concertina wire. Staying as far from the glow of the dim light as possible, we approached the fence.

Then we heard it again, a faint moan, almost like the sighing of the wind.

When we reached the fence, we glanced at one another, coming to an immediate unspoken agreement. Ernie crouched, cupped his laced fingers in front of me, and I stepped my right foot up into his hands. I grabbed the top of the fence and pulled as he hoisted me over. I slid over as quietly as I could and, once on the other side, slid as unobtrusively as I could along the edge of the fence and unlatched the small gate. Ernie slipped through, closing the gate behind him.

A small courtyard was lined with what appeared to be rusted moving equipment. The front door of the small building was made of heavy wood. We slipped quietly through the darkness.

And then we heard a scream.

-14-

Ernie kicked the wooden door in.

At first we couldn't see anything in the darkness but I pulled out my flashlight and pointed it toward a stairway that disappeared into the darkness. We clambered down the narrow passageway. At the bottom, another door was shut tight. We twisted the handle and shoved but it wouldn't open. Ernie stepped backed and kicked.

"Ow!"

It rattled some but didn't open. I shoved him out of the way, braced myself against the opposite wall, and raised my foot and lunged forward with the same movement. The door slammed open.

Moonlight streamed in through a window above us.

I waved the flashlight back and forth. We were in a basement, the walls lined with stacks of cardboard boxes that almost reached the ceiling. Some were rectangular with JAZZ CITY ALE logos printed on them and others labeled COLT 45. Nearby were yet more square boxes with the logos of various American-made brandies. Ernie stepped off to my right, still searching the dark, his hand on the hilt of the .45 inside his jacket. So far, nothing moved. Ahead of us sat a rumpled bed with ropes that had been cut. Beyond was a short flight of steps leading to an open window.

I jabbed my finger toward the dim light. Ernie nodded and moved forward. But before he did, a stack of boxes near the steps started to tilt, and that was when I realized that all the crates of liquor and cases of beer were stacked like gigantic dominoes. The top box fell and crashed toward the floor.

"Watch out!" I shouted.

Ernie leapt back out of the way, but a large figure darted across the top of the stairwell and the stack on the opposite side of the steps began to topple too. Suddenly, tons of cased beer and brandy and malt liquor were crashing down upon us. I leapt for the center of the floor. A small desk sat off to the left; I grabbed the closest leg and jerked it toward me. As one case fell onto my leg, I coiled up beneath the desk, and within seconds Ernie was crouching there next to me. Inkstones and coils of paper and writing brushes rolled on the floor beneath us.

What seemed like huge pyramidal stones thundered down around us. The little desk was hit hard more than once but held up admirably. Within seconds, the last case of beer had tumbled onto the floor, and Ernie and I pushed the desk away and stood up.

Amidst the dim light of the red bulbs outside, shadows moved through the window above us. I tried to climb toward it, but there was too much of a jumble beneath me and every time I hoisted my weight forward, more crates fell down around me. By the time I reached the stairwell, whoever had climbed out the window was gone.

Ernie returned to the doorway but it was blocked with crates of liquor. He started to shove some of them out of the way but stopped when he realized it would take an hour or more to clear a pathway. Meanwhile, climbing over the cardboard jumble, I had made some headway toward the window. Ernie followed. Outside, a heavy truck engine—maybe a three-quarter-ton—started up and roared away.

By the time I'd clawed my way over half a dozen crates, I shoved the window fully open and peered outside.

Nothing moved.

"Son of a *bastard*," Ernie said.

With some effort, we were able to climb out the window. A back door in the fence that circled the small annex building was wide open. We passed through into the open space between the warehouses and ran back to our jeep. When I asked the gate guard, he said someone had left—"*Migun*," he said, American soldier—but he didn't know who. And no, he hadn't jotted down the truck's unit designation because that wasn't part of his job. He did confirm, however, that it was a three-quarter-ton truck, US Army–issue. A GI was driving, but he hadn't seen anyone else in the cab.

"Then who screamed?" Ernie said.

We returned to the annex building for one last quick search. No one there. No trap doors, no secret closets, no dungeons beneath the floor.

"He took her with him," I said.

"Crouched down in front of the passenger seat," Ernie said.

"Easy," I said. "The gate guards wouldn't have seen her because they weren't looking."

All they wanted was to get through their shift and draw their pay. Whatever the crazy Americans did was up to them.

When we drove off from the 71st Transportation Company warehouse area, the gate guard was glad to see us go.

"Demoray aced us on that one," Ernie said.

We were already back on the main highway between Inchon and Seoul, exceeding the posted speed limit by at least fifteen kilometers per hour.

"How can you be sure it was Demoray?" I asked.

"Who else? The girl screaming, the writing desk with the ink and brushes, a Chinese wall of Colt 45. The Ville Rat sent us down there, but Demoray was probably tipped off by that damn gate guard. And he had his little escape plan set up for just such an eventuality."

"You're probably right."

"Yeah. So we're headed back to Seoul because I don't know where else to go. Got any ideas?"

"Keep going. Back to Seoul."

"Right. Good thinking." Ernie took his eyes of the road and twisted his head toward me. "Why?"

"He knows he's not going to get away with this."

"Okay." Ernie sped around a ROK Army military convoy.

"Even if he ditches the little *kisaeng* and we have trouble pinning Miss Hwang's murder on him, he knows we know about the game with the extra inventory."

"With the Colt 45 and the brandy and the other stuff."

"Right. That's over. And a record of all of it is on paper somewhere. Hard to find, maybe well hidden by the Comptroller's Office, but once we know it's there—and we do know—we'll be able to dig it up."

"So if he doesn't want to go to the Federal Pen," Ernie said, "he has to destroy those records."

"Precisely."

"But that's impossible. It would take him days, maybe weeks, to go back and pull all those invoices. Like Rick Mills said, this has been going on for years. Even if Demoray only goes back to when he got involved, it's a massive task."

"You're right about that." I waited for Ernie to say more, but his face was twisted in consternation. Still, he wound through the much slower traffic with the consummate ease of a driving virtuoso. "Unless Demoray takes a shortcut," I said.

Ernie glanced at me. "Shortcut? There's no shortcut. This is the fastest route to Seoul."

"Not that kind of shortcut."

"Then you mean with the records?"

"Yes."

I could see his expression change as he pieced it all together.

"I'll take the back gate," he said.

The back gate into South Post Yongsan Compound led us past the 121st Evacuation Hospital, along the edge of the 8th United States Army Golf Course, through the Embassy Housing Area, and finally into the main 8th Army Headquarters Logistics/Supply Command.

We pulled up in front of the 8th United States Army Non-Appropriated Fund Records Repository. A side door was wide open. Beyond it, a three-quarter-ton truck was parked. Holding his .45 at the ready, Ernie checked the truck and then shook his head. Empty. We entered the warehouse.

The lights were off, but there was enough moonlight streaming in through the windows and the doorway for us to realize that we were in the main office clerical area. We pushed past the same grey desks we'd seen recently with what appeared to be the same stacks of onionskin paperwork in their wire in-baskets.

When we stepped into the main records area, we stopped for a moment and listened. Above, moonlight filtered through the overhead windows, dimly illuminating the seemingly endless rows of metal stanchions and neatly aligned cardboard boxes of records. At first we heard nothing, but then Ernie motioned toward his right.

I listened carefully.

Splashing. The sound of liquid being poured, punctuated by intermittent gurgling. Vast quantities of liquid. And then, for the first time since we'd entered the warehouse, I took a deep breath.

"*Gas,*" Ernie whispered.

He motioned for me to go left as he moved toward the rows of records on the right. As I stepped deeper into the warehouse, I realized that many of the cardboard boxes on the wooden shelves were wet with gasoline. The air was saturated with its pungent smell. I reached into my pocket, wishing I had a handkerchief to tie around my nose. But I didn't. I thought of the .45 I hadn't checked out from the arms room. At a supply closet, I stopped to search with my flashlight and pulled out a broad-brushed broom, US Army–issue. I'd used millions of them in my day and knew how to detach the handle. I unscrewed it and when I left the supply closet, I had a sturdy walking stick in my hands. I held it with both hands, pointing it forward like I'd done with my rifle during bayonet drill.

When I reached the far end of the row, I squatted and listened.

Whimpering. The little *kisaeng*. She was just a few yards away. I stood up and walked toward the sound.

"Hold it!"

I froze. There was Demoray. Moonlight from the storm windows above shone down on him, and sitting next to him on a stool was the little *kisaeng*, her head bowed, her hair drenched with liquid. Gasoline.

Demoray held a lighter just above her head.

"Back off!" he shouted. "I want you both out of here *now*!"

Ernie was crouched about ten yards behind him, both fists aiming his .45 automatic dead into the center of Demoray's back. But the air was drenched with gasoline fumes. Certainly, if Ernie fired, this entire warehouse would explode into flame. The little *kisaeng*, Demoray, me, and Ernie with it.

"Hold it, Ernie," I said.

Ernie lowered his .45.

"What is it you want, Demoray?" I asked.

He stood up straighter, lowering the cigarette lighter slightly. "That's more like it," he said. "Showing a senior NCO a little respect for once."

"You don't deserve any respect," Ernie growled.

I waved him down.

"Name it, Demoray," I said. "What do you want?"

"First, I want you two assholes out of this warehouse."

I nodded toward the little *kisaeng*. "Only if she goes with us."

"She stays!" he shouted.

Ernie raised his .45 again.

"Burning her isn't going to do any good," I said. "Burning

yourself alive isn't going to do any good either. The game's over, Demoray. Best to keep your mouth shut and hire a good lawyer."

"Some Second Looey who doesn't know his ass from a hole in the ground?"

"You can hire a stateside lawyer," I said. "Other people have done it. You must have plenty of money."

"What do you know about money?"

"Not much," I admitted.

"Enough of the bull," Demoray said. "I want you and your partner out of here *now*." He raised the lighter, his hand on the striking wheel.

"Okay," I said. "We're moving."

I took a step backward and, as I did so, I flashed a hand signal to Ernie. We'd used them plenty of times in tight situations. They weren't regulation. You couldn't find them in any Army Field Manual, but they worked for us. This one said, "I'll distract him while you take him down."

I moved quickly to my left, stuck out my hand toward the little *kisaeng*, and said, *"Ka-ja,"* which in Korean means "Let's go." On cue, she rose to her feet. Demoray flinched and Ernie sprinted forward. Startled, Demoray swiveled at the sound of the footsteps, but he was too slow. Ernie plowed into him like an All-Pro linebacker. The lighter flew from Demoray's hand and skittered along the cement floor. I ran forward and pulled the little *kisaeng* behind me, then I crouched, dropping my right knee onto Demoray's thigh, grappling with one of his flailing arms, and simultaneously pulling my handcuffs out from behind my back. Within seconds we had him trussed up, lying facedown on the floor. I retrieved the lighter and placed it carefully into my pocket.

"Not so tough now, are you, Demoray?" Ernie said.

I started to walk toward the little *kisaeng*, expecting her to be relieved and happy, but instead of greeting me she stared off into the hallway to my left. Footsteps approached. Someone kicked my broom handle across cement and then a shadow emerged around the corner. Standing in front of us was Rick Mills, Executive Director of the Central Locker Fund.

Accompanying him, in all its macabre glory, was a double-barreled shotgun aimed straight at us.

-15-

"Don't even think about it, Bascom," Rick Mills said.

Ernie had his hand on the hilt of his holstered .45.

"Take off your jacket," Rick Mills said. Ernie did, and dropped it on the floor. "Now, unbuckle the leather. Without touching the weapon, drop the entire holster on top of the jacket." Ernie followed instructions.

"Now, gently," Rick Mills said, "using your feet, slide the jacket and the holster toward me. Ernie did, shoving it forward a few feet. "Now you, Sueño. Keep sliding it over here."

When it was close enough, Rick Mills told me to stop, then reached forward with his right foot and pulled Ernie's jacket right in front of him. By now, the jacket was soaked with gasoline. The little *kisaeng* had sat back down on her stool, both her hands now covering her face. Carefully keeping the shotgun aimed at us, Rick Mills crouched down, released Ernie's .45 from its holster, stood back up, and shoved the automatic into his front belt.

By now, Demoray had realized what was happening and was struggling to get up.

With the shotgun, Rick Mills motioned for me to move to my left. He also motioned for Ernie to step closer to me and the little *kisaeng*.

Then he said, "Demoray, can you hear me?"

"Yeah, boss. I'm okay now."

"These boys knocked you for a loop, eh?"

"They got lucky."

"I doubt that. They're just smarter than you. Why don't you admit it?"

Demoray didn't answer.

Mills said, "Come over here."

"I can't move, boss."

"Sure you can. Just wriggle forward a little bit at a time. You can do it."

"I can't."

"*Try*, goddamn it!"

Demoray tried. He made a few inches' progress. Then he made more.

"That's it," Rick Mills said. "Just keep coming like that. Like a big worm. The big worm that you are." He paused, stared at us, and then back at Demoray. "We had the perfect operation going," Mills said. "For years. Everybody was getting fat. The DACs were getting what they wanted, the generals were getting the swimming pools and golf courses, the ROK government was getting contracts and gifts every year, but nobody was getting greedy. Everybody played it cool, made sure the records stayed clean and questions weren't asked, and every Eighth Army inspector general was either handpicked by one of our commanders or kept busy with projects that kept him away from the Central Locker Fund. Everybody played it cool. Played it smart."

Demoray was just a few feet away from Rick Mills now, sweaty and smeared with gasoline. Like the worm Mills had suggested, Demoray looked up and said, "Get the keys, boss. Let me up."

Mills looked down at him, his lips twisted in disgust. Then he spit off to the side, took a step backward, and as fast as a striker kicking a ball toward the goal, his foot flashed forward. Demoray's head snapped back, and blood and flesh and what might've been molars flooded over his front lip.

"Dumb shit," Mills said.

The little *kisaeng* started to whimper.

"Can you shut her *up*?" Mills said. He shook his head. "Korean women used to be strong. My wife would never have whined like that. No matter what."

The little *kisaeng* stifled her crying.

"What now?" I asked Mills.

"Whadda you mean, *what now*?"

"I mean, you can shoot us. A lot of good it'll do you. The game's over now, Mills. You must've been listening when I gave Demoray advice. A good lawyer. You can definitely afford one, probably from one of those fancy law firms. Somebody who specializes in going up against the government. You know what Eighth Army JAG is like. You'll get a slap on the wrist. They won't just be intimidated by your legal representation; they don't particularly want the embarrassment of what's been going on beneath their noses for all these years."

Mills grinned. "You're a cynical bastard, aren't you?"

I shrugged.

"How about you," Mills said, turning to Ernie. "Do you agree with your partner here?"

"He's right about most things."

"But not everything."

"Nobody is," Ernie said. "Like how many cartridges do you have in that shotgun. Two? If you miss with one, either me or my partner will be on your ass."

I don't know how he managed it, but Ernie was somehow chomping on ginseng gum again.

Mills grinned even more broadly. "By God, I like your spirit. Shit, if I would've had guys like you working for me, instead of this piece of shit . . ." Demoray shook his head. ". . . we'd still be in business and going strong."

"We wouldn't work for you, Mills," I said.

"Why not. You don't like money?"

"I like money fine. I just don't like raping and torturing helpless women."

Mills frowned. Maybe it was my imagination, but I thought his finger tightened on the trigger of the shotgun. He glared at me. For a long minute, I held my breath. Mills was making a decision. Ernie felt it too. An aura of tension seemed to emanate from his body. I knew what he wanted to do. He wanted to attack. If he had to go down, he would at least go down fighting; but he was also weighing the odds. Rick Mills knew how to handle that shotgun. If either Ernie or I made a play for him, our guts would be blown out of our stomachs and splattered all over onionskin.

Finally, Rick Mills took his eyes off of mine and glanced at the little *kisaeng*.

"Get her out of here," he said.

I reached for her. She stood.

"That's what it was," Rick Mills said. "Not the money. Who gives a shit if wasted tax dollars land in my pocket or somebody else's? It was the arrogance. The cruelty. The thinking that we were better than the Koreans. So much better than their women that we could use them in the ways we saw fit. Ways that made us feel good. That's why this piece of shit deserves to die."

Demoray twisted his bloody mouth away from the floor, saying "Please."

Mills kicked him again.

"Go on," Mills said. "Get out. All three of you. Get out now."

Ernie grabbed the little *kisaeng* and started to back away.

I stepped backward, keeping my hands raised and my eyes on Rick Mills's shotgun. When I was almost out of range, I said, "You don't have to do this, Mills."

"Sure I do," he said.

"You'll be in trouble, sure," I said, "but you didn't kill anyone. You know how it works. You pay your dues and life goes on."

"I paid my dues," Mills said, "when my wife died."

"How about him?" I said, motioning toward Demoray. "You can't just shoot him."

"Why not?"

"You're not the judge and jury."

"I am now."

In the distance, a siren sounded. As we listened, it grew louder. "You better get out, Sueño. While you still can."

I backed away, stepped around the edge of the long row, and finally out of the line of fire. I leaned against the stanchion, breathing deeply, suddenly realizing that my knees were wobbly.

Apparently, Ernie'd already hustled the little *kisaeng* out of the warehouse. He ran toward me, grabbed my arm, and without a word yanked me toward the exit.

I followed.

We were just stepping outside the warehouse into the blessed fresh air when we heard it. A shotgun blast. And then, as we dived toward the ground, a huge *whoosh*, like a mighty monster inhaling all the oxygen in the world, and the 8th United States Army Non-Appropriated Fund Records Repository exploded into flame.

Orrin W. Penwold, the Ville Rat, was declared "persona non grata" by the ROK Ministry of the Interior, which meant that he'd never be allowed to return to the Republic of Korea. It took the KNPs a few days to find him, but eventually they did. The US Embassy bought him a one-way ticket back to the States.

Mr. Wilbur M. Robinson Sr., long-time Department of the Army Civilian with the 8th Army Comptroller's Office, decided to retire and discreetly took his leave.

The warehouse fire made some news, especially when the bodies of Master Sergeant Demoray and Noncommissioned Officer Rick Mills were found in the rubble. An Associated Press stringer did a story on it that not only appeared in Stateside newspapers, but was even cleared for publication in the Department of Defense official publication, the *Pacific Stars and Stripes*. It was a strictly factual story, however, and mentioned nothing about the long-term misappropriation of Non-Appropriated Fund merchandise.

Meanwhile, the Gunslinger was always good copy and the same AP stringer, tipped off by some anonymous source, got wind of the melee during the court-martial of Private First Class Clifton Threets. He reported on the shooting of Sergeant Orgwell and the official accusations against Threets, but the main focus of the story was the Gunslinger and how, according to eyewitnesses, he'd fired one of his pearl-handled revolvers into the ceiling of the courtroom. This made for quite a story back in the States, but since it couldn't be corroborated by official 8th Army sources, it didn't appear in the *Stars and Stripes*. Lieutenant Peggy Mendelson at 8th Army JAG never explained why, but after the story appeared, the charges against Threets changed from attempted homicide to aggravated assault. And when Second Lieutenant Bob Conroy threatened to fight even that, the charges were lowered to simple assault. Threets pled guilty to the charge, was sentenced to time served, and dismissed from the Army with a bad-conduct discharge.

Sergeant Orgwell was deemed no longer medically fit for duty and was granted disability retirement, including a lump-sum payment, a monthly pension for the rest of his life, and medical care provided by the Veterans Administration.

As per his wishes, Rick Mills was laid to rest in the burial mound he shared with his wife. Ernie and I attended the ceremony and even performed duties as ceremonial grave diggers, in accordance with Korean custom. Sure, Mills was a crook, but he'd also been a fellow soldier once, and in the end he'd conducted himself, if not with wisdom, at least with honor.

Mr. Kill, Chief Homicide Inspector for the Korean National Police, put a halt to the investigation of how many *kisaeng* Demoray had killed. A GI serial killer was not the type of story that either the Korean government or the United States wanted to hear about.

Miss Kwon, the little *kisaeng*, returned to her job as a hostess at the Bright Cloud Inn. Officer Oh, Inspector Kill's stalwart female assistant, was appointed to watch over her and make sure she made a successful readjustment to normal life. Or as normal as life gets in a *kisaeng* house.

Leah Prevault and I took a few days off work and traveled to a resort area in southern Korea on the island of Jindo, far from any military bases, or any Americans at all for that matter. We wandered along fishing wharfs and deserted beaches and ate platefuls of fresh fish and dried seaweed at well-lit restaurants at night. She made me tell her all about what happened and waited patiently as I tried to sort it all out. There's something to this head-shrinking stuff. Just speaking my thoughts aloud made me feel better. Especially when someone was there to listen.

Back in Seoul, Ernie and I entered the CID office together. Staff Sergeant Riley said, "Where in the hell you guys been?"

"None of your freaking business," Ernie told him.

Unfazed, Riley pulled out a sheaf of paperwork. "The provost marshal wants you both to sign this."

"What is it?" Ernie asked.

"Read it. You'll see."

"What *is* it?" Ernie repeated.

Riley turned away. "An apology to the Second Division commander."

"What?"

I grabbed the paperwork. It was two typed sheets, one with Ernie's name on it, one with mine. I skimmed it quickly. What it said, in essence, was that we were responsible for engendering a false impression that the 2nd Infantry Division had a race-relations problem in its ranks. It also said that we had spread false rumors that the Division had training and leadership problems. Finally, there was a statement to the effect that both Ernie and I were responsible for these transgressions and very sorry for having any hand in perpetuating said falsehoods.

"You've got to be kidding me," Ernie said.

"Nobody's kidding, Bascom," Riley said, hands on his hips. "You insulted the Second Infantry Division and the Second Infantry Division commander and now you're going to apologize."

"And if I don't?"

Riley's eyes narrowed. "Shit Detail City."

"I've been on shit details before," Ernie told him. He reached for the paper, crumpled it into a small ball, and tossed it into Riley's trash bin.

"You're going to regret this, Bascom," Riley said.

"Never."

Ernie stalked out of the office.

Both Sergeant Riley and Miss Kim, the secretary, stared at me. I lifted the paper and studied it. Instead of balling it up, I carried it across the room, set it on my wooden field desk, rolled a clean sheet of paper into my Remington manual, and started to type.

"What the hell you doing?" Riley growled.

"Preparing my rebuttal," I said.

Miss Kim brought me a cup of Black Dragon tea.

Continue reading for a sneak preview from the next
Sueño and Bascom mystery

PING-PONG HEART

-1-

Major Frederick Manfield Schultz appeared at the 8th Army Provost Marshal's office red-faced and enraged.

"She robbed me," he said.

I took the report, typing patiently as he explained.

"I met her at the UN Club. We started talking, I bought her a drink. Then we went back to her hooch."

"What's her name?" I asked.

"Miss Jo."

"Did you check her VD card?"

"I didn't think to."

"It's a good idea. If she's a freelancer without one, we might have trouble finding her."

This made him even angrier. "She stole my money, dammit. I want it back."

Miss Kim, the statuesque Admin secretary, pulled a tissue from the box in front of her, held it to her nose, rose from her chair, and walked out of the office. We listened as her high heels clicked down the hallway.

My name is George Sueño. I'm an agent for the 8th United States Army Criminal Investigation Division in Seoul, Republic of Korea. Reports of theft were routinely taken at the Yongsan Compound MP Station. But Major Schultz knew Colonel Brace, the Provost Marshal, and had gone to him directly with his complaint. Since he was a field grade officer, it was felt that allowing word of this incident to leak out to the hoi polloi of the Military Police would be detrimental to good order and discipline. So my partner Ernie Bascom and I—CID agents, not MP investigators—were given the job.

Schultz told me that he'd left the UN Club with Miss Jo and they'd walked back to her hooch near the old oak tree behind the Itaewon open-air market. In her room, he handed her fifty dollars' worth of crisp MPC, military payment certificates. She'd taken the bills, helped him off with his clothes and sat him down on the edge of the bed. Then she excused herself to use the outdoor *byonso*.

"I waited and waited," he told me, "until finally I got tired of waiting. So I slid open the door and looked out. Nothing. No light on in the *byonso*. I put on my clothes and went looking for her. She was gone. I pounded on the doors in the neighbors' hooches, but they just pretended not to speak English."

"Maybe they don't," I said.

This made him angry again. Full cheeks flushed red. Even beneath his blond crew cut, freckled skin burned crimson. "They live next door to a GI whore and they don't speak English?"

I shrugged. "So what'd you do?"

He knotted his fists. "I was tempted to tear the place down, rip up her clothes, smash the windows, throw the freaking radio and electric fan out into the mud. But I figured if I did, she might slap a SOFA charge on me."

SOFA. The Status of Forces Agreement between the United States and the Republic of Korea. One of its provisions is to adjudicate claims made by Korean civilians against US military personnel for damages suffered at their hands.

"It was almost midnight curfew," he said, "so I just put on my clothes and left."

"Smart move," I said.

He nodded. "I tell you, though, if I'd gotten my hands on her . . ."

We let the thought trail off.

"Are you on an accompanied tour?" I asked.

Unconsciously, he fondled the gold wedding band on his left hand. "No. The wife's back at Fort Hood." I continued to stare at him. "The kids are in school. We thought it was best not to move them."

I finished my typing, looked up at him and said, "Can you describe Miss Jo?"

He did. But it amounted to the same bargirl description we heard from most GIs: brunette, petite, cute foreign accent. Ernie looked at me and rolled his eyes. I stopped typing and asked Major Schultz to accompany us to the Itaewon Police Station. He agreed, and the three of us walked outside to Ernie's jeep.

Once there, I conferred with the on-duty Desk Sergeant. After a few minutes, he ushered us into a back room, pulled out a huge three-ring binder and plopped it on a wooden table. The book contained information gathered by the Yongsan District Public Health Service and was accompanied with snapshots of every waitress and barmaid and hostess who was authorized to work in the Itaewon nightclub district.

The girls are issued a wallet-sized card and are required to be checked monthly for communicable diseases. If they prove to be disease-free, the card is stamped in red ink. If they're sick, they are locked up in a Health Service Quarantine Center and forced to take whatever drugs the doctor prescribes. GIs call the wallet-sized folds of cardboard "VD cards." In official military training, soldiers are instructed to check that the card is up-to-date before having sexual relations. As you might imagine, few bother.

After the Desk Sergeant left, Major Schultz flipped through a few dozen pages of the book until he found the section marked *UN Club*. He stopped and pointed.

"That's her."

I studied the picture. She wasn't hard to look at. A face that could've belonged to a classic Korean heroine: a perfectly shaped oval with almond eyes and a clear complexion, and framed by straight black hair that fell to narrow shoulders. And maybe it was my imagination, but I thought she looked wistful, slightly ashamed at being photographed for a VD Card but resigned nevertheless to her fate. Next to the photo, written in *hangul*, were her name, date of birth, and National ID card number. I jotted down the info.

Major Schultz rose from his wooden chair. "When do you expect to catch her?"

"If she hasn't left town, it won't take long," I replied.

"It better not."

He turned and stalked out of the police station.

-2-

Ernie and I drove back to the CID office. Staff Sergeant Riley, the Admin Non-Commissioned Officer, sat behind a stack of neatly clipped paperwork.

"Where's Miss Kim?" I asked.

"Why?" Riley replied. "She doesn't work for you."

That was him. All charm.

"She seemed shaken up listening to Major Schultz."

Riley shrugged and returned to his paperwork. Ernie ignored our conversation, picked up the morning edition of the *Pacific Stars and Stripes*, sat down, and snapped it open to the sports page. Tissue was still wadded atop Miss Kim's desk and her full cup of green tea had grown cold.

I went to look for her.

I found her sitting on a wooden bench beside a small pagoda containing a bronze statue of the Maitreya Buddha. It had been set up years ago for the use of 8th Army's Korean employees, of which there were hundreds on this compound alone. A small grassy area in front of the shrine was well worn from spirited games of badminton that were held every day during lunch hour.

I sat down next to Miss Kim. "I'm sorry Major Schultz upset you," I told her.

She twisted her handkerchief, rolling pink embroidery around the edges. "It's not him," she said.

"Then what is it?"

She didn't answer. About a year ago, she and Ernie had been an item. She'd taken the relationship seriously. Ernie hadn't. He was tall, about six-foot-one, and had a pointed nose with green eyes that sat behind round-lensed glasses. Why women found him fascinating, I wasn't sure. Maybe it was his complete I-don't-give-a-damn attitude. Ernie'd served two tours in Vietnam, and having survived that, he figured every day was money won in a poker game; he spent them as such, taking any pleasure that came his way. When Miss Kim found out that he had other paramours, she dropped him flat. As far as I knew, she hadn't spoken to him since.

"If it's not Major Schultz that's bothering you," I asked, "then what is it?"

She shook her head, staring at the dirt in front of us. "Cruelty," she said. "So much of it."

I patted her hand. She dabbed her eyes with the handkerchief. I'd known her for well over a year now. I occasionally bought her gifts from the PX: a flower, small bottles of hand lotion, the type of breath mints I knew she liked. I suppose I was trying to make amends for the sins of my investigative partner. When she didn't continue, I said, "There's something else bothering you."

She laughed but stopped abruptly. "You notice things, don't you, Geogie?"

"I try to."

"There is something," she said.

"What?"

"It's nothing, really." She waved her hand in a dismissive gesture. "It's just that when I walk home, after the cannon goes off, somebody keeps staring at me."

Miss Kim was tall and slender and dressed well, which attracted a lot of attention on a compound full of horny GIs.

"Did he do anything?" I asked.

"Not exactly. While I'm heading toward the Main Gate, he follows me. And lately he's been walking up right beside me and when no one else is listening, he says things. Rude things. I ignore him, but he keeps doing it."

"How long has this been going on?"

"Maybe two or three weeks now."

"Describe him to me."

She shook her head vehemently. "No. I don't want trouble."

The Korean War had ended some twenty years ago. Seoul had been completely crushed, and only now was the Korean economy beginning to recover. A job on the American Army compound was considered an excellent employment opportunity, with good pay and job security. Miss Kim was afraid to jeopardize that in any way.

Then she turned on the bench and stared at me. "Don't do anything, Geogie. I can take care of it."

"Has this guy followed you off compound?"

"No. He always stops just before we reach the Pedestrian Exit."

"At Gate Five?" I asked.

"Yes."

"Where there are more people."

She nodded, then reached out and squeezed my hand. "Thank you, though," she said. Then she pointed at her nose. "I will take care of it."

We walked back to the CID office. Before we entered, she stopped and faced me again. "Promise you won't do anything?"

I nodded.

She smiled and trotted up the steps.

Before the cannon went off, Ernie and I found a hiding place amidst a grove of evergreen trees about twenty yards in front of the Pedestrian Exit at Gate Five. While we waited, just to pass the time, I needled him.

"You sure screwed up your chances with Miss Kim," I said.

He shrugged. "There's more fish in the Yellow Sea. Whole boat-loads of them."

"Not many like her."

He peeked around his tree, grinning. "You sweet on her, Sueño?"

"Sure, I'm sweet on her. Who wouldn't be? So are you, or you wouldn't be standing here in the cold, waiting to punch the sono-fabitch who's been bothering her."

Ernie unwrapped a stick of ginseng gum and popped it in his mouth. "Just out for a little fun," he said.

Which was probably true. Ernie loved conflict. The only time I saw him grin from ear to ear was when people were butting heads or, better yet, swinging big roundhouse rights at one another.

At what the military likes to call close-of-business, exactly seventeen hundred hours—5 P.M. to civilians—the cannon went off. In front of the headquarters building, the Honor Guard was lowering the Korean, American, and United Nations flags. We both looked around. What we were supposed to do, what every soldier was supposed to do, was stand at the position of attention and salute the flag, even if it was so far away you couldn't see it. Which was silly, but that's the Army for you. In the distance, we heard the retreat bugle blasting out of tinny speakers. Since no one was watching, we didn't bother to salute but remained slouched behind the pine trees. In less than a minute, the last notes of the electronic bugle subsided, and down the long row of brick buildings, doors opened and the first early-bird workers trotted down stone steps.

"Free at last," Ernie said.

Within minutes, a line of mostly Korean employees formed at the Pedestrian Exit. We watched down the walkway that led toward the CID office. After three or four more minutes, Miss Kim appeared in the distance. Just two feet behind her right shoulder walked an American in civilian clothes.

"There's the son of a biscuit," Ernie said. Like a hunting dog, his nose was pointed toward his prey.

I studied the guy. He was young, like a GI, but he wore a cheap plaid suit, his face was narrow and pasty and his hair, reddish-blond and curly, was too long for Army regulation.

"Is he a civilian?" Ernie asked.

"Maybe."

To get a better look, Ernie stepped out from behind his tree.

"Don't let her see you," I reminded him.

He waved me off. "Don't worry, Sueño. I got it." He ducked back into hiding.

Miss Kim was walking fast, clutching her handbag; her cloth

coat buttoned tightly, her arms crossed in front of her chest. Her head was down, her face grim. The guy stared straight ahead, as if he weren't talking to her directly but his mouth was moving, rapidly. His eyes were wide and glassy.

"He's getting his rocks off," Ernie said.

We were too far away to hear what he was saying, but gauging by Miss Kim's reaction, it wasn't good. The crowd surrounding them was of other Korean workers, and the guy appeared to be speaking softly enough that they couldn't hear what he was saying. Only his intended audience, Miss Kim, was receiving the full benefit of his blather.

Just before crossing the road that led to the Pedestrian Exit, the guy peeled off. As I'd hoped, he headed away from Gate 5, toward Main Post, using the sidewalk that passed the Moyer Recreation Center and the Main PX. Miss Kim disappeared into the flow of employees heading into the single-file line at the Pedestrian Exit.

Ernie smiled broadly. The guy was heading toward us, still mumbling to himself. Ernie reached into his jacket pocket and pulled out a set of brass knuckles.

"All mine," Ernie said, grinning from ear to ear.

"Not out in the open," I said. "Too many eyeballs."

We let the guy walk a few yards past us, and then we both scurried out of the trees and hustled close behind him.

"You drop this?" Ernie said.

The guy stopped and turned, a confused look on his face. "Drop what?"

"This," Ernie said, and stepped close and slammed an uppercut into his gut. Air erupted from his mouth. As he bent over, I grabbed his shoulders and straightened him out, then shoved him toward the shadows among the pine trees. Once safely behind lumber, Ernie slugged him again.

"Let's see some ID," Ernie said.

As the guy continued to grimace and clutch his stomach, I reached into his back pocket and pulled out his wallet. Ernie grabbed it from me and slid out our victim's military identification card, handing it to me. Quickly, I used my notebook to jot down his name, rank, and service number. *Fenton, Wilfred R., Specialist Four.* Next, Ernie handed me the guy's US Forces Korea Weapons Card. I read off the unit. "Five Oh First Military Intelligence Battalion. Headquarters Company."

"The Five Oh Worst," Ernie corrected and slugged the guy again. "Civilian clothes, hippie haircut. What are you, some kind of spook?"

"Counter-intel," the guy said. Counterintelligence.

"Caught any North Korean spies lately?"

"A few."

"Bull." Ernie slugged him again. "All you've caught is the clap."

When he recovered, Specialist Four Fenton pulled himself together enough to ask, "What's this all about?"

"It's about you harassing innocent women," Ernie told him.

"I'm not harassing anyone."

"What'd you just say to that woman you were walking next to?"

"What woman?"

Ernie slugged him again.

Fenton pressed his forearm against his rib. "I didn't say anything to her." Ernie pulled his fist back and Fenton flinched and said, "Nothing bad anyway."

Ernie let loose the punch.

"What the hell do you *want*?" Fenton said.

Ernie straightened him out and turned him toward me. I was six inches taller than him but leaned down close to his face, letting hot breath blast into his eyes. "We want you to stop pestering women who don't want anything to do with you. Maybe that's how you get your kicks, Fenton, but you're through doing it on this compound. No more," I said, pointing my forefinger at his nose. "You got that?"

He turned away.

Ernie shoved him against a tree. "Answer the man."

"I got it," Fenton replied sullenly.

"You better."

Ernie slugged him again, then took Fenton's wallet, turned it upside down, and pulled open the flaps. Calling cards and Military Payment Certificates and photographs fluttered toward the mud. Fenton leaned against a tree, arms folded firmly across his stomach. I tossed his military ID and weapons card into the mud with the rest of his documents.

Before we walked away, Ernie slapped him across the right cheek, gently. As we left, we heard Fenton spitting up something, maybe blood. When we were almost out of earshot he started to curse. Softly at first, then more loudly.

"I'll get you for this," he said.

"Like I'm worried about that, twerp," Ernie muttered.

"I'm with the Five Oh First MI!" Fenton ranted. "We're not called the Five Oh *Worst* for nothing."

Ernie rolled his eyes again. As we rounded the corner, leaving Fenton behind, Ernie waggled his forearms, pretending to shake. "I'm petrified," he said.

"We *never* lose!" Fenton shouted from the distance.

OTHER TITLES IN THE SOHO CRIME SERIES